It was hopeless

As far as the eye could see, there was no trail, no road, no evidence of man at all. Zach's gaze returned to Randy, and she chose that moment to look up from the map she was studying. He read the doubt in her eyes. "What is it?" he asked urgently.

"I'm not sure which route we should take," Randy began. "I—"

"What!" Zach seized her shoulders and swore hotly. "You'd better not be saying we're lost." His hands fell away as suddenly as he'd grabbed her. "I thought you knew what the hell you were doing!"

"I don't have to listen to this," Randy said fiercely. "I don't owe you anything, Zach Corbett. If you don't think I'm qualified, you're welcome to—"

She never got the chance to finish. From out of nowhere, an ear-shattering explosion rent the air.

The blast of gunfire....

ABOUT THE AUTHOR

The inspiration for Sandra James's sixth
Superromance came from a rousing game of
"What If." Sandra wanted to write a search-
and-rescue story, and the whole family
contributed to the brainstorming session. She
had to laugh at some of the story ideas her
husband and three school-age daughters
conjured up, but the final result was *North of
Eden*, an exciting and powerful story of
courage, adventure ... and love.

Books by Sandra James

HARLEQUIN SUPERROMANCE

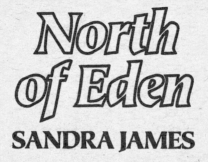

North of Eden

SANDRA JAMES

Harlequin Books

TORONTO • NEW YORK • LONDON
AMSTERDAM • PARIS • SYDNEY • HAMBURG
STOCKHOLM • ATHENS • TOKYO • MILAN

Published January 1990

First printing November 1989

ISBN 0-373-70386-4

For Valerie,
the kind of editor
every writer yearns for

PROLOGUE

Central Oregon
Late October

GHOSTLY SHADOWS RIPPLED across the surface of the mountain road. A dark sedan hugged the winding, twisting curves, burrowing ever deeper into the rugged high-country of the Cascade Mountains.

Three men occupied the sedan; one in the front seat, two in the back. The driver, Tom Phillips, glanced in the mirror, and spoke to the man directly behind him. "You're awfully quiet back there, Garrett. You miss that old cot you left behind already? Well, we've got another one just like it for you in Portland. No, sir-ree, I doubt you'll miss the Lake County jail at all."

Garrett sat still and silent. His large callused hands rested lightly on his legs. Inch-wide links of steel dangled from his handcuffs. His leg irons rattled slightly when he shifted and turned to stare out the window. Garrett's eyes glinted, the only sign he'd heard the driver's words.

Larry Robertson laughed and turned to the prisoner sitting beside him. He eyed his charge, his gaze sharp and piercing. "I wouldn't count on breakin' loose again if I were you, Garrett. Too bad it's so dark you can't take a good look around you. After your trial, it'll be a long, long time before you see any wide open spaces like this again."

All was silent as Tom Phillips turned his attention to the narrow ribbon of road before him. Cresting the top of a hill, the vehicle's nose dipped forward once more. His fingers tightened around the wheel in preparation for the next curve.

He never even saw the patch of ice that sent him to his death.

The vehicle spun out of control. It sailed from the roadway; the wheels left the ground as if it were airborne. The impact was horrendous as it plunged over the embankment and met the ground once more. Like a miniature toy, the sedan flipped end over end, skidding down a short but steep hillside until it finally came to rest against a burned-out tree trunk.

The silence was ominous and oppressive. The car's wheels spun crazily until at last they, too, ceased their restless motion. The rear door had been ripped off, leaving a jagged opening in the side of the car.

A low keening moan filled the air.

The sound came from Robertson. He'd been thrown from the vehicle's wreckage and lay sprawled facedown on the frigid landscape. Like a limp rag doll, his head lifted, then dropped forward again.

Nearby, a shadowy form slowly—painstakingly—pulled itself up and out of the wreckage. Dazed and disoriented, the man staggered and fell. Long moments later, he shook his shaggy head, gingerly flexed muscles and joints, and righted himself.

It was then he spotted the limp figure nearby. The leg irons scraped over the rocky landscape as he stumbled forward. He dropped to his knees, eyes straining, fingers searching frantically over Robertson's body. Within his bushy red beard, thin lips twisted into a sickening parody of a smile as he discovered the items he sought.

With a twist of a key, the metal cuffs around his wrists yawned wide; they clattered onto the ground along with the leg irons. The next instant his fingers grazed the cold hard steel of a gun barrel....

There was an explosive ricochet that sounded like thunder...but only the moon heard. The man glanced back at the winking lights of civilization.

And only the moon bore witness when he turned to gaze toward the mountainous wilderness.

Toward survival...and freedom.

CHAPTER ONE

THE NIGHT WAS ENDLESS . . . or was it day?

She wanted to lie back and relax. But she had to keep moving, wiggling fingers. Toes. She had to, or she would lose them.

Kevin! He lay motionless beside her, stiff with cold.

Don't lie still, Kevin! Keep your blood moving. . . .

The mists of darkness shifted. The filmy white shroud swirled and parted. Through a dreamworld, she saw herself crawling painfully to her knees, bending over a still, silent figure curled in a fetal position.

The cold was like nothing she'd ever felt before. Even the tears trickling down her numbed cheeks were like icy drops of crystal.

Don't leave me, Kevin! They'll find us . . . I know they will . . . I love you, Kevin! Oh, please don't leave me. Take me with you . . . Take me with you, please. . . .

The crystal teardrops shattered. Her heart froze. And she saw herself, curling next to her beloved as she lay down to join him in sleep eternal. . . .

RANDY PIERCE AWOKE SUDDENLY, her heart pumping with terror. Unthinkingly, she dug her fingers into her cheeks, knowing only that she needed desperately to *feel. . . .*

A moment later she slid abruptly from her bed. Her steps carried her straight to the window. Thrusting aside the lacy curtain, she stared out.

The Oregon dawn was a glorious one. The first faint fingerlings of sunlight pierced the low-hanging clouds gathered on the horizon. The sky was painted half a dozen breathtaking hues of purple and pink. But it was on the jagged outline of the craggy spire known as Mount Hope that her gaze lingered.

Mount Hope. Just thinking about it caused her to shiver. She had always found the virtuous name ironic, even before Kevin's death. All she had discovered there—all she remembered—was death.

Randy inhaled deeply, willing her heart to cease its furious drumroll. Her hands dropped away from the glass. The curtain fell back in place. It was then she realized her entire body was clammy, her forehead beaded with perspiration. Despite the chill of her bedroom, the nightshirt she wore was drenched through.

She glanced at the rumpled bedclothes. There was no point in going back to bed; she knew she would never sleep. She shed the knee-length jersey she wore and crossed to the closet for her robe. But her mind was still troubled.

She should have been surprised that the nightmare had returned, yet somehow she wasn't. After her last tragic climb, the nightmare had plagued her for months. She had dreaded closing her eyes for fear of the images seeping into her subconscious. It was only in the past year that she had given up the comfort of the night-light plugged into the socket at her bedside.

So what had spurred the unwelcome recurrence of her nemesis? The inevitable advent of winter?

Her fingers closed around the warm terry of her robe. She gripped a handful of material tightly, fighting the shadowy hold of darkness sliding over her.

But it was no use. She'd felt an elusive sense of danger last night in the midst of closing the outdoor sporting goods store she owned in town. Then later, after midnight, she'd heard the eerie wail of sirens heading out of town.

Coincidence? Randy expelled a slow, pent-up breath. She wanted to believe that's all it was, but she couldn't.

Again her gaze sought the rugged terrain dominating the skyline. Randy had once been like everyone else, totally captivated by the breathtaking panorama.

No more.

"One of these days," she said aloud, "I'm going to leave here, and I'm never coming back."

But she knew she wouldn't.

A half sad, half whimsical smile curled her lips as she turned away. She had only one employee at the store right now—Chuck Hall. The past two summers, she'd hired a young man from the area to lead hiking groups. This had been his last year, though.

Earlier in the week, Chuck had been showing three young men some of the latest ski equipment. One of them mentioned the trip they planned the next weekend. Before bad weather set in, they intended to hike up one of the most beautiful—and dangerous—peaks just outside of Bend.

She remembered thinking they were thrill-seekers—all of them. Both she and Chuck made no bones about vehemently discouraging them. "It's a difficult ascent," she had warned sternly. "Even for an experienced climber."

A slight shiver shook her. She prayed that this niggling feeling of apprehension had nothing to do with any of the three climbers.

Randy didn't wonder what made them crave the fevered excitement of such an adventure, the danger and thrill of conquest. She knew. The mountains were mystery and magic, offering an allure that inspired both excitement and fear. And this area of central Oregon was considered a winter playground, a summer vacationland, a sportsman's paradise.

Even paradise had its serpent.

ZACHARY CORBETT SWALLOWED his last antacid tablet and cursed the debilitating nausea. He was six feet two inches from the soles of his feet to the top of his blond head, and that was as close to the sky as he cared to come. He'd been that way since the day he'd had the fear of God—and heights—put into him by a woman who made Cinderella's wicked stepmother seem like a saint. Closing his eyes, Zach concentrated on drawing in deep, cleansing breaths of air.

He would have preferred to make the trip from Portland to Bend in an agency car, but the time simply couldn't be spared. Not when there was a potential killer on the loose. He'd caught the first flight out at seven that morning.

At the thought, his mouth tightened grimly. John Garrett's month-long spree of statewide bank robberies had ended several days ago. He'd finally been apprehended in Lakeview, not far from the state line. No doubt Garrett had intended to flee into either California or Nevada.

Tom Phillips and Larry Robertson had been assigned to transport Garrett from Lakeview to Portland to face federal charges. But the transport had turned out to be anything but routine.

Their departure had been delayed because of engine trouble. The pair were due in around ten o'clock that night. By eleven, Zach was battling a sickening sense of dread. There had been no contact from the two men for hours. The state police were called in to assist.

Then a call had come from the Deschutes County Sheriff's Office. Tom and Larry's vehicle had been located; it had crashed just outside of Bend. Whether the cause was accidental or otherwise, no one knew. But Phillips was dead. Robertson had been shot. And there was no sign of John Garrett.

Zach's palms were damp where he gripped the arms of the seat. When the small propjet finally touched down on the runway, every muscle in his body was rigid.

But there was no sign of weakness, physical or otherwise, when Zach crossed the tarmac and entered the terminal. His spine was straight, his posture strong and determined; he encompassed the driving spirit of a lawman from the previous century.

Gazing down the corridor, Zach spotted the drab brown of the sheriff's uniform as he came toward him.

"Zach Corbett?"

Zach nodded and extended his hand. "You must be Sheriff Parker." In the wink of an eye, Zach sized up the other man. Dan Parker was in his late fifties, with steely blue eyes and a sharp, watchful manner. He was several inches shorter than Zach, his build definitely, on the wiry side.

The two men shook hands. Parker had removed his hat, but before he replaced it, he rubbed his temples wearily. Something in the gesture told Zach this man had just been through one hell of a long night, the same kind of night he'd had.

And it wasn't over yet. This was only the beginning.

The pair left the terminal and made their way to a patrol vehicle parked at the curb. The sunny blue sky was in direct contrast to the layer of clouds he'd left behind in Portland. But the air was nippy, the wind brisk.

"What's the situation?" Zach asked once they were in the car.

Sheriff Parker started the engine. "Not much change," he said with a shake of his head. "We found Garrett's wrist and leg irons next to Robertson. Apparently he had no trouble finding his key and removing them."

"What about their weapons?"

Dan Parker grimaced. "Couldn't be located," he said briefly.

Zach swore under his breath. There was no doubt in his mind why they hadn't been found—Garrett had them.

The car sped forward. During the short drive to the brick building downtown where the sheriff's office was housed, Parker filled him in on the search for John Garrett.

There was a small silence. "What about Larry Robertson?" he asked finally. "Any word on his condition?" The question cost Zach no small amount of effort. Larry had been a close friend for years. Zach was godfather to his oldest son, Todd.

Parker hesitated. "I checked with the hospital just before I came after you. He was still in surgery."

Zach stared straight ahead, his face expressionless. "His wife is coming in sometime this morning."

"He's married?"

Zach nodded. He had been the one to tell Peggy last night that Larry had been shot. God, but it hurt to think of the disbelieving anguish on her face. His lips barely moved as he added, "They have two boys— eight and ten."

"Damn!" Parker muttered. "I hope to hell he makes it."

So do I, Zach echoed fervently.

There were no further words until after Parker led the way through the dispatch center and into a small private office. He'd no sooner dropped his hat onto the coat tree in the corner than a knock sounded at the door.

Zach heard only bits and pieces of the conversation that took place between the sheriff and a deputy.

The lines in Parker's face seemed to have deepened when he stepped back inside. "Bad news," he stated. "We just got a call from Dale McMillan, a rancher outside of town. About midnight someone broke into his house, threatened him, tied up the entire family and scared the living daylights out of all of them. One of the ranch hands found them this morning. They were all pretty shaken up." He seemed to hesitate. "McMillan was roughed up pretty bad."

The two men exchanged knowing looks. "Garrett," Zach muttered aloud.

"The description matches," Parker confirmed. "And the ranch isn't far from where he escaped."

Zach's mind was working furiously. "I'm surprised he didn't try to use them as hostages."

Parker sat down behind the desk. "He's got another motive," he murmured. "He knew exactly what he was after. Food. Warm clothing." There was a brief but significant pause. "A rifle and a couple hundred rounds of ammunition."

Zach's face tightened.

"I think," Parker added with slow deliberation, "I know where Garrett is headed."

Zach's gaze sharpened. There was something in the sheriff's manner that alerted him. "You know Garrett?"

The sheriff's smile held no mirth. "You might say John Garrett and I have had a long-standing relationship over the years." He pulled a file from the drawer next to him and tossed it onto the desktop in front of Zach. "He's the spittin' image of his daddy, and his daddy put me in the hospital for two weeks once. The old man's gone now, but every time he came down from the hills we could count on him hitting every bar in the county and tearing up at least one."

A muscle twitched in Zach's lean cheek. "And his son?" He already knew that Garrett had an arrest record a mile long, from petty theft to first-degree assault. And now with Larry, there was another. He prayed it wouldn't evolve into a murder charge.

"John was always half-wild. His father let him do as he pleased, and no one dared challenge either one of them. He's been on the wrong side of the law from the time he was ten years old." Dan leaned back in his chair, his expression grim. "He almost killed a game warden five years ago. When the judge put him behind bars, I hoped we'd seen the last of him." His tone had dropped. It was almost as if he were talking to himself.

Zach's jaw thrust out. "He's escaped from numerous county jails. It's my understanding he's been on parole less than two months. But he won't be free for long," he stated tersely. "I intend to make certain of that."

"Do you?" There was an odd light in Parker's eyes. "I'm afraid that's easier said than done." He rose and moved to the window, where he gestured out at the jagged skyline. "He's headed up into the mountains. I know it. I can feel it."

Zach stared at him. The other man sounded almost resigned. "Garrett isn't the first man who's tried to flee from custody." He thought of Peggy, her heart-broken sobbing last night, and his lips compressed into a thin line. "Wherever he is—" his voice echoed his grim determination "—I'll find him."

For the longest time Parker stared at him. Then he said softly, "I don't think you understand, son. Garrett is like a modern day mountain man."

The force of his emotions brought Zach to his feet. "So what are we supposed to do?" His fist crashed down on the desk. "He shot a federal officer—one of my closest friends, for God's sake. We can't let him get away with it.''

"I know that.'' The Sheriff's voice held a note of sharpness. ''There's a National Guard helicopter doing an aerial search right now, but you've got to realize what we're up against. The forest is unbelievably dense. You know damn well Garrett won't put himself in a position where he'll be easily spotted. And what if the weather takes a turn for the worse? It's suicidal to fly in bad weather. And if the visibility is hampered, there's about as much chance of sighting him as a jackrabbit in a snowstorm.''

"So what are you saying?'' Zach demanded. ''That we won't find him so why bother?''

Dan shot out of his chair like an arrow springing loose from a bow. ''Hell, no!'' he thundered. ''I know my job, boy, and I don't need somebody telling me how to do it!''

The younger man's back was ramrod stiff. ''That wasn't what I was trying to do.''

"Wasn't it?''

A grating silence prevailed as the two men confronted each other. Surprisingly Zach was the first to look away. He slumped back into his chair.

"All right,'' he relented, his voice very low. ''But you know I can't let Garrett walk away as if nothing happened.'' He closed his eyes and ran long-fingered hands through his hair, suppressing the urge to grind his teeth in frustration. ''It's not just my job.'' He attempted to explain his frustration. ''Larry's a friend, a damn good friend.''

Dan's expression softened slightly. He placed his hands on the desktop. ''And you have to understand," he stated very quietly, "that we have to be realistic about this. There must be hundreds of places a man like Garrett could hide out."

It was the last thing he needed to hear. Zach rose and walked toward the window. He stared sightlessly through the clear glass, his hands thrust into his pockets. "There's got to be more," he muttered. "There has to be something else that can be done."

Seeing Zach's bleak impotence, Dan experienced an odd kind of kinship. He knew what it was like to be kept waiting...and wondering.

He broke the silence with gentle insistence. "Everything that can be done *is* being done." The younger man's eyes flickered; if it wasn't for that, Dan might have thought the other man hadn't heard.

He hesitated, hoping he wasn't about to make matters worse. "The county search-and-rescue team is 150 miles north of here searching for a woman who was separated from her hiking group yesterday. But we sent out several teams this morning to search the woods and foothills."

Zach's voice was clipped. "Who?"

"Several groups of reserve deputies and Explorer scouts who've done this kind of thing before." When Zach said nothing, Dan's lips tightened slightly. "We have to be careful of volunteers in a case like this. If they're armed, there's the chance someone might panic and shoot at the first bush that rattled. Besides—" how he kept his voice from faltering, he never knew "—once you get up into the high country, the terrain is dangerous." He gestured toward the window. "Unless you know your way around, it's easy to get lost or hurt." *Or worse,* a little voice reminded him. Dan ignored the spasm of pain that shot through him.

Zach was silent for a long time. On one level, his mind was calmly detached. He understood Dan Parker's dilemma. His department was a small one; no doubt they had neither the money nor the manpower to launch a full-scale search for an indefinite length of time.

He fought back the coil of tension tightening his gut. Without looking back, he spoke. "So you think Garrett's headed up there—into the high country?"

Dan's eyes narrowed. "I do," he confirmed.

Zach turned slowly to face him. "Then it looks like I have no choice," he said softly. His gaze bored into the older man's. "I'm going after him."

In spite of himself, Dan gave a start of surprise. "Going after him!" He belatedly recognized the steely resolve in Zach's lean face. "But the teams have already left. Good God, man, you can't go alone!"

If anything, the fiercely determined light in Zach's eyes burned deeper. "I will if I have to." His voice dropped. It was almost as if he were speaking to himself. "Besides, maybe it's better this way. A group can cover more territory, but could be a liability if we got too close and Garrett realized we were onto him."

Dan Parker snorted. "*If* you get close," he pointed out. "Garrett has supplies now. Even if he didn't, people used to say his old man had dozens of different places in those mountains, where he hid flour and canned goods. He could probably hole up somewhere for the entire winter. And he knows those mountains like the back of his hand. Besides, didn't you hear what I just said? You could get lost and never find your way out. You could fall into a ravine and kill yourself. And keeping in radio contact won't do a damn bit of good if you don't know where in the hell you are!''

Zach's expression was challenging. "Then I'll need a damn good guide. The best man for the job, Sheriff.''

The best man for the job, Dan Parker echoed silently. He'd have laughed, if he weren't suddenly crying inside.

Because the best man for the job was a woman. And even if he'd approved—which he didn't—he wasn't sure there was any power on earth that would make her set foot in those mountains again.

But if anyone knew those mountains as well as Garrett, it was Randy Pierce. Maybe she would have some idea where he would go to weather the winter. She might even know of someone qualified to lead Zach Corbett after Garrett.

"Well, Sheriff?'' Zach's voice broke into his thoughts. "Do you have anybody in mind?''

Dan sent Zach a hard look. "No,'' he said shortly. He snatched his hat off the coat tree and jammed it onto his head. "But I know someone who might.''

CHAPTER TWO

RANDY WAS STILL WEARING her worn terry-cloth robe when she heard the crunch of gravel in her driveway. Peering out the kitchen window, she saw the brown-and-white patrol car roll to a halt. She wished she could have been surprised to see it. But even though she wasn't, her heart climbed to her throat and every nerve in her body grew taut with expectation.

Go away, she wanted to scream. *Go away and leave me out of whatever it is you're here for.*

She recognized Dan, of course. She's spent the first twenty-five years of her life in the house next to Dan and his wife, Marian. Dan's face was as familiar to her as her own.

It still caused a twinge of guilt when she recalled how she'd sold the big house on Elm Street. Her parents had signed it over to her when they'd moved to Arizona. But after losing Kevin, Randy had decided it was much too painful for all of them—herself, Dan and Marian—for her to continue living there.

And she knew she'd never be able to come face-to-face with Marian day after day. Since the morning they'd buried Kevin three years ago, Marian had cut her off cold. Randy loved Marian like a mother, but even when Marian had entered the hospital last winter for emergency surgery, Marian had refused to see her.

For Randy, knowing that Marian Parker still blamed her for Kevin's death was but one more bruise to an already battered heart—and the hardest cross of all to bear.

In spite of herself, she felt the unfamiliar prick of burning tears. Randy had to blink several times before she was able to focus on the man climbing onto the front porch, next to Dan. Unlike the sheriff, he wasn't dressed in a drab brown uniform. Instead he wore a sweater, slacks and a dark corduroy blazer.

Randy was at the screen door when Dan knocked. "Hello, Randy. Glad to see you're up."

"Morning, Dan." She returned the greeting, her smile as forced as his. If she hadn't suspected that something was wrong before, she certainly did now. Dan's laughing blue eyes, so much like Kevin's, were unusually somber.

She stepped back to let the pair inside, resisting the impulse to flatten her back against the wall. At five foot seven, Randy was no dainty flower about to topple over in the next breeze. But something about this tall stranger made her feel small and inconsequential.

She closed the door against the cool rush of air. Her hands moved to tighten the sash of her robe, and she realized she was garnering her defenses. It was an odd and unexpected response... or was it?

The stranger was glancing around her modestly furnished living room. There was an aura of danger that clung to the man, no hint of softness in the rugged profile he presented to her. His nose was too sharp, his chin too forceful, his lips too thin. As if that weren't enough, she experienced a sense of seething emotions held strongly in check.

She cleared her throat and glanced at Dan.

At the sound, the stranger turned to face her fully. Their eyes met for an instant. His were a strange opaque shade of grey, the color of shale. Randy registered the fleeting sensation of being weighed, stored, measured . . . and coming up lacking?

Her gaze flitted back to Dan. "Something tells me this isn't a social call," she said quietly.

"No." His agreement seemed to come reluctantly. He gestured between her and the stranger. "Randy Pierce, Zach Corbett. He's a federal marshal here from Portland."

The stranger's gaze had moved to the hallway. It lingered there a second or two, and Randy had the curious sensation he was waiting for someone else to appear.

But there was little time to dwell on the thought. Her mind was already reeling. What on earth was someone from the federal marshall's office doing here in Bend? And why on earth had Dan brought him here?

She suddenly realized the lapse in her manners. "How are you, Marshal?" she murmured. Clad in only her thick terry-cloth robe, Randy wasn't about to march across the room and offer her hand. But she didn't quite understand the faint relief that fluttered through her when he merely gave a cursory nod at her acknowledgment.

Dan dropped his hat onto the coffee table. "I think we'd all better sit down," he suggested, then glanced at Zach. "Especially you," he added, "since this will probably be your last chance for God only knows how long.''

But Zach remained where he was, and suddenly there was an ominous, almost deadly silence. His eyes slid accusingly to Dan's.

"Wait a minute," he said slowly. "You mean she's going to find someone to…" His voice trailed off, and he continued to look at the sheriff, his jaw hard.

Suddenly Randy wasn't sure she wanted to know what Federal Marshal Zach Corbett was doing here in Bend—or why Dan had brought him here. But like it or not, Randy was very much afraid she was about to find out.

She vaguely noted Dan rising to his feet. He looked as if he were about to square off for a knock-down-drag-out fight. "For your sake," she heard him say, a distinct challenge in his voice, "let's hope so."

Zach still hadn't moved. He'd appreciated Dan Parker's air of quiet authority and competence, but he had the feeling he'd just been royally duped.

He glared at the sheriff. *Next he'll be telling me she's going to lead me up there after Garrett!*

He stifled a sound of disgust. He'd already scrutinized Randy Pierce. Her hair was so dark it was only a shade lighter than black. She was slightly taller than average, and from what he could see of her body, her build was on the slender side. She wore that drab old robe as if she were a queen, but he could see the prominent bones of her shoulders beneath the worn material. Hell, she looked downright skinny! More than likely the only way she could traipse through a forest was if he carried her. She reminded him of a poor little church mouse. And with those huge dark blue eyes shining out of that narrow, high-cheekboned face, she looked about twelve years old.

It seemed as if Dan must have read his mind. "If I were in your place," he snorted, "Randy Pierce is the *only* one I'd ask to take me up into those mountains. She was on the search-and-rescue team for years. Hell, she trained almost every one of the members on the team today, including the leader!"

It was only too apparent that Zach had hit a nerve. But every time he thought about Garrett shooting Larry and leaving him for dead, his fury got the best of him. His gaze flickered to the woman. He could have sworn a look of panic flitted across her face, but his attention was reclaimed by the sound of Dan's voice.

"But," Dan added, "thank God that's not what we're here for." He glanced at Randy and paused, as if to choose his words with the utmost of care.

The tension in the air was like a knife-edge. Randy sat quietly, hands laced tightly in her lap to still their trembling. Under other circumstances, perhaps, the sight of usually unflappable Dan Parker nose to nose with this dark gold stranger might have made her smile.

But right now she was certain her face would splinter into a thousand pieces if she even tried. A tight knot of dread lay heavily in her stomach. It was an effort to make herself speak. "I think you'd better tell me what this is about," she said, looking at Dan.

Dan's expression did nothing to ease her peace of mind, however. In fact, it had quite the opposite effect. The knot in her stomach grew heavier. Harder.

"I guess that might help." His attempt at a smile met with failure. "The marshal and I have been up all night. I guess we're both a little on edge."

She sensed Dan's frustration as he thrust his fingers through his shock of steel-gray hair. And when he looked at her, she saw the one thing in his eyes she never expected to see.

Pity.

For all her outer calm, her insides were churning fiercely. "Tell me, Dan." She scarcely recognized the thin little voice as her own.

"All right," he said heavily. "You know the rash of bank robberies that's been in the news lately? The whole state's been hit from one end to the other."

Randy nodded. Her eyes never left Dan's face. "I thought the man responsible had been caught."

"He was. His name is John Garrett. The local police arrested him in Lakeview." Dan glanced at Zach. "Yesterday two U.S. marshals went there to pick him up and transport him to Portland to face federal charges. But last night something happened. We don't know if there was an accident or if Garrett overpowered the two marshals. But the car they were in crashed about twenty miles west of here. The driver was killed, and Garrett escaped." He paused before adding quietly, "He left the other marshal for dead."

She sucked in a sharp breath, her gaze traveling immediately to Zach. "And you're here after him."

The nod Zach gave was terse.

Dan sat down next to her. "Randy, I doubt if you know him, but John Garrett is from this area. He and his father, Isaac—"

Her eyes widened. "Dad mentioned him every once in a while," she murmured. "When I was just a kid, he came in once and tore up the store."

Dan glanced at Zach. "Randy's parents had a store specializing in outdoor sporting equipment," he explained. "When they moved to Arizona, she took it over."

Turning back to Randy, he reached out and gripped her hands. They were ice-cold. "Randy," he said very gently, "Garrett is still out there. We don't know where he is—if he's hiding out in the forest somewhere, or if he's headed up into the mountains."

Zach spoke, his voice low. "Garrett's already proved he's dangerous. He broke into a house last night and terrorized the family. And now he has food and weapons." His tone roughened. "The sheriff says he's skilled in wilderness survival. But he'll have to come out sometime, and when he does, there's no predicting what he'll do. He has to be found—now." His eyes met hers, cool and unreadable and opaque. "Before someone else gets hurt. Or killed."

If anything, Dan felt her hands grow colder still. He spoke quickly, before she had a chance to refuse. "Two things, Randy. You know those slopes as well as Garrett. I need you to think—think about anywhere in those mountains Garrett might be able to hide out."

Her lips parted. Dan saw the effort it took for her to speak. "And the other?"

There was a slight hesitation. "We need someone to take Corbett up into the high country," he told her. "We've got a couple of ground teams scouring the foothills, but the search-and-rescue team is up near

Mount Jefferson, searching for a lost hiker.'' Dan squeezed her hands, hoping to still the leap of fear in her eyes. ''The last few summers you had someone working for you in the store, taking groups of hikers up the trails in the mountains.''

Randy's lips barely moved. ''Hank. Hank Sullivan.''

''Sullivan! That's right! He lives in Tumalo, doesn't he?'' Dan's voice rose eagerly. ''Can you give me his—''

But Randy was shaking her head, her eyes dull. ''This was his last year working for me, Dan. He got a job with the forest service in Washington and moved last month.''

Dan's expression was pained. He didn't bother to hide his disappointment. ''Damn! Damn it all!'' He let go of her hands and slammed a fist into his palm. ''There's got to be someone else. There has to!'' He lurched to his feet and gestured impatiently at Zach. ''This damn fool says he's going, no matter what— even if he has to go alone!''

Randy's gaze flew to Dan's. ''He can't,'' she said jerkily. ''It's too risky. What if he got lost? Or what if he falls? He could lie there for days and . . .'' She gave a choked sound deep in her throat.

Zach watched the scene unfolding before him with mounting unease. He was tempted to jump in and tell them both that he didn't appreciate being talked about as if he weren't even there. But something was happening here; the atmosphere in the room was suddenly stifling. The sheriff's expression was no less tense than the woman's. He didn't understand the unspoken messages that passed between her and the older man. But whatever was going on between them, it didn't lessen the fact that Garrett was out there somewhere.

Vengeance had no part in this. But Zach was only human, and when he thought of Garrett's cold-blooded murder attempt on Larry, it was as if all the demons in hell had leaped inside him.

He wasn't even aware of the step that carried him forward. I don't see what the problem is," he stated tersely. "As long as I have a map—"

"A map!" Anger brought Randy to her feet. "Mister, we've seen your kind before. You think you're the conquering hero who doesn't need any advice and refuses to prepare for the worst. Do you know what happens to people like you? They're brought down on a stretcher—or in a body bag once the spring thaw starts! Besides, I doubt Garrett will be on any of the trails, and to do any traveling otherwise, you'll need a contour map!"

Zach's lips pressed together. He didn't dare look at Dan Parker for fear he'd be gloating.

Randy stepped forward. "Well?" Her eyes were snapping. "Do you know how to read a contour map?"

Zach's reply was almost grudging. "No," he conceded. He half expected to hear a triumphant "I knew it!" But instead he heard her say, "Weather conditions can change in minutes up there! If it snows you could be caught in a whiteout where you don't know up from down, right from left."

"Then what do you propose I do?" His jaw clenched. "If you know so much, maybe *you* should be the one taking me up there."

Zach wasn't prepared for the effect of his carelessly thrown out remark. He was so anxious and on edge about Larry and Garrett that he was only partially aware of what he'd just said. Dan Parker looked as if he'd throttle him without a second thought, but when Dan's gaze moved back to Randy, his face filled with pained resignation. Hers was completely drained of all color.

No one said a word. The silence was suffocating.

"Look," Zach injected tightly. "Garrett shot my best friend! Because of Garrett, he's lying in a hospital bed, and I still don't know if he's going to live or die. We're going to have to make some decisions here—"

It was Dan who spun him around by his shoulder and wheeled him toward the door with a strength that belied his size. "That's right," the sheriff said under his breath. He shoved the screen door open. "And I think you'd better let me handle this one, so just give Randy and I a minute alone."

Zach had a hard time biting back a blistering retort. He could feel the frustration and resentment building inside him with each minute that took Garrett farther and farther away from him. He was the first to admit his temper was never placid, but he'd always prided himself on his control. His stab of conscience told him he'd been wrong to lash out at both Randy and the sheriff.

"All right," he conceded shortly. "But make it quick. Garrett's not wasting time hightailing it away from here, and I'd better not, either."

CHAPTER THREE

"YOU SHOULD HAVE TOLD ME, Dan," Randy admonished quietly. "I had no idea Garrett had shot someone." She pulled her hands from his and moved toward the window, her eyes locked on the purple haze of the mountains.

She noted distantly that Zach Corbett had stripped off his coat and tossed it carelessly over his shoulder. The image of his chiseled features swam before her; he possessed a tough aggressiveness that some women might find attractive.

Zach Corbett was, she suspected, a hard man. As tall and rough as the mountains, and just as remote. But was he? an inner voice chided. It was concern for his friend that had prompted Zach's impatient reaction. She couldn't fault him for that, could she?

"How is he?" she asked Dan quietly.

"Who?" Dan frowned.

"His friend." Randy's eyes never wavered from Zach's figure. He stood with his hands thrust into his pockets, the wind tearing at his coat and his hair, but he paid no heed as he stared toward the ragged skyline. With his long legs braced slightly apart, his stance reminded her of loneliness and pride...and spirit. She could use a little of that spirit right now.

"Not good," Dan admitted finally. "The bullet lodged in his chest. They had no choice but to remove it right away, so he's still in surgery. The doctor wasn't sure he'd even make it through it."

Randy hugged her arms close to her body, as if to ward off a chill. There was a never-ending silence before she squeezed her eyes shut. "What should I do?" she murmured. "How can I go back up there after what happened?"

There had been a time when Randy would have thought it impossible to call herself a coward. Yet she had done so many times in the past three years.

Especially now.

She despised herself for her weakness, yet as always, her emotions won out against logic. The thought of climbing Mount Hope again—or any mountain— filled her with a pain that ran too deep to ever be forgotten. Three years ago she had lost her hopes and dreams along with the man she loved, and nothing would ever change that.

Behind her, Dan spoke quietly. "I can't tell you what to do, Randy. If it were a matter of personal choice, I wouldn't even be here. I don't like the idea of you anywhere near a man like Garrett."

She shook her head, the movement almost imperceptible. "There's probably more danger from the weather and terrain than there is from Garrett."

Dan didn't look convinced.

"I know how to use a gun, Dan. You taught me."

Dan's voice turned fierce and gruff. "I still don't like it. Dammit, if I could, I'd go up there myself and bring him back!"

Randy's heart leaped to her throat. The thought that Dan was serious didn't even bear thinking about. He'd suffered a minor heart attack about a year ago. But regardless, Dan was in no condition to take on such an attempt.

Whether that was what made up her mind, Randy wasn't sure. But she suddenly realized that if she refused, knowing what was at stake, she could never live with herself. Maybe they wouldn't find Garrett—perhaps they would. But either way, she'd have the satisfaction of knowing she had tried.

And maybe then she could stop calling herself a coward.

"The marshal was right, you know." Her half smile was whimsical. "Although I think he was surprised to hear himself say it." She paused. "But I *should* be the one to take him up there. Besides, there isn't time to find someone else."

The silence spun out for a moment. Dan came up behind her and touched her shoulder. The words he spoke were not what she expected.

"You know you're wasting away here, girl. I've often wondered why you stayed within a hundred miles of this place, why you didn't move to Arizona with your parents."

Her smile held a trace of sadness. "I've wondered the same thing about you and Marian. You could have retired at the last election."

Dan sighed, his gaze drawn toward Mount Hope. "Sometimes I doubt either one of us will ever leave here—or ever forget what happened up there." He was silent for a moment. "And sometimes I think leaving here and never looking back would be the best thing for all of us.''

When he turned to her again, she saw that the lines in his features had eased slightly. ''You know,'' he said with tender gruffness, ''that you're the daughter I never had.''

No, she thought with a pang that speared her heart. *I'm the daughter you* should *have had...and* would *have had if I'd married Kevin.*

She lifted herself on tiptoe to kiss his lined cheek. At that precise moment, they heard someone thump twice on the front door.

''Drat the man,'' Dan grumbled. ''He sure as hell didn't give us much time.''

But it was Randy who ushered Zach Corbett inside again. The moment she closed the door, she lifted her eyes and confronted him with a directness that caught Zach off guard.

''Are you sure you're up to this?'' she asked evenly. ''This won't be a stroll in the park.''

Zach cocked an eyebrow. In spite of what he'd said, had he really expected her to help him go after Garrett? The question was moot. She was the best he could hope for, and so be it.

He was secretly surprised she'd decided to take up the gauntlet. It appeared that Randy Pierce was no church mouse after all, he decided, looking her over. She wasn't smiling, but her eyes held a challenging gleam that reminded him of a mountain lion. Well, better this than passive lassitude.

He folded his arms and met her gaze head-on. ''I'm as ready as you are.''

The merest hint of a smile curved her lips. In the back of his mind, Zach wondered what the real thing would look like. She might even be pretty....

But everything else was wiped from his mind as he found himself the object of a very careful scrutiny. Her gaze lingered on his shoulders, his arms, the lean strength of his legs. There was nothing the least bit coy or sexual in her examination, and he found himself wishing there was! He was a lot better equipped to handle a subtle or not-so-subtle come-on. But Randy Pierce looked at him as if he were a bug under a microscope, and it made him just a little ill at ease...hell, he felt downright uncomfortable!

"Are you now?" she finally returned coolly. "What kind of shape are you in?"

He was a little disconcerted by the question. "Well, I...do a little jogging now and then."

"Now and then? And I suppose you pump a little iron, shoot a few baskets with the boys occasionally? A weekend athlete, Marshal?"

Zach glanced at Dan. Judging from his expression, the sheriff was finding this rather amusing. Clearly he'd find no help in that direction.

He cleared his throat. "I wouldn't quite say that."

"But you're not on any kind of regular regimen? Daily?"

He shook his head. "A couple times a week is more like it," he admitted, feeling rather sheepish and not quite knowing why.

"Well, that's better than nothing." Randy sighed. "You'll be sore, though. And don't be surprised if your muscles spasm."

By now, Zach had made up his mind that if he did get sore, he certainly wouldn't admit it. He wouldn't put it past her to gloat!

She was all business now that she'd given her consent, and he couldn't fault her for that. But he stiffened when he noted her considering look again.

"You probably didn't come prepared for something like this," she murmured.

"If you mean clothing—" Zach shook his head "—no, I didn't. At least, not if we run into snow."

He could have sworn he saw her flinch, but she spoke so quickly he decided he must have been mistaken. "That's a possibility. The weather can be very unpredictable this time of year." She glanced at Dan. "You'll have to take him down to the store. Chuck can fit him with what he needs while I get things together here."

Dan nodded. "Something else, too," he said, his voice low. "I don't like the idea of you two going out on such a wild-goose chase. What if Garrett isn't below timberline?" His eyes fixed on Randy. "Where could he go to weather the winter? Is there any place that might offer enough shelter?"

Randy felt her whole body go numb. Her mind zeroed in on the abandoned gold mine not far from the summit of Mount Hope. Few people even knew of its existence. She had stumbled on it by accident only after she'd climbed to the summit countless times.

She'd talked about it so much that Kevin finally decided he had to see for himself. And it was there where Kevin had fallen and pulled a muscle. If it hadn't been for that, they could have made it down the mountain hours earlier, before the storm blew in.

If it hadn't been for that, Kevin might still be *alive....*

But no...*no!* She wouldn't give in to the veil of darkness waiting to snatch her in its grasp. It was going to take all her strength to gather the courage to set foot in those mountains again. Strength she wasn't sure she had.

"Possibly," she said at last, reaching for the map he'd pulled out. "I'll show you."

Zach didn't miss the look she exchanged with Dan. They spread the map out on the dining room table, but just before she bent over it, some elusive emotion flickered over her face. Pain? Fear? A little of both?

He thought of her reaction when Dan told her Garrett had probably escaped to the mountains. But now, he balked at calling it a display of weakness.

He scrutinized her closely, taking advantage of her preoccupied concentration. Whatever it was that had come over her earlier had vanished, which meant she had an amazing amount of self-control. He was a little ashamed for having thought of her as a church mouse. But he also had the curious sensation that Randy Pierce was not an easy woman to get close to.

And indeed, there was a kind of stoic aloofness etched on her features. The stark daylight filtering through the window highlighted a bone structure that hinted at a hidden sensuality rather than prettiness.

Nor was she as young as he'd first thought. There were faint lines fanning out from her eyes; he placed her age at somewhere near thirty, a few years younger than he was.

He listened distractedly to the low-voiced conversation between Randy and the sheriff. Dan showed her the place where the accident had occurred and Garrett had escaped, as well as the McMillan ranch Garrett had robbed. She shifted and stretched to indicate an area farther north on the map. The movement outlined the unexpectedly tempting swell of her rounded hips . . . not such a skinny-minny, either.

"Marshal!"

With a start he realized he'd been staring. Randy had straightened, and judging from the disapproval snapping in her eyes, she was only too aware of the direction his eyes had taken.

No harm in looking, he wanted to say. Instead he summoned a faint smile.

Randy sent him an arch look. "How soon do you plan on leaving?"

Zach countered with a question of his own. "How soon can you be ready?"

There was a lot to be done. Randy's mind worked furiously. Food, sorting through gear, the meticulous job of packing . . . a flurry of panic set in. It had been so long since she'd done any of this! What if she forgot some essential item? What if her skills weren't as sharp as they had been?

Once she and Zach Corbett headed out, there was no turning back. She was responsible, not only for her own safety, but his, as well.

Responsible. The word rang in her head almost like a death knell. Kevin had trusted her; he had no doubts about placing his faith in her. But Kevin was dead. And Marian had screamed that she—Randy—was *responsible* for the death of her son. . . .

Randy couldn't help it. She longed to fling the map back at both men, to tell them to find someone else, someone who wasn't plagued by nightmares and fears of the dark.

But suddenly she remembered what Dan had said: "Dammit, if I could, I'd go up there myself and bring him back."

Could she take the chance it wasn't just idle talk? Dan was the sheriff, and there was no one else available. No doubt he would consider it his duty to assist Zach Corbett in tracking down Garrett. And if Dan did that simply because Randy was too *cowardly*, Marian would never forgive her if anything happened to him.

But who was she kidding? an inner voice mocked. Marian still hadn't forgiven her for Kevin.

Zach was waiting expectantly for her reply. Bravado was a wonderful tool, and it was this that made Randy lift her chin and inform him evenly, "I can be ready in about three hours."

"Three hours!" His voice reflected his impatience. "Dammit, if Garret left the McMillan ranch just before dawn, he already has a hell of a head start on us. That's going to put us at least six hours behind him."

"Look, I'm sorry." She cut him off sharply, but to her horror, her vision began to mist. She averted her head, her teeth digging into her lower lip as she struggled for control.

"I'm sorry," she said again when she was finally able to speak. Her low tone carried both a warning and a quiet petition for understanding. "But most of my equipment has been packed away for...a while." He didn't seem to notice her slight faltering. She forced her gaze to meet his. "I need to make sure nothing's been damaged since it was last used. I'll do it as quickly as possible.''

Zach fought his impatience. "I suppose it'll have to do," he muttered curtly.

Randy made a quick call to Chuck, advising him of the situation and asking him to be there when Dan brought Zach in. She then arranged to meet them at the sheriff's office as soon as she was ready.

Randy watched the patrol car leave a few minutes later. She shivered as if an icy mountain wind had swept into the room. But unlike the feeling that had awakened her earlier that morning, it was not the chill of remembrance, or even the chill of fear. It was the cold of foreboding, and she found her gaze drawn helplessly toward the mountains...and Mount Hope. A fugitive—a potential killer—was out there somewhere, and she and Zach Corbett were going after him. Three people...

Randy didn't believe in spirits; she didn't believe in ESP or anything remotely like it. But she couldn't shake the feeling that one of them would never come back.

CHAPTER FOUR

As THEY DROVE AWAY from the house, Dan was aware of the eyes burning into him from the other side of the car. His sigh carried a multitude of emotions, the least of which was impatience.

"Well?" he prodded, his tone gruff. "If there's something on your mind, then say it, man."

Each drew a deep breath. There was a healthy coil of some indefinable emotion fired low in his belly. "You could have told me she was a woman," he charged flatly.

Dan grinned unexpectedly, remembering the look of shock that had passed over Zach's face. "Knocked you over with a feather, eh?"

Zach was not amused. He pulled his attention away from the other man and scowled. "Let me say that again. You *should* have told me."

Dan's grin vanished. This time his look was tinged with a hint of stubbornness. "What difference does it make that she's a woman? I went to Randy for advice because she was the most qualified to give it. And you were the one who spoke up and goaded her into taking you up there."

Goaded? Zach grimaced. The word wasn't one he particularly liked; but he had to admit he had backed himself into a corner with his unwitting challenge to

Randy Pierce. He only hoped he didn't live to regret it.

"Under any other circumstances, I'd say it wouldn't make any difference at all." Zach made the admission grudgingly. "But it's bad enough to be forced to look to a civilian in a situation like this, let alone a woman. Things could get pretty hairy up there. What if she falls apart?"

A spasm of pain twisted the older man's lips. The idea of Randy Pierce falling apart was utterly laughable, and laughing was the last thing he felt like doing.

But the thought was sobering in more ways than one. Maybe that was exactly what Randy needed...not to fall apart, but to let loose some of the pain bottled up inside her. Dan hadn't seen her often these past few years, yet he had always known intuitively what she was feeling. But it was what he *didn't* see that nagged at him. Randy had always worn her every thought like stars in her eyes, there for everyone to see. But now her face was wiped of all emotion...and so hauntingly empty that Dan wanted to die of shame.

It hurt to see her like this, a mere shadow of the warm, vibrant woman she'd once been.

His heart twisted. And then there was Marian....

His knuckles tightened around the steering wheel. "Randy won't fall apart, take my word for it." His lips barely moved as he spoke. "I have the feeling you two are like a couple of sticks of dynamite, but you better watch out for her all the same."

Zach was unreasonably annoyed. The last thing he needed was to play nursemaid to someone. "I just hope she knows what the hell she's doing," he muttered.

He knew as soon as he turned his head that he'd hit a nerve. The sheriff was bristling visibly. His voice cracked like a whip. "Seems to me you ought to be counting your blessings, Marshal. Randy Pierce was a climbing instructor for more than seven years, so don't even think she isn't qualified."

Zach's features turned stony. Qualified or not, he knew Randy Pierce hadn't wanted to guide him. From somewhere deep inside, he also sensed this wasn't going to be easy for her—it might even be an ordeal. As much as he would have liked to sympathize, he couldn't.

He thought of the cold clamminess of his hands on the plane this morning. It was just like that day all those years ago when his stepmother had locked him outside on that damned balcony. He'd been terrified then, as terrified as he'd been this morning. And now—unbelievably—he was about to undertake some of the highest peaks in the area. This search would be no less an ordeal for him.

But the sheriff was right on several accounts, Zach agreed silently. He would have to watch out for his reluctant savior once they got close to Garrett—and they would, he promised himself fiercely. And he and Randy Pierce hadn't exactly hit it off well together, either. He had been edgy and impatient, and she had been understandably wary.

"Look," he began evenly, "you can tell me this is none of my business if you want, but I have the feeling there's something you're not telling me. You said she *was* a climbing instructor. She's not anymore?"

For an instant, all the wind seemed to go out of Dan Parker. "No," he admitted resignedly. "It's been over three years since Randy did any climbing."

"She hasn't climbed at all lately?" It was less a question than a demand.

Dan's reply was a long time in coming. "That's right."

Zach's jaw clamped shut. She had said it had been a while since she'd used her equipment—but three years! And she'd had the nerve to chide him about being out of shape. How he kept from hitting the ceiling, he didn't know.

"Why did she quit?"

Dan stared straight ahead. "She had her reasons."

Zach felt as if he'd been locked in a dark closet at midnight. More than ever, he was certain there was something going on that he should be aware of. "What reasons?"

There was a long, uncomfortable silence. For a moment Zach thought the sheriff would refuse to tell him.

Dan's voice was choppy when he finally spoke. "Someone she knew was involved in . . . an accident."

Zach's eyes narrowed. "And she called it quits?"

"It was a bad one," the sheriff conceded. "What made it worse is that it was someone—" Dan stumbled over the words "—someone close to her." He gestured vaguely. "She's been through a lot," he added, his voice low. "I know what you're up against, but go easy on her."

Zach was sorely tempted to press further, but the closed look on the sheriff's face warned him that any attempt would be futile.

He swore silently, the harsh words directed at himself. Why the hell was he snapping at the sheriff anyway? Maybe he was overtired. He closed his eyes and opened them, trying to clear the grittiness from his vision. Dan Parker was, he acknowledged, doing the best he could, but under the worst of circumstances.

"I'm sorry," he said quietly. "I don't mean to take this out on you." He grimaced. "It's just that it's all so—"

There was no need to go on. "I know," Dan put in quietly. He gave a halfhearted smile. "I've been in similar spots a time or two myself." He fell silent for a moment. When he resumed, his tone was very low. "But I'd appreciate it if you'd remember what I said. Randy's been through a lot, so go easy on her."

Zach was reminded of the strange undercurrent running between Randy Pierce and the sheriff. There was a kind of invisible bond between them. Yet he sensed it was one they both would have preferred to forget.

With a shrug, he turned his attention elsewhere. It was just as Dan had said. He admitted to being a little skeptical of Randy Pierce the guide, but Randy Pierce the woman was none of his business. Besides, he sure as hell didn't need any more problems. With Garrett on the loose, he had enough of his own.

FIVE MINUTES AFTER Dan had left, Randy was still standing at the kitchen window looking out the window toward Mount Hope. She felt curiously warm, except for the throbbing in her temples.

It was the headache that finally spurred her on toward the bathroom. She reached into the medicine cabinet, dumped two aspirin into her palm and downed them quickly.

She showered quickly and dressed in khaki pants and a light flannel shirt. It really was amazing, she thought, tossing her nightgown onto the bed. Two aspirin—her mother's cure-all for headache to backache—and the dull pounding in her head was nearly gone.

If only such a miracle drug existed to wipe away the ache in her heart. Oh, it was duller now. Less sharp, less piercing. She succeeded in blocking it out most of the time. But it was still there.

In that moment, all her fears returned, swamping her like a thick cloud of snow. She sank to the bed, giving in to the bleakness in her soul.

She gripped her hands together tightly in front of her chest, as if in prayer. How could she go back out there? The day Kevin died, she had sworn she would never again set foot in those mountains. She thought of all the equipment stored in her attic. Why hadn't she gotten rid of it long ago? Given it away. Better yet, *burned* it!

A flurry of panic gripped her. She couldn't go back there. She couldn't! The allure that once held her captive was no more; there was no silent, irresistible beckoning to come and conquer.

Her fingers clenched. The mountains gave life to so many of God's creatures. And they took it away....

It came to her then, in a sudden wash of reckoning. She wasn't doing this for Dan, for the memory of the man she'd loved or even for Zach Corbett.

"I'm doing this for me," she said aloud.

And that triumph, however small, gave Randy the strength she so desperately needed.

IT WAS LATE THAT MORNING when her car rolled to a halt in the small parking lot adjacent to the county offices. Randy hurriedly dropped her keys into her pocket and stepped out. It had taken longer than she'd expected to sort through her equipment and pull out everything she needed. Then she'd called Chuck at the store to give some last-minute instructions. It was Chuck who had told her Zach Corbett had left nearly an hour earlier, headed for the hospital. No doubt he'd gone there to see his friend Larry Robertson. Randy didn't know if he was back or not, but she quickened her pace nonetheless.

Sure enough, he hadn't lingered at the hospital. She spotted him almost immediately. He stood near a teletype machine, talking to one of the deputies. She approached him quietly.

Just then he glanced up and saw her. As she expected, his expression was marked by just a hint of impatience. She thought she saw his glance flicker to the clock on the wall, but he said nothing. He made one last comment to the deputy and turned his attention to her.

"Got everything together?"

Randy nodded. Unthinkingly she ran a discerning eye over his clothing—roomy pants, long-sleeved shirt, ankle-high hiking boots. Chuck had outfitted him exactly as she would have. But for just an instant, Randy was taken aback. He seemed bigger, broader than ever, his shoulders stretching the material of the shirt he wore. Even his legs seemed impossibly long.

Zach lifted an eyebrow. For the second time that morning, she was making him feel like a bug under a microscope. Her eyes made the return trip to his face. "Well?" he prompted. "What's the verdict?"

"You'll do." There was an unfamiliar dryness in her throat. The words were crisp and to the point—and all she could manage.

"Good." His businesslike tone matched hers. "Why don't you let the sheriff know you're here? I need to make a quick call to my office in Portland and then we can leave."

Randy nodded and started to move toward Dan's office. Before she could raise a hand to knock, the door opened. "Randy! You're here." His greeting was a good deal warmer than Zach Corbett's had been.

Randy let him pull her inside and close the door. "You're sure you're up to this?" He peered at her intently.

His eyes were filled with both warmth and an odd resignation. A bittersweet regret filled her chest as she absorbed his look. Not for the first time, she acknowledged how grateful she was that Dan had not turned her away as Marian had.

"I'll be fine," she told him softly, summoning a smile. Outwardly she was calm, but inside she was a seething whirlwind of emotions. But she couldn't let Dan know. Not dear, sweet Dan, who had clung to his unswerving faith in her in spite of everything.

You can't fail him, she told herself fiercely. *You can't.*

Dan studied her face a moment longer. Then, apparently satisfied with what he saw, he dropped her hands and moved back around his desk.

He held up a small portable radio. "We want to stay in radio contact with you as much as possible, so we're sending you up with a pair of these. One for the marshal, one for you. And some spare batteries, too." He pushed both across the desk toward her. "Marshal Corbett will show you how it works."

Randy made a mental note to store the batteries in the waterproof compartment of her backpack. "Has there been any further word on Garrett?"

The worn leather chair behind the desk creaked as Dan sat down. "I made a few calls to some old-timers after we left your place. A couple of men said they heard Garrett and his father used to spend a lot of time up on one of the peaks just west of here. The trouble is, nobody seems to know which one."

Randy slid her hands into the front pockets of her pants. "That's a lot of territory to cover," she remarked quietly. She thought of Zach Corbett. He wasn't a seasoned climber or hiker, and she wasn't in top condition, either. It could be a tough, grueling trip for both of them.

Dan sighed. "I only hope you two aren't going on a wild-goose chase. But at least with the radio we'll be able to keep in contact with you and keep you posted." He passed her a mug shot across the desk. "This is Garrett."

A prickle ran down Randy's spine as she stared at the bewhiskered man in the picture. With his shaggy hair and beard, John Garrett looked ruthless and dangerous.

Dan's eyes avoided hers as she handed it back. "I don't have to tell you to be careful out there, do I?" he asked.

Randy smiled slightly, but it was a smile that was tinged with poignancy.

When he rose, Randy knew it was time to leave. Dan skirted the desk and would have passed by her, but she stopped him with a hand on his forearm.

She looked into his eyes. "You know I couldn't love you any more if Kevin and I *had* gotten married."

Dan's throat grew tight. First he had gone all sloppy and sentimental at Randy's place. Now it appeared it was her turn.

"I know." He pressed his lips gently to her forehead. "But it's good to hear you say it. But—" he wagged a finger at her and Randy knew he was trying to lighten the air "—this isn't goodbye, you know."

Wasn't it? Randy suppressed a shiver, recalling her premonition that once again, the mountains would soon lay claim to another human life.

His tone turned dry. "If Zach Corbett has anything to say about it, you two will be back before the dust even settles around here—and you won't be alone. In fact, I *hope* that's what happens." A faint frown creased his forehead. "One more thing, Randy. Zach Corbett wants Garrett and he wants him bad. I just hope he doesn't get reckless and put both of you in danger."

Reckless? It wasn't quite the word Randy would have used to describe Zach Corbett. Dangerous, perhaps. And there was no doubt that he was driven by raw emotion in his quest for Garrett. But she also sensed that beneath his predatory guise of the moment lurked a cool, calculating man who wouldn't risk any mistakes. She murmured as much to Dan.

He quirked an eyebrow. "All I can say is this. Heaven help anyone who gets in his way. Zach Corbett isn't the type to mince words." He paused. "But you and I both know that with what the two of you are about to do, the quickest way isn't always the best."

True enough, Randy acknowledged silently. In fact, what appeared to be the quickest route was often the most hazardous. Nor was she surprised to learn that Zach Corbett didn't hesitate to speak his mind. Well, that was fine with her—but if they happened to cross swords, she fully intended to return the favor.

Dan started to reach for the doorknob, then abruptly turned back to her. "Just be careful, girl," he warned.

"I will," she promised. She injected a lightness she was far from feeling into her tone. "You just make sure we get all the latest weather reports."

"Done." He clicked his heels and saluted smartly.

Randy smiled, but shook her head ruefully and her eyes were somber.

Suddenly there was a knock on the door. Randy was the closest, and she reached for it instinctively.

"Dan?" A woman's voice came through the opening door. "Your secretary said she thought you were alone—"

There wasn't time to move. There wasn't time to think or issue a warning of any kind.

Suddenly Randy found herself face-to-face with Marian Parker.

CHAPTER FIVE

THE ENSUING SILENCE was terrible. Randy stood numbly, rooted to the floor. She couldn't move. She couldn't even breathe.

Looking at Marian was like seeing a mirror image of herself. Randy knew the same shock that registered on Marian's face was reflected on her own. But unlike her, Marian's expression underwent a lightning transformation that changed her initial surprise into something else entirely.

The door clicked shut, closing out the sounds of the outer office...and closing the three of them inside. Suddenly it was as if the air had been charged with a deadly current of electricity.

Marian stared at her unblinkingly.

Randy wanted to wither up and die.

The older woman's eyes swiveled almost accusingly to Dan. "What," she demanded of her husband, "is she doing here?" Her voice was very low. The lack of any emotion whatsoever was conspicuous.

Randy felt Marian's angry gaze all through her. She stifled the almost-hysterical impulse to laugh. Anger? Marian wasn't angry with her. She hated her! She hated her for killing her son!

And Randy knew that if Marian hadn't forgiven her by now, she never would.

Dan stepped between them. Randy's heart went out to him, knowing how trapped and helpless he must be feeling. "She's here to see me," he said quietly. "She's helping us look for the man that escaped last night." He laid a hand on his wife's arm, silently pleading with her. Marian shook his hand off.

"A case?" The question was clipped. "What kind of case?"

With a minimum of words, Dan explained about Garrett.

Marian whirled on Randy. "I thought you weren't doing that kind of thing anymore. I heard you've been hiding away in that store of yours."

Dan's lids closed wearily. *Hiding away?* he echoed silently. *If she is, she's not the only one.*

Randy tried to still her inner trembling. Why was this happening? she agonized. She'd blocked out much of what had happened that horrible week three years ago and rarely allowed herself to think of it—and Kevin. But because of this wild-goose chase for Garrett, it was all coming back with a vengeance.

She couldn't handle an out-and-out confrontation with Marian, not now. Since Kevin's death, encounters between them had been rare, but they *had* run into each other. Oddly enough, Randy would have preferred that Marian ignore her—pretend she saw right through her—as she had those other times.

With a strength she hadn't known she possessed, Randy looked straight into Marian's brown eyes. "It's something that has to be done, Marian. I want to help Dan—"

"Dan? Because you think you owe him? Well, think again, young lady. Nothing will make up for what you did . . . nothing!"

The words were starkly—horribly—familiar. Jagged bursts of phrases crowded in her brain, drowning out all else. *You took him up there . . . Kevin, my only son . . . he had no business being up on that mountain and you took him . . . as far as I'm concerned, you killed him with your own hands. . . .*

Countless times before, Randy had asked herself the question that once again sprang into her mind. What would Marian have her do? An eye for an eye? A life for a life? This time, as before, she had no answer.

Dan stepped closer toward his wife. "Marian," he began sharply.

Randy shook her head and silently stopped him. "Why are you doing this?" she asked very quietly. "Do you think you're the only one who misses Kevin? The only one who loved him? Do you think I didn't love him, too? That losing him didn't hurt me just as much as it hurt you?"

Marian's lips pressed together. "I was his mother! He was my son!"

Randy refused to back down under her furious glare. She thanked God for the saving anger that flowed into her, washing away the hurt. Because if it hadn't, she was desperately afraid she'd have fallen apart.

"And I would have been his wife, so don't tell me I didn't love him, Marian." The words were low and controlled. "Of all the people in the world, *you* should understand how I felt. I grew up knowing Kevin as well as I know myself." Hard as she tried to prevent it, the pain in her heart brought agony to her voice. "When Kevin died, he took a part of me with him."

"And you think that's not how I felt?" Marian's cry was straight from the heart.

Dan stood as if paralyzed. He had the strangest urge to shout in frustration as their angry voices drifted through his mind. It was like watching some sick sort of competition, where one player was determined to outdo the other. Who loved Kevin the most . . . Who *grieved* for him more? This was a contest in which he had no desire to find out the winner.

It wasn't until Marian stepped toward Randy, fists clenched, her expression outraged, that Dan was galvanized into action.

He grabbed his wife's hand and stepped next to her. "That's enough!" he cried hoarsely. "Both of you just . . . just don't say any more!"

His warning gaze traveled from one woman to the other. They both looked as if they'd been frozen, eyes locked on each other in some grisly kind of combat. The atmosphere was stifling. No one said a word.

There was a rap on the door. As if in relief, three pair of eyes swung toward the sound.

Zach Corbett stepped into the room. "Everything's all set," he announced. He glanced at Randy. "Are you ready?"

Randy drew a deep, cleansing breath and nodded, all the while praying that no one would see the glitter of tears in her eyes.

Dan saw Zach's gaze flicker curiously toward Marian. Dan quickly introduced his wife; Marian extended her hand, but her greeting was anything but standard.

"So you're the one she's taking up there." Marian left no doubt in anyone's mind who "she" was. "Well, good luck, mister. You're going to need it." She sent a last, withering look at Randy and left the office.

If Zach noticed anything amiss, he said nothing. The trio quickly took care of the last-minute preparations, and then they were heading out the door. Dan had arranged for a deputy to accompany them to the drop-off point in Randy's car. Neither he nor Zach was prepared to take the chance that Garrett might see them leave a police vehicle, no matter how unlikely the possibility. Once there, the deputy would return with her car.

Zach drew the sheriff aside for a moment. "Can you do something for me?"

Dan nodded.

"Will you check on Larry and keep me posted?"

Dan's expression softened. "Sure. I've already arranged for someone to pick his wife up at the airport."

"Thanks." Zach was grateful, but the moment was an awkward one. He shifted uncomfortably. "Sheriff—" there was a slight hesitation "—about this morning..."

Dan waved aside his apology. "It's forgotten," he said briefly. "I know the strain you're under. I just hope to hell you two find Garrett and get him behind bars where he belongs."

Zach's eyes glinted. "That," he stated in a voice of unrelenting intention, "is exactly what I intend to do."

And looking at Zach Corbett, Dan didn't doubt it in the least. He looked very strong, very sure of himself. But looking at Randy...well, that was another story.

THE RIDE OUT OF TOWN and toward the mountains seemed to take forever. The three occupants of the car were silent, each submerged in a separate world. Zach's thoughts drifted to the woman next to him. Randy Pierce was a good driver, he noted absently. He had no qualms about being a passenger with her, though the road soon twisted and turned, climbing and bouncing over the hills like a game of leapfrog.

He studied her profile wordlessly. She'd pulled her hair into a long braid that hung down her back. Her expression was impassive; she appeared intent on her driving. Still, he couldn't help but think she seemed strangely subdued, almost...beaten.

Beaten. It was an odd word to come to mind, Zach decided, yet it was the only one that was fitting.

He sensed her tension. She'd been tense ever since they'd left the sheriff...no. No, that wasn't right. She had been tense *in* the sheriff's office, when he'd interrupted them.

He turned this over in his mind. The ease with which she spoke to Dan Parker hinted at a long relationship. Yet with Dan's wife on the scene, that wasn't the case at all. Come to think of it, hadn't they *all* seemed a little edgy? And then there was Marian Parker's cryptic parting remark.

He was still puzzling over it when the car rolled to a halt. Zach lifted his eyes.

"End of the line," Randy said lightly. She opened the door and hopped out. The deputy followed.

Zach glanced around. She turned off onto a gravel road some time back, and he saw that it literally *was* the end of the road. Just beyond the gravel, the jumble of green forest began, stretching out and before him as far as the eye could see.

His gaze flickered to the craggy mountain peaks that loomed above. Another time, another place, and he might have taken a moment to gratefully fill his lungs with the heady fragrance of pungent evergreen and clean fresh air.

"This is as far as we can go?" He couldn't mask his disappointment.

To Randy's ears, however, it sounded very much like ill-concealed annoyance. She skirted the front fender and walked toward the trunk. "The road doesn't go any higher than this. And this is where Dan's expecting us to return three days from now," she stated quietly.

Zach frowned. He'd wanted to make it at least five, but Dan had insisted on three. Randy had remained quiet throughout the discussion, but once again, he'd had the feeling that she and the sheriff were communicating on some unspoken level.

"Three days," he murmured, then voiced his thoughts aloud. "Unless we get close to Garrett."

Randy plunged the key into the trunk's lock more forcefully than necessary. "If I were you, Marshal, I'd remember that nature makes the rules around here."

The bite in her tone was thinly disguised. Zach decided to ignore it. "You might as well call me Zach," he murmured. "There's no need to be so formal out here."

When Randy said nothing, he wondered idly if he'd said something that rubbed her the wrong way. He watched as the lid to the trunk popped open. There were two large framed backpacks neatly stowed inside. A sleeping bag was tied to the bottom of each. She hauled out the closest and handed it to him, then turned back to rummage through a zippered pouch. Zach caught a glimpse of a compass and a flash of what was probably a knife. She bent and slid the entire pouch into another zippered compartment.

Zach had already begun the process of shrugging into his backpack. His eyes widened as its weight settled on his shoulders. It must have weighed at least fifty pounds! Not only that, but he was taken aback by its bulk. It reached all the way down to his hips; he felt stiff as a board with it strapped to his back.

"How far are we from the place where the car crashed?" he asked.

"Give me a few minutes and I'll show you," he heard her mutter beneath the lid of the trunk.

Randy straightened and slammed the lid closed. He eyed her covertly. She was tall, but even so, she didn't look as if she could handle her backpack! He opened his mouth, prepared to be gallant and lend her a hand, but she pulled the pack up and on before he could say a word.

The deputy had gone around to the driver's seat. Zach watched Randy wave as he drove off.

He found himself pricked by a tiny feeling of guilt. Could it be that he had underestimated her? In spite of Dan's assurance, there was a part of him that inwardly scoffed at her abilities. Zach's tiny deprecating smile was directed at himself. He chalked it up to a little male chauvinism he was humble enough to admit to. And as the sheriff had continually reminded him, he really had no other choice but to rely on Randy.

He followed her as she headed into the woods. They'd been walking for about five minutes when Zach recalled that she hadn't answered his question about the site of the accident. He was just about to remind her, when they came to a small ridge. The hillside below was riddled with burned-out tree stumps, affording a view of the land they'd left behind.

Randy stopped and turned around. "You can see the general area where the crash happened from here," she said, nodding her head to the right.

Zach shielded his eyes against the glare of the sun. Some distance away, the road climbed gently from the flatland and coiled up the sloping terrain. "I'm not sure where you mean."

The step she took brought her next to him. Her shoulder brushed his as she leaned very close to point. "Pretend there's a straight line out from my fingertip. See where the road disappears around the bluff?"

He squinted slightly. "Yes . . . yes, now I see it."

"That's where it happened. You can't see it from here, but there's a hill on the other side."

The noonday sun glinted off the gold of the gently rolling landscape. Combined with the incredible blue of the clear skies overhead, it looked like a pastoral scene straight out of a travel magazine. For a fraction of a second, Zach's stomach churned sickeningly, but he didn't blame his fear of heights. They weren't high enough yet, and there was solid ground beneath his feet. He'd just spotted the treacherous embankment next to the roadway. It was only too easy to visualize a car tumbling down that incline, end over end.

A burning resentment licked through his veins. He wasn't aware of his fingers clenching. Why Tom Phillips? he despaired silently. Why had his life been taken, and not Garrett's?

Randy's voice brought him back to the present. She'd dropped her hand, but they still stood shoulder to shoulder. "You see that house and barn, the one between the bluff and the edge of the forest?" He gave a slight nod, and she quietly added. "That's the McMillan ranch."

Zach's eyes narrowed. "The one Garrett broke into?"

This time it was Randy who nodded wordlessly.

Zach rubbed his chin. "And it's between here and the place the crash occurred," he murmured. "It makes sense to think that maybe he skipped to the mountains."

Randy gazed sightlessly ahead. "But he also could have veered to the north or south when he got into the woods."

"True enough," he admitted. "But I'll let the ground teams take care of that possibility." He hitched the backpack a little higher on his shoulders. "You think he could have come this way?"

Randy hesitated. "Possibly. If he's headed into high country, this is the easiest way to get there."

Damn! Zach made a sound of impatience. Garrett wouldn't go where he thought they might be looking for him.

"But it's not the quickest way, and this trail isn't used much this time of year. And it's out of sight of the road."

Now that was more like it. Ever since he'd received word that Garrett had escaped, there had been one frustration after another. But for the first time that day, Zach felt they stood a real chance of making some progress. It filled him with a primitive sense of excitement, like the fever of battle pumping through his veins.

The woman at his side might have vanished into thin air. His every thought, every fiber of his body, was consumed by just one thing. Finding Garrett.

"You'd better be looking over your shoulder," he muttered aloud, "'cause I'm right behind you."

Randy watched Zach scan the distant horizon. She shivered, in spite of the warmth of the noonday sun. His expression was hard as a rock, just like his voice. She, too, had but one thought. Zach Corbett looked like a man possessed.

DAN APPROACHED THE PORCH steps slowly. Lord, but he was bushed. There had been no sleep for him last night. His body was just too old and weary to adapt to that kind of stress, the way it once had. He paused for a moment, blinking to clear the grittiness from his vision.

His eyes lifted. This old house that had been his home for over thirty years. His gaze traveled over the wide porch, the slatted pink shutters framing the windows. He waited for the familiar feeling of pride and welcome to sweep through him as it had so often in the past.

It didn't come. With a pang, Dan realized he couldn't even remember the last time he'd felt that way. Instead, he experienced only a yawning bleakness.

He loved this house, but he acknowledged that it was too big for just the two of them, him and Marian. They used to talk of finding a smaller place once Kevin was grown and off by himself; they had stayed because of Kevin and Randy.

It hurt to think of how he and Marian had looked forward to their son's marriage. Both of them wanted nothing more than to hear once more the pitter-patter of little footsteps running down the halls, and laughing squeals of children—Kevin's children—bouncing off the walls.

But there would be no laughter. There would be no grandchildren. And now the house was as stark and barren as a deserted old shack in the middle of nowhere.

But Marian would never leave this house—because Kevin had lived here. Dan knew better than to even suggest it. To this day, Marian kept Kevin's room exactly as he had left it. Though Marian didn't seem to realize it, all they had left now was each other.

Dan blew out a long weary sigh and trudged up the steps. His mind veered to his wife and her visit this morning. Under any other circumstance he'd have been delighted to see Marian. It seemed she got out so rarely these days. But the timing couldn't have been worse.

It made him rather unsure about his welcome. Unsure? He snorted inwardly. *Dreaded* was more like it.

He found her in the kitchen, hunched over the stove. He stood in the doorway for a few seconds, studying her wordlessly. Her short cap of dark hair was peppered with gray. She was thinner than she'd been a year ago. His heart twisted. And the lines bracketing her mouth...had they always been so deep?

Marian glanced up just then and saw him. Her lips pursed together. Why, she looked as if she were pouting! The thought made him want to laugh. Did fifty-five-year-old women pout?

"Hello to you, too," he murmured. He tried to kiss her but she pulled away. He closed his eyes. My God, he despaired silently, will it never end?

When he opened them, Marian was noisily pulling plates and cups from the cupboard. Dan sat down at the table, his expression tolerant but pained.

"All right, Marian." He sighed. "Let's just get this over with, shall we?"

Marian didn't pretend to misunderstand. "You've seen her before, haven't you?"

Dan paused. He suspected he would be damned no matter how he responded. "Yes," he admitted, his tone even. "I have seen Randy from time to time."

Marian thumped a pan on the stove. She still hadn't faced him fully. "You know what I think of her, Dan Parker!"

The words hung in the air. Dan was silent for a very long time. When he finally spoke, his voice was low and very deliberate. "I do." There was a significant pause. "I also know you used to think the world of her."

His wife whirled around. "That was before she killed my boy!"

"Marian—" his voice sounded as if he had the weight of the world on his shoulders "—we've been over this before. Randy was not responsible for Kevin's death. She had no way of knowing that Kevin would fall. They'd have been clear of the storm if it weren't for that. It was an accident, Marian, a tragic accident."

But as always, there was no reasoning with Marian—not when it came to Randy. Dan had tried often enough. He'd finally realized how useless it was. Marian blamed Randy for taking Kevin up on Mount Hope, and she would until her dying day.

Marian's thin shoulders trembled with outrage. She clutched a thick wooden spoon as if it were a weapon. "Why are you on her side?" she cried. "How can you betray Kevin? He was your son, too, Dan!"

Dan couldn't even summon the strength to feel angry or indignant. He and Marian had once been so close, he thought helplessly. How had they drifted so far apart? He felt as if the gulf between them had stretched into an ocean.

Marian's gaze seemed to burn into him, and he shook his head in mute despair. But he flinched when Marian threw the spoon down and ran from the kitchen. Pounding footsteps echoed hollowly through the house as she ran up the stairs. Dan wanted to clap his hands to his ears to shut out the sound. But the footsteps abruptly stopped in the room directly over his head. Kevin's room.

"No," he whispered finally. "I haven't forgotten."

And Marian couldn't forget. That was the whole problem, he thought listlessly. Neither she nor Randy could forget how—or perhaps more importantly *why*—Kevin had died.

Much as he'd loved his only son, Dan was well aware he wasn't the one who'd been hardest hit. That, he decided grimly, was a toss-up between Randy and Marian. The pain of losing Kevin had been building in both women ever since Kevin died, like steam in a kettle, bubbling and blistering. Pain like that needed an outlet, *any* kind of outlet. But what would happen when the pressure burst?

He wasn't sure he wanted to know. God help him, but he didn't.

Dan rose to pour a cup of coffee. He sat back down at the table, but made no move to drink his coffee. Instead he stared into the cup, seeing only the distorted images of Randy and Marian swimming in the muddy-colored liquid.

Why did they stand so proud and aloof? He racked his brain for an answer, but as always, he found none. Both women could have had him, someone to cling to, someone to share the burden. All of them could have had each other.

A sad smile curled his lips. They didn't know it, but Randy and Marian were so much alike.

And so very alone.

CHAPTER SIX

H OW FAR IS IT before we start gaining any altitude?''

They'd been weaving steadily through cool, shady stands of fir, cedar and hemlock. Zach tried to disguise his impatience as he called out to Randy, walking on ahead of him.

Apparently his attempt wasn't very successful. She stopped and looked back at him. A tiny smile of amused indulgence curved her lips. It was the first time he'd seen her smile.

The realization surprised him. It also annoyed him, and his irritation with himself increased when he discovered he liked the way she looked when she smiled. Sweeter, and softer. On second thought, though, maybe he shouldn't have been so surprised. His only distraction the past hour had been when he'd noticed the smooth, fluid ease with which she walked.

"It's about five miles from where we started to the base of the mountains." She tipped her head to the side and added softly, "Another hour and we'll be out of the flats."

Zach nodded, but by the end of another hour, he wished he hadn't asked. Every time he caught sight of the craggy peaks looming above the treetops, a stab of apprehension shot through him. He'd feel a hell of a lot better about going after Garrett if he didn't have this damn fear of heights.

He also wished he felt as comfortable as Randy looked carrying that heavy pack. Just as she'd promised, the terrain had begun a gentle ascent. He kept apace with her, but it wasn't easy. It was his damn pack, he decided disgustedly. If he could chuck it and move unencumbered and unrestricted, he'd have no problem at all. So why was it that the pack presented no hindrance at all to his female companion? She moved so naturally that the backpack seemed merely an extension of her body.

She chose that moment to stop and glance back at him. "How are you doing?"

Zach gave her back look for innocent look. "Fine," he lied.

Her gaze traveled over him with the same microscopic intensity she'd given him that morning—and it induced the same blistering reaction from Zach.

She made a slight adjustment on the padded strap going over her shoulder. "I can slow down if you want. Or maybe we should stop for a few minutes for something to eat—"

"I'll never catch up with Garrett if we do!" The words came out more sharply than he intended. Randy stared back at him, wide-eyed and unblinking, but for just an instant, the expression in her eyes reminded him of a wounded animal, hurt and defenseless.

Zach didn't like knowing he'd put that look on her face. He wasn't proud of his behavior. He and Randy Pierce seemed destined to strike sparks off each other, and he didn't understand it. He sensed that she was dangerous somehow. It was only in the past year that he'd finally stopped feeling guilty over his divorce from Suzanne. And now here was Randy Pierce threatening his newfound peace of mind.

He wanted to apologize. He *knew* he should apologize. The words just wouldn't come.

But it was his turn to stare when Randy slid the pack off her back and dropped it to the ground. She ripped open one of the zippered compartments and yanked out a candy bar. Straightening, she leveled a blazing glare at him.

"I suppose you don't want one of these, either!" she snapped.

Zach shook his head wordlessly. He was too stunned by the display to do anything else.

"Fine," she muttered. She heaved the pack onto her shoulders again. With nary a look or a word to him, she whirled and stalked forward again.

Zach was surprised to find the makings of a rueful grin catching at the corners of his mouth. Amazingly his ire had vanished and he felt oddly cheered. No, he thought again, feeling unaccountably pleased. Randy Pierce was definitely no church mouse.

RANDY BIT OFF THE END of the sweet, smooth chocolate and chewed furiously. She hoped Zach Corbett was starving by the time they made camp tonight. He had to be the most stubborn and uncivil man that she'd ever had the misfortune to meet.

In her anger, she set off at a grueling pace. She wasn't about to let Zach Corbett accuse her of being the stone in his path when it came to his quest for Garrett.

How much time had elapsed, Randy was never certain. At a bend in the trail, an unobtrusive glance behind her revealed the strain she'd subjected him to. A fine sheen of perspiration dotted his forehead and upper lip. The air was cool, the temperature only in the mid-fifties, but he'd unbuttoned his flannel shirt and tugged it loose from his pants. Randy's stomach gave a peculiar lurch; she was glad he was wearing a knit undershirt.

It was then that Randy realized his legs must surely feel like pillars of lead. Hers did, and though she hadn't done any climbing, she still jogged nearly every day. Old habits were hard to break.

She shortened her stride a little, hoping Zach wouldn't notice—or if he did, that he wouldn't say anything. Instinct told her he was a man who'd been given no shortage of the substance known as male pride, and she really didn't care to test just how much or how little he really possessed.

Randy's feet conveyed the change in the rocky trail before her consciousness noted it. She noticed they had come to a small flat meadow. In the summer, the sun-bleached grasses were dotted with patches of Indian paintbrush and blue lupine. Now the fall rains had mellowed the color to a rich green. She wasn't sure what drew her gaze back to the trailhead, but what she saw there made her pull up short.

Zach plowed right into her, causing her to lose her balance. Tired and hungry, he bit back his exasperation and reached out a hand to steady her. It was then that he noticed the questioning expression on her face. His gaze followed the direction of hers.

There was a large boulder several yards ahead of them. The grass around it lay trampled and askance. But there, in a patch of soft bare earth, was the unmistakable imprint of a lug-soled boot.

Zach's eyes narrowed. Randy saw his gaze travel fleetingly to the soles of her hiking boots before returning to the footprint. It was long and wide, the indentation sinking into the earth nearly an inch.

"How big," she asked quietly, "is Garrett?"

"He's a moose," Zach said bluntly. "Six feet. Over two hundred pounds. And—" he bent down to study the footprint more closely "—there was a pair of boots stolen from the ranch he broke into."

Randy could sense his mounting excitement. At the realization the print might belong to Garrett, an eerie tingle ran up her spine.

"This is a recent print," Zach murmured. His voice turned low and urgent. "You're positive this trail isn't used all that much?"

Randy nodded. "The trail leading in from the southeast is touted by the forest service, so it's the one most hikers and climbers take."

Zach stood. He still looked tired, but the determined gleam was back in his eyes again. "I figured if Garrett left the McMillan ranch just before dawn this morning, that would have put him a good six or seven hours ahead of us. But I'd say this print isn't more than a few hours old. We may not be as far behind him as I thought."

"That's true," she said slowly. "But we're going to have to find a place to camp for the night soon."

"How soon?" He couldn't keep the edge from his voice.

She glanced at the sun, sinking lower into the sky with every minute. "An hour. Maybe a little more. Besides—" she hesitated "—we can't go much farther anyway. There's a ridge up ahead that's too rocky and windy to make a good campsite."

His lips compressed into a thin line.

"We can't travel at night," she reminded him. "And I don't think even Garrett would be foolish enough to try it."

She fully expected an argument, but at her words, she detected a slight relaxation in the muscles around his mouth. He nodded, and they set off once again.

They found one more set of footprints, but they didn't linger for long. Once Zach was convinced the print matched the other, they moved ahead.

When they came upon a small level clearing bordered by a thick stand of fir trees on one side, a narrow gurgling stream on the other, Randy glanced around. "I think we should stop here," she announced. "This is a good place to spend the night."

Their eyes met. She could read the conflict she knew was roiling away inside him, but again, he said nothing.

She wasted no time setting up camp. Darkness was fast approaching, and it would be easier if they'd eaten before it was fully dark. Zach helped her clear the rocks and twigs from a small square of ground. Sinking down where she'd dropped her backpack, she searched for the lightweight tent inside.

She began unfolding the small tight square of material. "Would you mind gathering some of the dead wood and other small branches around so we can have a fire?"

There was a flat silence.

Randy brushed distractedly at a stray hair before glancing up. Zach was gazing down at her.

"No," he said finally. "No fire."

She blinked. "But it'll be dark soon—"

He cut her off abruptly. "I won't take the chance that Garrett will see it and know we're after him." Only his expression softened the blunt words; it was an odd mixture of regret and determination.

Zach took a deep breath, wondering a little at her reaction. She had scrambled to her feet. She was staring at him, her eyes wide and filled with dismay. "I know it may make it harder when it comes to meals," he began.

"No." Her voice was faint. "I brought a small camp stove."

"Then it really won't be a problem, will it?" His tone was quiet but firm. Was it his imagination, or had she turned pale? And why the hell did he feel as if he'd suddenly been cast in the role of villain?

Randy turned away, determined he wouldn't discover the stricken look she was certain she wore. "No," she murmured, more to herself than to him. "I guess it won't."

She deliberately blanked her mind and set to work again. The tent had been pitched, a canned stew warming on the tiny burner before she became aware of just how quickly the old routine had come back to her. But the abrupt realization was tinged with bitterness. All this had once been second nature to her. Her father had taken her with him on weekend trips like this from the time she was three years old.

She was uncomfortably aware of Zach prowling around the site like a restless soldier waiting for the inevitable battle cry. His shadow fell over her. She glanced up through the screen of her lashes and saw him walk to the edge of the clearing. His manner was preoccupied; he studied the ground intently.

He must have sensed her eyes upon him, because he turned and started toward her. "It's too bad there's no snow on the ground," he said with a frown. "If Garrett had been through here, his tracks would be easy to spot."

Her indrawn breath ended in a hiss. Just the thought of snow was enough to set her heart pounding furiously.

"Snow would only complicate things, not make it easier." Randy was scarcely aware of speaking until she heard the words pour forth. "So don't say that. Don't even think it!"

Her vehement response startled him. Randy could see it as his eyes locked on her, his frown deepening. She could almost hear the questions running through his mind, and she felt foolish—very foolish indeed.

She confined her attention to what she'd been doing before—dishing up the stew. For a moment there was only the strident sound of metal scraping metal. She didn't look at him as she handed him a fully laden steaming plate.

It didn't help matters that he was obviously ravenous. Randy found she had no appetite at all, though she ate to keep her strength up. Her mind was fraught with worry. All afternoon she'd managed to keep thoughts of Kevin at bay—her disagreeable companion had seen to that! But now that the night loomed before her, thoughts of Kevin returned with a vengeance.

The dinner she'd just consumed sat like a cold hard lump in her stomach. She tipped her head back and tried in vain to will away the shrouded visions of the past. But as if she'd been commanded from afar, her gaze was drawn helplessly to the west...to Mount Hope.

Like a lonely sentinel it loomed, a huge black beast. Shadowy. Majestic. Mysterious.

It was this, she acknowledged with heartsick dread, that lay behind her decision to never climb again. The fear of old memories...and remembered heartache. She had been so afraid this might happen! It was why she had never returned, why she had never even let herself think of coming back to these mountains. Yet here she was...in the shadow of Mount Hope.

Beside her, Zach stirred. Against her will, her wayward mind homed in on his presence, clinging and refusing to let go. Kevin's image wavered in her mind's eyes, only to be replaced by another.

Zach Corbett was very different from Kevin—broad where Kevin had been slender; as blond as Kevin had been dark; harsh and unyielding where Kevin was the gentlest, most sensitive man she had ever known.

She found it ironic that *she* was the supposed expert here. This morning, she had unwittingly compared Zach Corbett to the same mountains that now surrounded him. Her eyes ran over his profile, stark and strong. He looked totally content, completely at home in what she knew to be an alien setting. Yet it was almost as if he belonged there.

But he didn't belong here, a niggling voice reminded her. And as it did, she was doused with a very cold wave of reality.

Her stomach muscles tightened. What if something happened? Garrett never even entered her mind; it was as if he posed no danger at all. What if there was an accident? If Zach Corbett was hurt—if *she* was! Could he find his way out again...alive? She damned him silently for his casual mention of snow. What if a storm blew in! Would he, too, look to her for help? For salvation? For his life?

But at the moment, it seemed that all he required of her was something to drink. With a start she realized it was the second time he'd posed the question to her.

Randy set aside her plate and reached for her pack. Quick as a wink, she produced several tea bags and bouillon cubes.

Zach was left feeling a little deprived, though not because of the choices she offered. Watching her slender but surprisingly well curved derriere upended for those few seconds provided the best view he'd had all day.

"I'm afraid I didn't bring any coffee." Her tone was apologetic.

He shrugged. "That's all right." The truth was, nothing would have tasted better right now than a nice hot cup of coffee.

"But there's powdered juice mix if you'd rather have something cold. And hot chocolate."

"Powdered, too, I'll bet."

There was a wry undertone in his voice that made Randy's eyes bounce up to his. He reached for one of the tiny packets of bouillon, and she was startled to find a flare of humor in his eyes. She was even more startled at the tiny quiver that shot the entire length of her arm when their fingertips brushed.

He crouched forward to fill one of the two mugs from the small pot of water on the stove. He handed one to her, then filled the other. Randy found herself captivated by the taut symmetrical lines of his back and shoulders. Her attention was diverted when he resumed his place against the rough bark of the fir tree Randy had claimed. Their shoulders were separated by only an inch or two. He'd buttoned his shirt and tucked it back in, but the sleeves of his shirt and undershirt were now rolled up past his elbows. Her heartbeat quickened. His forearms were strong, but not heavy, layered with a dense coating of silky-looking golden-brown hair.

Zach settled back against the tree trunk and crossed his arms over his chest. After the hectic pressures of the day, it felt good to stretch out his legs and watch the stars come out, one by one. Hard ground and all, he was looking forward to a good night's sleep.

He nodded at her backpack. "I really hadn't given much thought to eating out here. What else do you have in there?"

Randy had been feeling just a little flustered, but the current of tension that had marked the day appeared to have vanished. She found herself responding in kind.

"If you're thinking of breakfast, you'll probably be disappointed. I'm afraid it's going to be cold cereal."

His reaction was predictable. "Wonderful." He was clearly less than enthusiastic. "I don't mind cold cereal, but cereal without milk is another story."

Randy hid a smile. "But there is milk."

"There is?" His tone reflected his surprise. "Won't it spoil with nothing to keep it cold?"

"Nope." Her voice was ripe with satisfaction—and not without a hint of laughter, as well.

Something of her smugness must have shown, because he eyed her suspiciously. In the midst of raising his mug to his lips, he suddenly brought it down to his legs. "Don't tell me," he said slowly. "The milk is powdered, too?"

She nodded.

"In that case, I'll take everything I can get right now. Can I have that candy bar I turned down earlier?"

He was, she discovered, trying as hard as she was not to smile. But he was also serious. The little-boy plaintiveness in his voice attested to that.

Even if she'd wanted, she couldn't have refused. She moved to pull a chocolate bar from a small pouch on the outside of her pack.

Zach practically pounced on it.

"Now if I really wanted to give you a hard time about this," she teased, "I'd tell you to raid the cache of snacks in your own pack."

The wrapper was already stripped off and a third of the bar gone. His eyes widened as he hastily swallowed a mouthful of chocolate. His expression was so precious that Randy decided she'd gotten her revenge for the hard times he'd given her today. But when he spoke, his words weren't at all what she expected.

"This is yours?"

Randy hesitated. He seemed to be enjoying the chocolate so much she hated to spoil it for him. "Yes," she said finally.

"Then the least I can do is share it with you." He broke off a sizable chunk and handed it to her.

Randy chuckled. "We'll both probably regret this tomorrow," she murmured, taking a small bite. "Sweets provide quick energy on the trail."

"So that's what the snacks are for? A little pick-me-up?"

"Yes. And you don't have to stop to eat them."

"Well," he murmured, popping the last chunk into his mouth. His eyes gleamed as they caught hers. "It's nice to know there's more in my pack."

Randy laughed and conceded this round to him after all.

Darkness had long since spread its veil over the wilderness. More than ever Randy longed for the cheeriness of a fire. She could see the hazy outline of Zach's profile, but just barely. She'd included a lantern in their supplies, but she was strangely reluctant to risk shattering their newfound peace.

"You've known Dan Parker a long time, haven't you?"

Where the question came from, Zach wasn't really sure. One minute he was admiring the star-studded sky, marveling over their number and brilliance. The next he found his attention cornered by the woman beside him. The question slipped out before he was even aware of it, but he glanced at Randy curiously and waited.

Randy felt his eyes on her and wet her lips. It was an innocent enough question, yet she felt something inside holding her back. Talking about Dan meant thinking of Kevin.

"Yes," she said finally. "While I was growing up, Dan and his wife were our neighbors." Her voice grew halting. "Dan is...was...like a second father to me."

Zach studied her quietly. He wished he could see her better. "But you've lost touch lately?"

Did she only imagine the underlying gentleness in his tone? Perhaps, if she got to know him, she might even like Zach Corbett.

But in the darkness, Randy's smile was bittersweet. Losing touch. That was one way of putting it.

"Yes."

"And his wife?"

"Marian?" She sound startled.

"Yes. Marian."

The name hung in the air between them. Zach didn't have to see Randy to know that her head had whipped around. He felt her stare like a tiny needle going into his skin.

"What about her?"

Randy's voice was carefully neutral. Zach suddenly wondered if he'd overstepped his bounds. He sensed her wariness keenly, just as he sensed she was trying to hide it. He also felt compelled to make some kind of explanation for his curiosity, however lame it might be.

"I'm not sure," he said after a moment. "I only saw her those few minutes in the sheriff's office. I hadn't thought about it at all before that, but she wasn't what I expected. She seemed so much different than Dan. I don't know...harder somehow."

Harder. He'd hit the nail on the head exactly. It was an effort to keep her voice even, but Randy found herself defending Marian. "She's had some hard times lately. And people change. We can't control what happens to us. And we can't always control our responses when something does happen."

Instinct told Zach there was more—a lot more. She'd said Dan Parker was like a second father to her, but what about Marian? She'd said nothing of her relationship with Marian. In fact, she'd aroused more questions than she'd answered. No, there was no love lost between Randy and Marian Parker—that he was certain of.

He also admitted his first impression of the woman hadn't been a good one. When he'd stepped inside Dan's office earlier, the atmosphere was crackling, like a bomb about to explode. No, he hadn't liked Marian Parker at all.

And he knew why, too. She reminded him of his stepmother. Tough. Hard. Aggressive.

The lull that followed was the first uncomfortable moment tonight. Zach was just as aware of it as Randy, and perhaps it was this reminder that made him think of Larry.

"Do you have a flashlight? We should probably radio the sheriff's office and let them know our position."

Randy was only too willing to turn her attention elsewhere. The conversation had taken a disturbing turn; when Zach had asked about Marian, she hadn't meant to wax philosophical.

She found the flashlight and the small hand-held radio. She listened quietly while Zach made contact.

She gave him the logistics of their position when he asked; he relayed them quickly. His next words were about his friend.

"How's Larry Robertson?"

Randy decided it was a good time to give him a little privacy. She slipped inside the tent and laid out their sleeping bags. By the time she finished, Zach was through with the radio and had replaced it in the backpack.

"How is your friend?" she asked softly.

At the sound of her voice, he spun around to face her.

"He'd just come out of surgery when I saw him this morning." The voice that reached her ears was pitched very low. "The doctor said then his condition was pretty touch and go." His hands slid into the back pockets of his khakis. He glanced away and out into the night. "That hasn't changed."

Something caught in Randy's chest, something that made her hurt as she knew he was hurting. She wanted to go to him, to wrap her arms around him and chase away his pain. But there was something stoic and proud in the way he held his shoulders, staring out into the night-shrouded darkness. She suspected he wouldn't welcome her comfort.

"And Garrett? Has there been any news?" She almost hated herself for asking.

He turned back to her, but his expression was hidden by the darkness. There was no trace of emotion in his voice as he told her, "None. None of the search teams have found a trace of him."

She thought of the footprints they'd discovered. "Then maybe we're on the right track after all."

Zach said nothing, but it was a silence that communicated his helpless disappointment over his friend, his frustration over Garrett. Randy was glad she'd made him smile earlier, if only for a moment.

"I think I'll turn in now," Zach said. "How about you?"

Randy's heart leaped. She dreaded the moment she had to crawl into the tent—and it didn't have a thing to do with spending the night in such close quarters with this man or any other man.

"I think I'll stay up a while."

Zach nodded and came closer. Her eyes came up when he stopped before her. She found herself holding her breath, sensing he wanted to say something.

"Good night, Randy," he said finally and disappeared through the opening in the tent.

Randy stared after him, her lips parted. Her name on his lips startled her. It rushed through her mind that she liked the way he said it, all soft and husky.

She dropped back against the tree and curled her arms around her legs, disgusted with herself for being so fanciful. Drat the man anyway! she thought crossly. Her reactions to him were confusing enough without him compounding the issue. First he'd been suspicious of her, and that hadn't earned him any points in her book. Then, for a time tonight, the brief glimpse of humor he allowed her completely disarmed her. She recalled the tingle of sensation she'd felt when their hands had brushed, and she was appalled at the conclusion that entered her mind. Surely she wasn't attracted to him!

It was even stranger that it was somehow comforting to know she wouldn't be alone tonight. And it was that which gave Randy the courage to step inside the tent. She carefully closed the flap and secured it.

Her eyes hadn't had time yet to adjust to the darkness. She got down on all fours and felt her way tentatively. Zach had taken the sleeping bag closest to the far wall. He appeared to be asleep, his breathing deep and even. One arm was thrown out behind his head.

She sat down and unlaced her boots, pulled off her socks and set them aside. Her shirt and jeans came next, leaving her clad in a fleecy pair of long johns. Moving very quietly, she slipped inside the sleeping bag and pulled it to her chin, willing her tense muscles to relax.

She released a slow, pent-up breath, wishing she could forget she was smack dab in the middle of the wilderness, the place she'd vowed she'd never return to.

But she had survived her first day back. She'd had a few bad moments, but it wasn't as awful as she expected. Still, the night was yet to come. She shivered and prayed that sleep would come quickly.

She prayed for naught.

It wasn't from lack of comfort, since there was a pad beneath her sleeping bag. Her body also staunchly remembered the hundreds of other nights she'd slept on the trail. But her mind stubbornly refused the balm of sleep. She could have relaxed if it wasn't for the tumult of the day.

Or so she told herself.

She lay on her back, staring at the point where the steep pitch of the tent joined sides...or where it should have been.

It was pitch-black inside the little tent. Outside, the mountains were deathly quiet. Even the wind had ceased its restless path across the earth.

She wanted to move, to rise and throw back the flap and let in a precious sliver of moonlight, no matter how fleeting. When she'd fastened it, she told herself she was closing the darkness out. But she'd succeeded only in closing the night demons in.

She fancied she could see the trees in the encampment crowding in, coming closer. Her eyes strained frantically through the inky shadows, searching for something—anything! But the walls were closing in, the ceiling coming closer, the inky darkness thick and heavy and threatening to smother her.... Fear was clawing inside her, the fear she'd thought she'd conquered. In some distant corner of her mind, she knew her imagination was simply working overtime.

She nearly jumped out of her skin when Zach rolled over. Damn him, she thought furiously. Damn him anyway! How can he sleep so peacefully while I...

Her breathing came fast, then slow, then fast again. She struggled against the cloying sensation of being smothered. And now her fingertips, obsessively clutching the sleeping bag to her chin, were growing cold....

A tiny moan broke from her throat. *I can't do this,* she thought in panic. *I can't! I've got to get out where I can breathe...!*

CHAPTER SEVEN

ZACH WOKE SUDDENLY, as if someone had flipped on a light switch. His eyelids snapped open. It was blacker than sin inside the little tent. But he was instantly alert, instantly wary, eyes and ears straining for whatever it was that had snatched him from slumber.

Something reached his ears—the sound of jagged panting, like someone running a marathon. Then all hell seemed to break loose.

He knew Randy lay next to him. He felt rather than saw her violent movement as she lunged from her sleeping bag.

It was instinct, pure and simple, that made his arms shoot out. He caught her by the ankle, cursing roundly when he heard her come down heavily.

He bolted upright. "What the hell are you—"

He got no further. "Let me go!" she yelled. "Damn you, let me go!"

She shot up again, wrenching herself over and yanking her ankle from his grasp. She started to lurch up, but Zach was there again. This time he succeeded in wrapping his arms around her. The force of his body sent them both crashing to the ground, knocking the wind from her lungs and wringing a grunt from Zach.

He didn't know how long she'd be still this time, so he took unfair advantage and yanked her over on her side. Using his arms and legs, he pinned her against him. "Are you crazy?" he grated out. "What the hell are you doing?"

Randy was half sobbing, almost hysterical, fighting the binding arms around her and fighting for air to fill her tortured lungs.

"It's so dark," she choked hoarsely. "So dark . . . I can't breathe in here!" She latched onto his shirt with both hands. Whether it was to push him away or plead with him was beyond her comprehension. She knew only that she was terrified.

Zach swore softly. Still holding her with one arm, he fumbled for the flashlight he'd placed at the head of his sleeping bag and switched it on.

He didn't know what he'd been expecting, but it wasn't what he saw. Her eyes were wild and filled with terror, as if she had just glimpsed all the horrors of hell. He was too stunned to do anything but stare at her in shocked silence.

She closed her eyes. "Please," she whispered.

A dozen different emotions rushed at him from all sides, and each was tinged with contradiction. He was bewildered and puzzled, at a total loss to explain her hysteria. He was also madder than hell that she'd awakened him from the blessed oblivion of sleep he so desperately needed.

But the sound of that pathetic little voice cut into him like a knife blade. He let her go.

Stony faced, Zach watched her scramble to her feet. She half dragged, half shoved her sleeping gear through the little opening and outside.

He jerked on his pants, grabbed the flashlight and followed her outside, muttering under his breath.

The moon emerged from behind a cloud. In the silvery half-light, he saw that she was busy arranging the sleeping bag on the ground, near the spot where they had eaten. Her movements were quick and jerky; he sensed the nervous tension that still plagued her. He wanted to reach out a hand to touch her, to soothe her. But right now he was probably the last person she'd want comfort from.

He knew she was aware of his presence, but she simply ignored him, straightening here, smoothing a fold there.

When she finally turned to him, his gaze fastened on her like a hawk. "Mind telling me what that was all about?"

Randy swallowed dryly. For all its softness, the demand in his voice was implicit, the look in his eyes implacable.

She lowered her eyes and laced her hands together tightly in front of her to still their trembling. "We couldn't have a fire." The words were half hurt, half accusing.

Zach bit off an impatient exclamation. "I told you why. I don't want to alert Garrett to our presence. If I can catch him, the best way to do it is with him off guard and not expecting anything."

Randy bit her lip, aware she was acting like a child. No doubt to him her fear was unreasoning, but to her it was as real as all her past nightmares.

She drew a long, shaky breath. "I know." Her voice was a mere thread of sound. "But you don't understand—"

"You're right," he said shortly. "I don't. So why don't you just tell me what the problem is?" He was more frustrated than angry. Why did everything come out all wrong around this woman?

Randy's fingers strained against each other. She still felt ridiculously near tears. Oh, God, why did this man affect her like this?

"I'm sorry. I didn't mean to wake you up, I swear. I was just trying to get *out*!" Once started, she couldn't seem to stop. "It was so dark in there, and so *close*...I—I felt like I was being swallowed up...." Whatever else she said, she had no idea. She knew only that when she'd finished, Zach was staring at her as if he couldn't believe his ears.

"That's all?" He sound incredulous. "You're afraid of the dark?"

"I..." She floundered helplessly. She felt awkward and exposed. Shamed. If only she could be angry! "Yes," she said miserably.

There was a weighty pause. "Something left over from childhood?"

Randy stiffened. "No." Her tone was as short as his had been moments ago. His question was just the impetus she needed to summon her pride. She was fine now and determined to show him so.

She turned her back on him and prepared to slide into her bed. A hand on her arm stopped her.

"You might as well wait for me." He sent her a pointed look before he stalked back into the tent. He reappeared a second later with his arms heaped full of his own sleeping gear.

Her chin lifted. "What," she asked coolly, "are you doing?"

"Damned if I know," he grumbled. The sleeping bag dropped in an untidy mound at her feet.

"There's no reason for you to put yourself out. I didn't ask you to stay out here with me."

Zach glanced up at the star-filled sky. It promised to be a long night. He was still tired and definitely not looking forward to sleeping out in the cold, unsheltered night air.

"Don't I know it," he muttered. He dropped to his knees and yanked at the zipper on his bag. "It'll be warmer if we zip these together."

Her lips tightened. "Didn't you hear me? I said you don't need to stay out here with me. In fact, I don't want you to. Besides, it would hardly be the first time I've spent the night out in the open!"

She sounded so pious, so righteously indignant that Zach felt a laugh coming on. But he suspected he was on her hit list already. He didn't dare give in to temptation.

He deliberately ignored her protest. Her pride was talking now, which was all right with him. He was secretly glad she'd gotten some of her starch back. He also suspected that his pity was the last thing she wanted—or needed.

But Zach couldn't deny that seeing her as he had, her eyes glazed with some unknown terror, had shaken him considerably. Something inside stabbed at him as he thought of it. Childhood fear or otherwise, he had no right to chide her about it, not when he was petrified of heights and therefore just as guilty.

At the memory, his stepmother's face swam before him. When his father had died, he'd spent too many long, lonely years by himself, yearning for just a touch—a hand on his—any sign of human warmth or compassion from the woman who was all the family he had left. Granted, this situation with Randy was different. But he wouldn't willingly let her suffer alone, even if it meant sacrificing some of his own comfort.

He glanced up at her. "Want to give me a hand? I'm getting cold out here."

Randy shivered. So was she, but she wouldn't admit it. It didn't occur to her until then what a ridiculous picture she must look to him, standing outside in the dead of night in long underwear and stockinged feet.

She adjusted the flashlight and ducked back into the tent. She came out a few seconds later with something tucked under her arm. "Here," she said crossly. "Wear this then." She repositioned the flashlight again and dropped down across from him.

Zach pulled on the woolen cap she'd tossed his way. He was glad the darkness hid his smile. She wouldn't like it if she thought he was gloating.

She zipped the bags together much more quickly and with far more dexterity than he'd displayed. The next thing he knew she'd dropped a thermal blanket in front of him.

She was busy tucking her hair beneath a cap identical to his. "You can wrap this around you if you need it. Or you can put it over you, but you'll be warmer if you do it under the sleeping bag."

She waited for him to unroll the blanket and lay it inside. When they slid within the folds of the sleeping bag, Zach held out a corner of the blanket, a silent indication for her to cover herself, as well.

Randy hesitated, then shook her head. She wasn't cold, not yet anyway. Zach raised his eyebrows but said nothing. He merely reached out to switch off the flashlight.

Randy clenched her jaw, every nerve in her body humming as she waited for the thick gloom of the night to swallow her up once again. But the feeling never came.

She relaxed her muscles, one by one. She turned her head and saw the shadowed hump that was Zach. He'd rolled over onto his side so that he faced her. She knew intuitively that his eyes were closed.

Her own began to droop. Why she suddenly felt so comforted, she had no idea. Maybe because he was so close, close enough that she had only to stretch out her fingertips to touch him.

On that thought, she slept.

THE EARTH AND SKY SPUN crazily when Zach opened his eyes the next morning. His mind befuddled with sleep, he couldn't place the anemic, tepid sunshine. Nor could he figure out why his backside was cold, while the front of him was blasting with a furnacelike heat.

He came awake instantly when he discovered the reason. He and Randy were curled up together like a pair of spoons. His chest was sealed to her back like jam to bread. The sweetly curved derriere that he'd taken so much pleasure in eyeing yesterday was cuddled against a part of him that shouted loud and clear that—church mouse or no—she'd managed to kindle an unexpected but very potent male response in him.

His mouth quirked. It was no wonder he'd sought her warmth. His head was bare, and sometime during the night she had commandeered his blanket! His arm was curled perilously near the lower swell of her breast, clearly outlined beneath the soft shirt she wore.

He sucked in a harsh breath, unable to still the leap his heart took. Unless he was mistaken—which he very much doubted—she wasn't wearing anything underneath it.

He tried to ignore the tight knot of awareness in the pit of his stomach. Randy was the last woman on earth he'd thought would stir his blood. She was too tall and slender. Too stoic and distant and strong. He liked a woman who looked like a woman—liquid eyes and warm, inviting lips. A woman who was full, soft and lush.

His mind balked at the obvious—that he was simply desperate for a woman—any woman. He'd had no lasting relationships since he'd divorced Suzanne four years ago. He was used to periods of celibacy.

Randy stirred against his body, instinctively nestling toward the heat of his body. It was an almost painful reminder that she wasn't as hard as she appeared. Last night had shown him that.

He ground his teeth, angry at his lack of control. He had no time for feelings like this. No time for anything but finding Garrett.

On that note, Zach eased away from her. He'd been tempted to linger a little longer, and now he knew why. He slid from the sleeping bag, every major muscle in his body screaming a protest as he stood up. His legs felt as though someone had tied them in knots. Even his shoulders were stiff and sore. Never again would he take for granted the soothing benefits of a long hot shower. His choice of a quick wash in a frigid mountain stream was as good as no choice at all.

He remained where he was for a moment, curiously reluctant to leave Randy alone. His gaze lingered. She looked like a child, lying there huddled under the covers. Her cap had come off and her braid was loosened. Dark, silky tendrils of hair clung to her temples and cheeks. She wore no makeup, and her skin looked fresh and soft and immensely touchable. Zach had to fight the urge to bend over and brush the hair from her cheek; to discover for himself if it was as soft as it looked.

Damn! He sounded like some moonstruck adolescent youth! Annoyed with himself, he clenched his jaw.

"Randy." He bent over and shook her shoulder.

She released a long bubbly sigh. She slowly opened her eyes and stared straight up into his face. She looked just as surprised to see him as he'd been to find himself glued to her back this morning. Zach was not amused. Her unguarded reaction made her seem far too innocent and vulnerable for his peace of mind. He was already well on the road to discovering she was a woman of contradictions, and he didn't need any more unwelcome reminders.

What he needed was to get underway. The sun was well into the eastern sky. They'd never find Garrett at this rate.

His voice was low and gritty. "It's getting late. We need to leave." He watched her bound to her feet. The ease of her lithe movements grated. Clearly she hadn't suffered the same ill effects of yesterday's hike that he had.

He spun away with a scowl. "I'm going to go down to the stream and wash up."

Hands on her hips, Randy tossed her braid over her shoulder and stared after him. "Well, good morning to you, too!" she muttered. It was apparent the night's sleep hadn't improved his disposition any. She winced inwardly. Would a night of good, solid, *uninterrupted* sleep have made any difference? She turned and kicked at a stray pebble. She doubted it.

He was right though. They did need to get moving. She washed with one of the premoistened towelettes she'd brought, then hurriedly brushed and rebraided her hair, secretly glad she was alone. After her shameful weakness last night, she wasn't yet ready to face Zach. Although, she told herself wryly, she needn't have worried about being uncomfortable or embarrassed at the prospect of facing him this morning. He'd succeeded only in pricking her irritation!

By the time he returned, their breakfast was ready. Within fifteen minutes their gear was packed. Randy had just buckled the strap from her pack around her waist when she felt a hand on her arm.

"Yes?" Her voice was calm and matter-of-fact, as cool as he had been this morning.

His eyes roamed her face intently, as if looking for something hidden and elusive. She grew uncomfortable beneath his searching regard, and his reasons were suddenly all too clear.

Hot betraying color rushed into her cheeks. She had to force herself to meet his gaze. "If you're worried about a repeat of last night's performance," she stated curtly, "don't. It won't happen again, I promise."

Zach's lips thinned as she marched off, her back as stiff as a soldier's. He'd been about to apologize for his shortness this morning, but why bother? She'd probably fling it back in his face.

He had no choice but to follow her. The silence they maintained was anything but comfortable.

There was no trace of any more footsteps. Since they were off the trail, the terrain was rocky and uneven, sometimes tricky to negotiate. Next to her, Zach lost his footing several times, but he didn't ask her to slow down. He simply plodded along next to her, his expression one of dogged determination. It was just like a man to suffer in silence! Randy shook her head. Zach Corbett was as stubborn as he was annoying!

She called a halt after nearly two hours. The sky was far less brilliant than yesterday. But the cloud cover appeared to be diminishing. The clouds looked high and far away, not very thick.

She stripped off her backpack and dropped it to the ground near a towering boulder. "Whew." She let out a breath and flexed her weary shoulders. "Are your legs as tired as mine?"

Zach glanced at her sharply. Was she making a dig at him? He detected no trace of mockery in her expression, though. He eased his pack to the ground beside hers and shrugged. "When I woke up I thought I'd be in pain all the way up to my eyebrows. But once we were up and moving, I was okay." He rubbed his hand across his forehead. "I'm more winded than anything," he admitted.

"Don't feel bad," Randy said lightly. "I am, too. It's been a while since I've done this."

It was the wrong thing to say. She knew it the minute she caught his expression. He said nothing, but she could almost see the doubts creeping into his mind, one by one. She couldn't help but be a little resentful. She'd had this reaction before. Mountaineering was a man's sport. It was rare to find a woman involved in it, and that automatically made her abilities suspect.

Randy didn't want to start another argument, though. No doubt she'd say something she'd regret. Her best bet was simply to ignore him.

She stopped and pulled a map from her pack, pinpointing their position. There was an abandoned logging camp on the flank of the next mountain that could make a good hideout. But there was also a cave on the opposite side. Her brow furrowed. The route to the cave was narrow and treacherous. Would Zach be able to handle it? Plus that area right around the cave was prone to rock slides. It was even possible the entrance to the cave had been blocked.

A sense of hopelessness swept through her. Searching for caves that might or might not be there... searching for a man who might be miles away... It was like trying to find an ant in a maze.

Zach dug out the binoculars and scanned the vast panorama that spread before him. The forest seemed to stretch all the way to the Pacific. They hadn't gained much altitude, twisting and turning, but they were high enough that he could see for miles. An involuntary shiver ran through him. As far as the eye could see, there was no trail, no road, no evidence of man at all.

His gaze returned to Randy. She was still studying the map, oblivious to his presence. She frowned deeply once, and a niggling suspicion edged its way along his spine. She chose that moment to glance up at him. Though she quickly tried to cover it, he read the doubt in her eyes.

"What? What is it?" His tone was urgent. The uncertain look on her features scared him.

Randy sighed. "I'm not sure which route we should take," she began. "I—"

But she got no further. Zach had already drawn his own conclusion.

"What!" He seized her shoulder and swore hotly. "You better not be saying that we're lost!" His hands fell away as suddenly as he'd grabbed her. "Damn! Why couldn't Dan Parker send me up here with somebody who knew what the hell he was doing!"

Randy sucked in a sharp breath. Knowing he thought it was one thing, but hearing him say it was another. It hurt—more than it should have, even more so because it came from this man. But with that feeling came another, and in her anger she struck out.

Her eyes sparked like a lighted fuse. One furious step forward brought her so close to him their boots touched. She flipped the map in the air and jammed a finger into his chest.

"I don't have to listen to this," she said fiercely. "I don't owe you anything, Zach Corbett. I'm doing this for Dan, not you! Now if you don't think I'm qualified, you're welcome to go your own way. But I wasn't kidding when I said they'd bring you out in a body bag if you tried this on your own! My guess is you'd never make it back to where we started! Furthermore—"

She never got the chance to finish. From out of nowhere, an ear-shattering explosion rent the air.

The blast of gunfire.

CHAPTER EIGHT

ANOTHER BLAST FOLLOWED.

For an instant Randy thought she'd been hit. Her body slammed sideways, and she hurtled through the air, landing on her back with a dull thud, her breath ripped from her lungs. Her head hit the ground and a kaleidoscope of lights danced before her eyes.

It took a moment to realize that the heavy bulk of the body weighing her down belonged to Zach. Her heart lurched. He was so still!

"Zach!" she cried frantically. She lifted her head, afraid he'd been hit. "Are you—"

The words were crammed down her throat as he clamped a hand over her mouth. "Shh!" he hissed in her ear.

When Zach saw that she meant to be quiet, he removed his hand, but his fingers tangled in her hair kept her head on the ground. He placed his lips next to her hair. "You're not hurt, are you?"

She gave a tiny shake of her head, her eyes huge. He could feel her heart thudding wildly against his own. He knew she had to be frightened out of her wits, if not from the gunshot, then from his instinctive reaction. Her skin was pale, but he knew she wasn't going to fall apart. Another time, perhaps, and he might have admired the inner calm he sensed in her.

Even if she'd wanted to, Randy couldn't have said another word. She was sandwiched so tightly between the base of the boulder and Zach's body that she could hardly breathe. His expression was harsh, blindly intent as he scanned the area. It frightened her to acknowledge the thought running through both their minds. Had they stumbled upon Garrett? Was he the one who had fired the shot?

Above her, Zach's body lifted in a half crouch. Her eyes widened when he pulled a deadly looking revolver from his waist. Stunned, she watched him lunge forward and around the huge boulder, out of her sight. There were the unmistakable sounds of a scuffle, a muffled grunt and a groan. Scarcely aware of what she was doing, Randy dug in her pocket for her pocketknife and flipped out the blade. It flashed through her mind that she wasn't about to sit back and make herself an easy target. And if Zach was in trouble, she wasn't about to lie back helplessly, either!

She charged around the boulder only to stop short at what she saw. Zach had just reholstered his revolver. He stepped over and extended a hand to a dazed-looking man struggling to his feet.

"Geez, I was sure it was time to meet my Maker! I thought you were a bear coming at me!"

Randy remained where she was, several yards away from the scene. She saw now that the other man was a hunter. He wore a red cap, a plaid jacket and an orange down vest.

"I'm really sorry." Zach bent and handed him his rifle. "But your shots were close and I thought you were shooting at us."

The man pointed down toward a gully. "I spotted a buck down there." He shook his head. "First one I've seen in four days. And wouldn't you know it, the damn thing got away! My buddy and I planned to stay a week, but at this rate we might as well head home now!"

"That might not be a bad idea," Zach said slowly. "There's a felon on the loose somewhere up in these mountains. He escaped from custody almost two days ago."

The man whistled. "Dangerous?"

"He's already shot one man."

"And you're looking for him?"

Zach's gaze briefly met Randy's. "Yes." A frown furrowed his brow. "You said you've been here four days?"

The man nodded.

"Have you seen anyone else up here the past day or two?"

The hunter nudged the bill of his cap. "As a matter of fact, I did see someone yesterday afternoon," he said earnestly. "My buddy and I didn't think anything of it at the time—thought it was just another hunter, but we knew it wasn't one of us because we've both stayed south of here. He was alone, too, I'm sure of it."

"What did he look like?" Zach's voice sharpened. "Big? Red haired with a beard?"

"I really couldn't say. He was too far away. I saw him through my binoculars, and he was walking the opposite direction."

Randy stepped forward. "Where was this?"

He gestured to the relatively flat area between the two peaks just ahead. "Up there near the saddle." He paused, then added, "There's an old logging camp up there. Shouldn't be more than a day's hike from here."

"I know." Randy smiled at the man. "Thank you. You've been a big help."

"Yes, you have." Zach's voice was low and deep. "I appreciate it, though I'm sorry about being so rough on you."

The man slung the rifle over his back and shrugged. "An understandable mistake. You don't need to worry though. As soon as I get back to camp, I'm heading home. I'd rather go home without my buck than run into the fella you're after." He tipped his hat and was gone.

Randy's eyes followed the stranger. "The tracks we found yesterday were probably his," she said.

Zach sighed. "I know. I took a good look at his boots." He rubbed his chin thoughtfully. "That logging camp he mentioned. Think Garrett could have decided to hole up there?"

She pivoted. "Why, Marshal," she drawled, her voice dripping with sarcasm. "Are you actually soliciting my opinion?"

His gaze slid away. It did her a world of good to think that he was embarrassed. He could use a taste of humble pie.

She planted her feet firmly apart and faced him squarely. "In fact," she added tightly, "before we heard those shots, I was about to tell you we can go one of two ways. To the logging camp, or to a cave on the opposite side. From here, it's about the same distance to either place. The cave is a much harder climb.''

Zach flinched, but he didn't back down before the silent accusation in her eyes. He'd done her a great disservice by doubting her. He didn't realize just how much until that moment.

"I'm sorry," he said quietly. "I shouldn't have said what I did. The truth is—" he hesitated "—I wouldn't have come at all if I'd thought you weren't capable."

Randy's anger had faded, but not the hurt, and that confused her. It shouldn't have mattered what Zach thought of her, but it did.

In spite of what he'd just said, she recalled that he'd been ready to charge out and pursue Garrett entirely on his own. It frightened her to think what lengths he would go to to find Garrett. But looking at Zach now, she was surprised to find a glint of humor in his eyes.

"Should we call a truce?" he asked lightly. His gaze lowered, lingering at the pocketknife she clutched in her right hand. "I sincerely hope you don't think you need that to convince me further."

Randy glanced down, stunned to find she was still holding the knife. She quickly folded the blade. "When you ran around the boulder and I heard you scuffling with that hunter, I thought it was Garrett. And I—I couldn't think of anything else to use," she explained. Her half smile was sheepish. "But I guess it wouldn't be much good against a man with a gun."

The light in Zach's eyes faded. His expression turned unexpectedly sober. "Don't be so sure. A gun isn't much good at all if you're charged by someone with a knife, even from as far away as twenty feet."

He read her disbelief, but his smile held no mirth. "Believe it, Randy. It's true."

His words were chilling. It seemed obscene to think of her knife as dangerous—as a weapon. To those who braved the wilderness, a knife was a friend, often a lifesaving tool.

She dropped the knife into her pocket as if she'd been burned. As she did so, a quiver of premonition sneaked up her spine. Losing Kevin had forever changed her view of the wilderness. And Zach had just now changed her view of a lifesaving tool. What other changes lay ahead of her?

A coil of dread tightened her stomach. Her gaze was drawn helplessly toward the mountains—huge, black, forbidding. They had sapped her strength and her courage.

And they weren't through with her yet. Because Randy knew, with a sick certainty she couldn't deny, that whatever game fate had chosen to play with her would be played out here....

In the shadow of Mount Hope.

ONCE THEY GATHERED up their gear again, Zach turned to her. "Was that hunter right when he said we could reach the logging camp in a day?"

Her response was guarded. "You can reach the summit of most of these peaks in a day in warm sunny weather. But if it's a winter climb, you're looking at several days instead. And the logging camp is on the east side of the slope. From here, the easiest way to get to it is to take a circular route around the lower flanks before hiking up to the saddle."

"I'm not interested in easy. I'm interested in quick."

His jaw was tense. Randy wasn't sure she liked the hard glint in his eye. "What are you getting at?"

"Can you show me—roughly—where the logging camp is? And the cave, too?"

She did, and kept her peace while he surveyed the map carefully. Finally he circled a small area with his finger. "This looks like it would be midway between the two."

"I'd say so, too."

His head lifted. "Is there anywhere we could set up a temporary camp for a few days? Somewhere between both points?"

"There is," she said slowly. "But we wouldn't be able to see both places. But we'd still be in a good position to scout around in either direction."

"That's good enough." He squeezed her shoulder, his eyes gleaming. "We're getting close. I can feel it."

Randy had caught his excitement, but when she glanced toward the summit, a stab of pain pricked her. The peak they were on wasn't a terribly difficult ascent, but it wasn't a particularly easy one either, especially for a beginner.

"You're positive this is what you want?" She probed gently. "To head *over* the summit rather than around?"

"It is." His tone reflected his resolution.

"Can I offer some advice then?"

He smiled slightly. "Sure."

"When the climbing gets steep, don't let yourself lean in. If you do, it's a lot more likely that your feet will slip out from under you. Try to keep your weight over your feet and let your legs do most of the work. Use your hands for balance and support."

Zach nodded and slipped into his backpack, not wanting to see the concern in her eyes. Talking about it wasn't going to make the ascent any easier. But as long as he kept his mind on Garrett and the fact he was closing in on him, he'd be okay.

He hoped.

THE CLIMB BEGAN with deceptive ease. The terrain angled gently higher, not nearly as steep as Zach had feared. They took a brief break for lunch and started off again. It was then that he began to understand Randy's warning.

The trees were thinner here than at the base of the mountain, seeking a tenuous hold at every opportunity. They picked and weaved their way around huge angular boulders that looked as if they'd been tossed from the heavens by a giant hand. The air was much cooler here, too. He could hear the wind moaning from the summit.

Since they'd left the hunter, the atmosphere had been far less strained than it had been throughout their journey. Neither he nor Randy kept up a running commentary, but when they talked, it was much freer and easier than it had been before.

Randy stopped to slip a nylon jacket over her shirt. Shoving her arm into the sleeve, she glanced down at Zach. "How are you doing so far?"

"All right."

It wasn't much of an answer. She peered at him closely. He'd propped his shoulder against an outcrop of rock. His eyes were shut, his lashes fanned out against sharply angled cheekbones.

Her decision wasn't even a conscious one. "Let's take a breather here—" she began.

His eyes snapped open. "No!" His hand shot out and gripped her wrist, preventing her from sliding her pack from her shoulders. "You don't have to baby me. I said I was all right, so let's keep moving."

"Fine with me!" Randy glared at him and snatched her wrist away. He was impossible, utterly impossible! The sooner their little escapade was finished, the better—if only to part company with this man!

They continued on, maintaining a tense silence. For a time Zach kept pace with her. Then he dropped back to follow behind her.

It was midafternoon when they approached the summit. Snow softened the contours of the rugged terrain. Ahead was a long, spiny ridge that angled sharply around a corner, then broadened out into the small fat dome that capped the peak.

"It's not much farther to the top," she called back to Zach. "Another ten minutes and we'll be there." She got no answer, but she really hadn't expected one, either. She strode forward and knew from the crunch of his boots that he wasn't far behind.

She didn't glance back at him until she reached the place where the ridge cornered sharply to the right. He had come to a halt several yards behind her, his gaze riveted on the lower reaches of the valley.

Her brows shot up. It was fine when he wanted to stop, she thought disgustedly, yet let her say a word, and he was up in arms. But she held her peace and let him enjoy the view, while she did the same.

Holding very still, her senses slowly absorbed the rhythm of the land. Below, the earth was a checkerboard of color, blanketed with deep green forest, blue-bowled lakes and patches of glistening white snow.

The wind shifted and the spell was broken. Randy sighed and turned to Zach. She felt as if she'd been struck by lightning.

He still hadn't moved. He stood as if he were frozen in place, his skin a pasty shade of white. Beads of perspiration dotted his upper lip.

A horrible suspicion had formed in her mind. "Zach?" She touched his arm gently.

Nothing. He didn't even blink.

Stunned disbelief washed over her. He was afraid of heights! Randy found herself torn by two very different emotions. She felt sorry for him, but as soon as she was able, she was going to take great pleasure in wringing his neck!

She closed her eyes and racked her brain. In all her years of climbing, this was something she had never encountered. A man afraid of heights, tackling a mountain? She'd have laughed if it wasn't so heart wrenching.

She finally stepped in front of him, her movements very slow and deliberate. His reaction—or lack of it— made her wince. It was eerie, the way he continued to look . . . not *at* her, but through her.

Her hands gripped his forearms. His muscles were tense and rigid. She wished he would tremble or cry or scream—anything but that dazed, blank look of horror.

She injected every ounce of authority she possessed into her voice. "Look at me, Zach."

His eyes were glazed. He gave no sign he'd heard her.

Her nails dug like talons into his skin. She knew she was inflicting pain, but she didn't know how else to reach him. "Zach, look at me!"

She didn't realize she'd screamed until the sound echoed hollowly in the air.

Slowly, miraculously, his gaze lifted to hers.

She felt like crying with relief. Her hands slid down to grip his. "Listen to me, Zach." Her voice was very clear, very calm. "There's a solid wall of rock behind you, nothing to be scared of. I want you to step back to it. Okay? I'm right with you."

She saw his Adam's apple bob. Long, painful seconds passed while he stared at her. At last, he inched backward. When his back touched the wall, he slumped down to the ground, his knees bending as if in slow motion.

Randy followed him down. She watched his chest rise and fall raggedly. He'd closed his eyes, and she waited until his harsh breathing evened out before she spoke.

"I know how you feel," she began quietly.

"You don't!"

The violence in his words stunned her—and angered her, too. "I do," she contested hotly. "Do you think I don't know what fear is? How do you think I felt last night? I'm afraid of the dark—"

"And what did you do? Are you going to tell me you conquered your fear of the dark? You ran from it, Randy! Not far, but you couldn't hack it so you ran!"

His eyes were blazing now. Well, she had what she wanted. All his attention was focused on her, but it wasn't turning out the way she'd expected. A part of her wanted to cry out, to deny what he said, to match his anger with her own.

But he was right. Dear God, he was right.

Then all at once, it didn't matter. She felt a tremor shake his entire body, and then he went absolutely still. She stared into a face gone numb and ashen.

"There's nowhere for me to run here," he whispered. "Nowhere..."

His tone, as much as the words, made her blood run cold.

She shook his shoulders, struggling to keep him out of the shadows threatening to claim him once more.

"Zach, it's only a little farther, and then we'll be on our way down!" Urgently she sought to reassure him. "It's better after that, I promise you. I'll hold on to you and we'll move along the wall. The path here is fifteen feet from where the drop-off begins, so you're in no danger of falling. If you'll just keep your eyes on me you'll be fine—" She could have bitten her tongue when his eyes veered beyond her shoulder to the yawning chasm below.

His hands closed around hers so tightly she almost cried out. "I can't do it," he whispered. "I can't."

"You can't stay here, either!" she cried wildly. "You have no choice, Zach! You have to come with me!"

He shook his head, over and over and over.

Randy had never felt so helpless. Nothing she said made any difference. There was nothing she could do to make him see....

She had only one choice left—and it was a hell of a gamble. She and Zach had already engaged in quite a few skirmishes. If this worked, it might even spawn an all-out war . . . but she'd worry about that when—and if—it happened.

"Fine, Zach, just fine!" She shoved his hands away and stood up. "You want to act like a kid who doesn't have the sense he was born with, go right ahead! Just how long do you plan on sitting there anyway? A day? A week? You won't let me help you, so if you want to leave here, you're going to have to do it yourself."

She walked away and didn't look back.

Zach turned his head and gaped at her, unable to believe his eyes. He tried to call her name, but it wouldn't pass the tight constriction in his chest.

He tilted his head and looked up, hoping it would ease the tightness in his stomach. But the granite wall swelled ominously overhead. It was nearly as bad as the yawning valley below. He knew it was simply his fear taking hold, but whenever he glanced down, his panic sharpened. It was like gazing into a bottomless pit. He didn't feel he was on top of the world. He felt he was about to go tumbling end over end into the farthest depths of hell.

It was as if he'd been plunged back in time. He couldn't move. He couldn't think. His stepmother's face swam before him, her smile tinged with spite as she shoved him onto that wretchedly tiny balcony he'd always hated for some unknown reason. He remembered rushing to the door, screaming and crying as he pounded on the door. But she didn't come. . . . She left him there . . . *alone*. And in his mind's eye, he saw the little boy he'd once been finally slump back against the door, shaking and counting the hours until she came back, terrified that if he moved he'd find himself hurtling toward the sidewalk. . . .

Reality staked its claim once more. Zach blinked
and focused his vision on his bent knees, willing his
inner trembling to stop. It hit him like a ton of rubble
just how *alone* he was again now that Randy was gone.
Cripes! She'd really done it. She'd actually left him!

But the more he thought about it, the more it infu-
riated him, especially her high-and-mighty little
speech. She'd called him a senseless kid. He hadn't left
her alone last night when she'd been so afraid. *She* was
the one who was practically in tears. Who the hell did
she think she was?

"Dammit, Randy, when I catch up with you, you'll
be sorry!" Where the strength for his war cry came
from, Zach never knew. But he'd no sooner closed his
mouth than she appeared before him, a finger pressed
to her lips.

"Hush!" she warned in a low whisper. "What if
Garrett should hear you?"

Zach muttered furiously under his breath.

She watched him struggle to his feet. The hint of a
dimple appeared beside her mouth. "Did you really
think I'd leave you here?"

"Hell, yes!" he said hoarsely.

Her smile deepened. She extended her hand wordlessly. His fingers closed around hers; it was almost as
if he could feel her strength flowing into him.

It wasn't easy. He clung to the low soothing voice at
his side, murmuring encouragement, telling him how
glaciers had eroded the top of this once-mighty peak.
There was more, but he scarcely heard.

They didn't stop until the land flattened out again.
Zach wasn't sure whether to laugh or cry or shake her

silly for the scare she'd put him through when she left him!

Instead his arms closed around her, almost frighteningly strong, crushing her to his chest. Giddy with relief, his knees gave way. He collapsed onto the rocky ground, but neither seemed to notice—or care.

She lifted her head. Her eyes glittered with moisture. She was crying, Zach realized numbly. She made no effort to brush away the tears. She merely clung to him and hugged him even more fiercely as he stared down at her.

He couldn't remember when—if ever—a woman had cried for him. A bittersweet pain ripped through him, but along with the pain was a curious feeling of joy. He felt oddly proud yet humbled by her sensitivity.

Gently, wonderingly, he touched her cheek.

She raised her face and smiled tremulously. "You did it," she whispered simply. "I knew you could."

CHAPTER NINE

IT WAS ODD how things changed after that, Zach reflected later that afternoon. He didn't understand how or why, but it was as if an invisible bond had been forged between them. He wasn't quite sure how he felt about it yet, just as he wasn't entirely comfortable knowing that Randy had seen a part of him never exposed to anyone else. But he couldn't ignore it, either. The feeling that had formed inside him was too strong, too...compelling.

At least she knew now that he wasn't as hard and unyielding as he appeared. He was just as human, just as vulnerable, as she.

And Zach knew that she wasn't as cool and distant as he had first perceived. She could hurt, and she could bleed...and she possessed an empathy that was all too rare in today's world.

But something inside told him that she was dangerous to his well-being. In her own way, perhaps just as dangerous as Garrett.

They reached their destination late that afternoon with no further trouble. Zach guessed from Randy's anxious glance at the rapidly lowering sun that she wanted to set up camp as quickly as possible. It wasn't until they'd finished that he took a good look at his surroundings.

The high mountain meadow was like an alpine sanctuary, quiet and peaceful. The scent of pine was thick and heavy, teasing his nostrils. He envisioned the meadow as it might look in the spring and summer, masses of brightly colored flowers clustered on the gentle slopes.

Randy handed him a plate of stew. His expression must have hinted at his thoughts. "It's beautiful here, isn't it?" she said softly.

Zach nodded, easing down to the ground to balance his plate on his knees. He smiled slightly. "I was wondering what it was like here in the summer."

For just an instant her face glowed. Then, just as quickly, the warmth died out. Zach had the feeling her smile was forced.

"It's wonderful. Lots of flowers. Lots of wildlife. I saw a doe with her fawn here once." She gazed at him beneath the screen of her lashes. "Of course, I wouldn't say it's likely you'll discover it for yourself."

The faint censure in her voice made him look up from his meal. Her slender brows were raised rather haughtily, but he didn't mind. "You're probably right." He gave a sheepish grin and went back to his meal, unaware of her frown.

"I still can't believe you didn't tell me you were afraid of heights."

He took another bite of stew. "You know," he remarked in a conversational tone, "this is pretty good. And I know these vegetables can't be powdered."

"They're dried. And don't think you can get off the hook by changing the subject, Marshal Corbett."

"I thought we agreed you'd call me Zach."

"We did," she began in exasperation.

"They why aren't you doing it? I've called you Randy. A number of times, in fact."

"As I recall," she stated grimly, "you bellowed it for the whole world to hear!"

Zach was having a hard time understanding his feelings himself. He should have been embarrassed—after all, he'd made a first-class fool of himself today. Or maybe he should have been grateful to her for getting through it. Why was it he only felt . . . relieved?

"Drastic circumstances call for drastic measures," he assured her around a mouthful of stew.

Randy heaved a sigh. It was hard to stay angry or indignant. But she had to admit, she liked seeing this gentle, teasing side of him. It was different from the intense, driven man she'd seen so far.

She put aside her plate. "I'm serious, Zach. You should have told me you were afraid of heights."

He hesitated, then came to a quick decision. "All right." He placed his empty plate atop hers and studied her. "What if I had? Would you have brought me here after Garrett?"

"Of course not!" She sounded horrified.

"And you didn't tell me I'd have to spend the night freezing my tail off when we could have been snug and warm inside the tent, just because you're afraid of the dark. I'd say that makes us even."

His utter calm was infuriating. "It's not the same thing and you know it!"

"Do I? Besides, I'd say it is the same. I flew down here from Portland, Randy. And I got past the ledge today. It'll be easier next time. I know it. If I just take it one step at a time, I'll make it."

Randy stared at him in dismay. He didn't sound arrogant or boastful. She almost wished he did! He said it would be easier next time, but would it? She had given up her nightlight months ago and considered her fear of the dark all but conquered, only to discover that wasn't the case at all. As for Zach, that ledge today was like a walk in the park compared to the climb he had ahead of him.

Or was she simply being silly? Overreacting? She sighed and absently turned her attention to cleaning up their supper. They would find out soon enough.

A few minutes later, she pulled the tent from her backpack. Zach glanced over in surprise. "Hey," he said softly. "I'll admit I was trying to prove a point a few minutes ago, but I wasn't trying to push you into anything. We don't have to use the tent if you don't want to. We can sleep under the stars instead."

His expression was compassionate but not pitying; his pity was something Randy couldn't have withstood. And it was tempting, so tempting, to go along with him. But if she did, she would be losing the battle against her fear. Worse, she wouldn't even be putting up a fight.

"No." Her voice was low but even. "It should be up. We can stow our gear in it, and we won't be so cold tonight."

Zach slanted her an odd look, but he remained silent for several seconds. "I think it's time we made radio contact," he murmured. He seemed to hesitate. "I'm going to tell them the rendezvous we originally set is off." He watched her closely. "Is that all right with you?"

Randy went very still inside. Ever since Zach had suggested setting up a temporary camp, she'd suspected this was coming. Well, at least he hadn't caught her unprepared. "We have enough food for a little over a week," she warned quietly. "And please ask them to make sure we're kept posted on the latest weather reports."

She bent over and prepared to assemble the small tent, but she couldn't stop thinking about what he'd said. Dread wrapped around her chest, making it difficult to breathe. How could she stand to stay up here for a week? There were too many reminders of all the ghosts she thought she'd laid to rest. There was too much guilt and too much pain. Only one thought eased her anxiety at all: it could be worse, much worse, indeed. They could be up on Mount Hope instead.

Zach handed her the radio when she stepped back outside. "Here's the weather report."

Randy listened quietly while the deputy relayed the information. It wasn't bad, but neither was it as good as she'd hoped for. A band of high cloud cover was expected to move into the area in several days. She also quietly inquired about Zach's friend Larry and learned he was in critical condition. There had been nothing on Garrett.

From the corner of her eye, she saw Zach move away. When she'd finished with the transmission, her gaze instinctively sought to find him.

The wind moaned a sad, lonely sound that caught at her heart, even as her breath caught at the sight of Zach. He stood a few feet away, his face lifted skyward. His profile was stark and unyielding, his dark blond hair tousled and windblown. He looked tough and rugged and totally in harmony with the rough, unpredictable wilderness.

His voice reached her clearly. He sounded half sad, half wistful. "It's funny," he murmured. "I've never been much of a stargazer, but then I've never seen stars like this. Up here they look—"

"Different? Brighter than anything you've ever seen before? And closer? So close you feel you could reach out and touch them?"

She wasn't aware that she spoke until he turned his head. Through the darkness, their eyes met.

"You feel it, too," he said gently.

She took a deep, unsteady breath. "No, not anymore."

A note of unmistakable bitterness had crept into her voice. Zach stared at her. "But you did once." It wasn't a question, it was a quiet statement of fact.

She inclined her head. "Yes," she admitted, her voice barely audible. "I felt it once."

Zach's hand came out and gripped hers. His other hand on her shoulder, he guided her down onto a large flat boulder. Then he sat cross-legged on the ground before her. "Tell me," he said very quietly. "It's something I've never understood...why a man—or woman—feels the need to climb." He paused. "Dan said you were an instructor once. I take it climbing wasn't simply a weekend hobby?"

She wondered vaguely if he knew of the inner struggle he'd just caused. Climbing was the last thing she wanted to talk about. Yet she rationalized that it was better to tell him why...than why *not*.

"No," she said finally. "It wasn't a hobby, although it began that way. My father loved to hike and climb, and he started me out when I was fairly young. Even then I loved it, and it wasn't just the challenge. It's so quiet up here, so peaceful and untouched."

Zach had gone over to fill a cup with hot tea. He pressed it into her hands and resumed his place at her feet. "But what about fear? There must have been a time when you were scared."

"Of course I was scared. I wouldn't be human if I said I wasn't. But as for why I climb, I'm not sure I can explain it in words." She smiled slightly. "There's a saying among climbers—that every man knows his limits when he's climbing. It's not just physical strength. It's more the will to achieve, because after a while, all the effort takes place inside, driving you on. It makes you feel...like an explorer. You can be exhausted and cold and frightened to death, but all of a sudden it doesn't matter how many people might have been there before you."

Zach's gaze drifted to the distant peak beyond. Stars outlined the summit like a glittering crown of silver against a background of midnight blue. Incredibly beautiful, he thought, but still daunting.

His gaze returned to the woman before him. "But you don't feel that way anymore."

"No." Her throat grew achingly tight. That one word was all she could manage.

He removed the cup from her hands and pulled her to her feet. His look was so deep and searching, she felt she'd been turned inside out. "Why, Randy? What made you decide to stop climbing? Dan mentioned that someone you knew had an accident."

He would have said more, but something in her expression stopped him. The seconds ticked by slowly.

It was almost as if he could see her disappearing deep within herself.

His hands closed around her shoulders. She would have pulled away, but his grip tightened just enough to remind her she wasn't free.

She stared at him through eyes gone dull and lifeless. "It doesn't matter, Zach. It happened a long time ago, and it doesn't concern you."

"Maybe not," he argued. "You didn't ask why I'm afraid of heights, but I'll tell you anyway. When I was six years old, my stepmother punished me by locking me out on a balcony outside while she went to work. I was four stories up, but to my mind it was more like forty. I sat huddled against the door because every time I looked down I got sick. I was afraid I'd fall if I moved even an inch. It scared the hell out of me and I've never gotten over it, but it didn't stop me from coming out here—" his arm swept in a wide arc "—to find Garrett."

"So what do you expect?" She didn't bother to hide the bite in her tone. "A medal for bravery? Personally I think you're a fool for taking such a harebrained risk. It's the kind of thing that gets people killed!"

"I'm trying to understand and I'm trying to make a point. You don't strike me as the kind of woman to roll over and play dead because of one mistake. If you loved climbing so much, why give it up just because of one accident?"

Perhaps it was his choice of words . . . *roll over and play dead*. Randy suddenly felt as if an arctic wind had blown across her heart. "I don't see why it matters to you." Her tone was weary. "My reasons are my own and that's the way it's going to stay."

This time when she pulled away, Zach let her go. He stared after her, frustrated and confused. She was right. It shouldn't have mattered. But it did. Dammit, it did!

He thought of how she had faced him earlier today, fearlessly, her shoulders stiff with pride. No, she was no coward. If anything, Randy was a woman with an enormous amount of self-control. She possessed a quiet dignity, but she was almost too subdued. It was as if there were a spark missing.

She didn't want to be here. She'd made it perfectly clear that day at her house. Yet here she was.

Someone—or perhaps something—had hurt her deeply. Zach was compelled to find the mystery in her heart.

Hell, he thought angrily. *Hell!* "I don't need this," he muttered aloud. "I shouldn't even be thinking about her. I ought to be concentrating on finding Garrett!"

And that, Zach promised himself grimly, was exactly what he planned to do from now on.

FOR THE SECOND NIGHT in a row, sleep eluded Randy, while the man beside her slumbered peacefully. This time, though, it wasn't the darkness that kept her awake. Her mind was caught up in the tumult of the past hour.

Zach had wanted to know about Kevin. Should she have told him? She hadn't, because she was afraid. *Of what?* a voice asked.

I don't know!... He's different, different from Kevin, different from any man I've ever known....

Then she realized she was desperately afraid that to talk—or touch—would open up her soul to him. Already he'd made her feel and remember things she didn't want to feel. And that was a risk she wasn't prepared to take, for Randy was a woman through with taking chances. She would tempt Providence no more.

Yet she couldn't stop thinking of Zach, of a frightened little boy huddled against a door, terrified to look down for fear he'd fall. A wrenching pain ripped through her. His stepmother, he'd said. What kind of woman would do that to a child?

She shuddered to think what else he might have suffered, what other invisible scars he bore. She wondered too what had shaped him into the man he was today. If he was sometimes hard or cruel, could she blame him?

Her eyes squeezed shut. Her breath caught painfully. She recalled the way he had looked when they set off yesterday after Garrett. She had compared him once before to the mountains, and his eyes had been like mountain granite, hard as stone.

But was he? She remembered with stark clarity how he had clung to her this afternoon. It seemed ridiculous to think of such a man rousing such melting protectiveness in her. Yet he had needed her strength, her courage.

Whether she liked it or not, Zach had in that moment kindled a new awareness of him. Seeing Zach, so frightened, so alone in his terror, her heart was like ice. But with his arms around her, she experienced a budding warmth, as if something inside had begun to melt. It frightened her, this feeling. It was strange and unfamiliar and made her feel even more vulnerable to him, which was exactly what she didn't need.

No, he wasn't a cold man. Just very determined. Maybe even a little ruthless.

She was jolted back to the present by a violent exclamation. She felt as well as heard the lurching motion of Zach's body. Knowing instinctively that something was wrong, she scrambled for the flashlight.

His face was eerie in the muted light, a tight grimace of pain. He had bolted upright and heaved to his feet, only to collapse back onto the sleeping bag.

"What is it?" she asked urgently. "Your leg?"

"Yes!" He gasped and pointed to his left leg. "I tried to stand up but it only made it worse."

Randy didn't give a second thought to what she was about to do; she simply acted. She knelt between his feet and ran her hands down his leg.

His calf felt as if it had been tied and knotted by a giant hand. His breath hissed through his teeth when her fingers clamped onto the muscle. Rhythmically, methodically, she began to stroke and knead, massaging away the tightness. Zach leaned back and closed his eyes.

After a few minutes, the muscles began to relax. The cramp had eased. Her fingers registered the warmth of his flesh, the faint roughness of his hair-covered skin. In her haste to ease his pain, his clothing, or lack of it, had failed to penetrate her mind. But now she realized that Zach wasn't wearing his long underwear. Instead he wore only a rather scanty pair of men's briefs that revealed more than they concealed. She rocked back on her heels, her hands jerking away from him as if she'd been burned.

Zach propped himself up on his elbows and opened his eyes in protest. "Hey," he began. Her high color and bemused expression made him pull up short. He followed the direction of her gaze.

"Cripes," he muttered. "This is a hell of a time to turn modest on me. Aren't you forgetting we slept in the same sleeping bag last night?"

Randy's eyes flashed up to his. He sounded more wounded than amused, but she wasn't about to admit how shaken she was by his state of undress. A little indignation proved a wonderful tool to cover her uncertainty.

Her chin tilted. She gave him a rather pointed and thorough once-over, but Zach didn't seem to mind in the least. He still lay sprawled before her in indolent grace, legs spread-eagled, his torso angled slightly upward as they confronted each other. After a few seconds, it was her turn to find herself tied up in knots. Her eyes strayed helplessly downward. Her gaze touched the hardness of his arms; his biceps looked strong and corded. A surprisingly dark layer of body hair matted his chest and abdomen, reaching clear down to the edge of his briefs and beyond.

Where she found the strength to speak, she never knew. "Forgive me if I'm mistaken," she said in a voice of utter politeness. "But weren't you complaining earlier about 'freezing your tail off'? If you're cold, it seems to me you deserve it!"

He sighed and reached for the pile of underwear he'd shoved into the corner. "Boy, but you're testy tonight," he grumbled, thrusting his legs into the bottoms. "What's the matter? Afraid to go to sleep because the bogeyman might get you?"

The words were a mistake. Zach knew it the instant he glanced back at her. She looked ready to cry. He truly hadn't meant anything by the comment, but at the sudden silence that descended, he realized he'd hurt her feelings.

He sat very still, experiencing a rare uncertainty. She refused to look at him, her gaze focused on her hands. His fingers reached out to touch her jaw before his hands settled on her shoulders. In some distant corner of his mind he marveled at the texture of her skin—like a sun-warmed peach. Slowly he guided her eyes to him.

"I'm sorry, Randy. I shouldn't have said that. I didn't mean anything by it, I swear."

His eyes, like his tone, were infinitely gentle. Randy found herself totally disarmed, caught wholly off guard.

"You're not angry, are you?"

There was a heartbeat of silence while they stared at each other. Through her own sensitive awareness, she could feel his closeness, and it set every nerve in her body aquiver. Something was happening here, she thought fuzzily. Something strange. Something wonderful.

She shook her head; it was all the answer she could manage.

His gaze bore into her. "Are you sure?"

His eyes were like liquid silver. Randy couldn't have torn her gaze away if she'd wanted to—and she didn't. It was a revelation as startling as it was disturbing.

"I'm sure," she whispered.

"Then come back to bed." His hands deserted her shoulders, leaving her feeling inexplicably exposed . . . and so very alone. She watched Zach slide back into his sleeping bag. To her surprise, he turned on his side, as if to make room for her.

Her hands, resting on her thighs, were suddenly far from steady. Sleeping with him with their bags zipped together was one thing; this was quite another. Her mind balked, but to her horror, her body suddenly craved the warm security of his.

Zach chuckled silently. He suspected Randy wouldn't be pleased if she knew how expressive those huge blue eyes of hers really were. He could practically read every last thought running through her mind.

He held out his hand. "If my intentions are ever less than honorable, I'll be sure to warn you first."

Her eyes sought his. There was a faint smile on his lips, but his expression held nothing to alarm her. He might be teasing a little, but he wasn't making fun of her.

Randy took his hand and slid in beside him. They lay side by side, their linked hands the only point of contact between them. It was pitch-black inside the tent, yet his touch kept the shadows of the night at bay. As if he were aware of her thoughts, his fingers twined more tightly about her own, long and lean and strong, his palm pleasantly rough against hers. Her eyes closed. Her heart and mind curiously at peace, she slept.

Zach was amazed how quickly she fell asleep. After a while, she turned and curled against his side, in-

stinctively seeking his warmth. He stiffened for an instant. Then his arms closed slowly around her, and all
at once it seemed the most natural thing in the world
to tuck her head into the hollow of his shoulder.

His hand drifted up and down the length of her
back, his fingers unconsciously gauging her body,
charting the narrowness of her waist, the slight deli-
neation of each rib. She was tall enough to fit against
him perfectly, slender but wiry.

His fingertips encountered the rounded plumpness
of her breast, and something utterly male reared its
head. His hand stilled. He held his breath, fairly aching with the need to plunder and shape the soft velvet
mound beneath his palm. But the dictates of his mind
overruled the sudden pulse of desire.

Zach sensed the moment was infinitely precious. He
didn't understand it. He didn't know how or why, he
just knew, and Zach was a man used to relying on instinct. He liked feeling her softness, her strength, the
way her body shaped to the hard contours of his. He
liked the way her hair tickled his chin, the sweet
womanly smell of her. He enjoyed listening to her
steady breathing, her breath pooling warmly against
his neck. He was strangely reluctant to clutter up the
moment with feelings of sex or awareness.

Outside the wind howled eerily. A faint chill in-
vaded the air, and he gathered her closer.

She slept on, as if she had turned herself over to him
in complete and utter faith. If he had any sense, he'd
untangle himself, turn his back and put her out of his
mind completely. Where women were concerned, he'd
seen both sides of the coin and precious little in between. He knew what it was like to be controlled and

manipulated, to be crushed like a stone underfoot. That was all he'd been to his stepmother—dirt. He also knew what it was like to have someone wholly dependent upon him; weak and passive and clinging to his neck until he thought he would strangle. Zach wasn't sure which was worse.

Randy had taught him already how wrong he'd been about her. Unwillingly, reluctantly, Zach smiled to himself. He found it hard to believe he'd ever thought her a church mouse. No, more than likely, Randy came from the same barrel as his stepmother.

But Zach was curiously loath to leave her alone with her fears, and very much confounded by his reluctance. But, no—no, that wasn't right. It wasn't just Randy he was thinking of. He was feeling rather selfish, he realized. His arms unconsciously tightened. He felt strangely possessive—even protective—with Randy lying curled against him. He couldn't remember when he'd ever experienced such deep contentment or found such pleasure in simply touching and holding.

He felt her stir against him, nuzzling closer, like a kitten before the fire. His lips pressed against her forehead. He cupped her cheek in his palm, his fingers gently brushing her lower lip and marveling over its satin texture. His warm breath stirred her hair as he whispered, "Shh, it's okay. Go back to sleep."

Her body pressed closer still. She gave a breathy little sigh. Against his fingertips, she smiled. "Kevin," she murmured.

Zach froze. He'd never have dreamed it possible a moment earlier. In one blinding second, between one breath and the next, his pleasure died a quick and painful death.

He didn't understand his sudden bleakness, any more than he understood why he couldn't let her go. And so Randy slept on in his arms, while Zach stared into the darkness of the night....

RANDY AND ZACH WEREN'T the only ones out that night, their eyes lifted heavenward. Dan Parker stood on his porch, a solitary figure. Only he wasn't looking at the stars. His attention was commanded by the jagged outline of the mountains. Silver moonlight touched the distant peaks, barely visible on the horizon.

There was a faint bite to the wind, a forewarning of winter. He shivered a little with cold. Once, Marian wouldn't have let him step out of the house on a night like this without bundling him into a thick warm sweater. And once, she would have joined him out here. She would have slipped her hand into his and smiled at him, her face full of love and warmth and laughter.

But Marian didn't laugh anymore. She didn't smile. And sometimes Dan was convinced she no longer loved him.

Just thinking about it made his heart squeeze tight. Marian had once been a very intense, passionate woman. *She still is!* a voice in his head scoffed.

Dan smiled sadly. "But only in hate," he murmured aloud. "Only in hate."

Or was his imagination simply running wild? There were times when he felt he would burst with trying to withhold the emotions roiling away inside him. He had only to see Marian gazing listlessly into space, and the simmering resentment began rearing up inside him.

He hated himself then for being jealous of his son. Dear God, his *dead* son.

A hot tear spilled down his weathered cheek. Then another, and another. Dan made no move to wipe them away. "Forgive me, Kevin," he whispered. "You were my son and I loved you just as much as your mother. But she never thinks of me anymore. She thinks only of you. And sometimes it makes me feel she must have loved you far more than she ever loved me."

It was a long time later when Dan trudged inside. Marian sat at the kitchen table, her hands curled in her lap. Her husband received only the briefest of glances as he moved by her.

He poured himself a cup of coffee and sat down across from her. A brittle silence prevailed, until the wind blew a smattering of leaves against the pane. Dan lifted his head toward the sound, staring out into the night. He sat very still, absorbed in his thoughts.

Marian's voice startled him. "For heaven's sake," she snapped, "you've been brooding for two days now. I don't know what you're so worried for."

It was a struggle to keep the anger from showing in his voice. "There's an escapee out there, Marian. I won't rest easy until he's behind bars again."

"That may be," Marian snorted, "but he's not the one you were thinking of just now, was he?"

The atmosphere was suddenly stifling.

"There was an accident today, Marian. Two members of one of the search parties slid into a ravine and were hurt. Not critically, but one broke his collarbone." Quiet as his voice was, it contained a hint of challenge as he regarded his wife. "And yes, it made me think of Randy. I'm worried about her. Is that so wrong?"

Marian's palms slapped hard on the table. "I don't know why. You, better than anybody, should know that if trouble comes along, she'll be looking out for herself and to hell with anybody else."

Dan was appalled—and so angry his voice was shaking. "My God, Marian, it makes me ashamed to hear you say that! From the time she was two years old, Randy sat at this very table more times than I can remember, just like one of the family. She *was* family, and as far as I'm concerned, she still is. I don't see how you can be so cold."

For just an instant, Dan could have sworn he saw a flicker of guilt pass across Marian's face.

She gathered her sweater around her shoulders and stood up. She glared at him, her eyes both angry and tormented. "And I don't see how you can forgive her, Dan Parker!"

Dan's heart wrenched. When Kevin died, he'd lost not only his son, but his wife. And if Marian had her way, he would lose Randy, too.

"You don't understand," he whispered. "How can I not forgive her?"

But Marian didn't hear. She was already gone.

CHAPTER TEN

RANDY AWOKE VERY SLOWLY the next morning, caught in a nebulous world between sleep and wakefulness. In some far-off corner of her mind, she knew she'd spent the night on the cold, hard ground, yet she couldn't recall when she'd been so comfortably toasty and warm....

It took a minute to register the lean hard length of Zach's body lying flush against her own. She froze, her senses tangled in a flurry of sensations. Her head was pillowed on a sinewy bare arm. Muscled thighs bonded with hers. But it was the undeniably male feel of what lay between those thighs that flooded her body with an entirely different kind of heat.

She lay very still, her mind in a panic. Sometime during the night, Zach had flung his free arm over her. His fingertips merely grazed the shallow indentation of her spine, but to Randy his touch was like a brand burning into her flesh. How could she free herself without waking him?

The thought never progressed any further. She slowly raised her head... only to find Zach's eyes staring straight into hers.

Randy's heart began to pound. The air was suddenly filled with a shattering awareness. They were so close, so close they might have been lovers who'd spent a long and fulfilling night making love over and over... Randy searched for something glib, something cute to break the tension of the moment.

"Zach—"

"Don't," he said. "Don't say anything."

There was something in his tone she couldn't identify. A warning? Or a plea? She stared back at him warily, stunned to discover the same wariness within him.

Zach seemed upset, maybe even angry. She could almost feel the tension flowing through him as the hand at her waist tightened with an almost convulsive force. His eyes roamed her face as if he wanted to devour her.

Don't, her mind screamed. *Oh, Zach, don't do this to me.*

The dark intensity of his expression made her want to run and hide. She was just as frightened by the dark thrill that ran through her.

His head lowered. Randy couldn't tear her eyes away from his mouth, so hard and yet so sensual.

Don't, she thought again. *Don't touch me. Don't look at me....*

His mouth came down on hers. She gave a whimper—or did she only imagine it? She lifted her hands to push him away, only to find herself clinging tightly to his shoulders.

His lips were hard and hungry, but far from hurtful. He kissed her as if he were starved for the taste of her, and she sensed an almost frantic desperation in him that made her heart cry out for him. He wasn't taking from her. It was as if he were seeking something instead....

Zach, she thought. *Oh, Zach, what are you doing to me?*

Her mind was spinning. She couldn't breathe, she couldn't even think. She could only feel, and what she felt was a shocking instantaneous arousal unlike anything she'd ever experienced. His nearness surrounded her, took hold of her, possessed her. Her eyes squeezed shut against a pleasure so acute it was almost painful.

Her hands moved without conscious volition. Her fingertips dug into the sinewed binding of his arms, absorbing the latent power, the feel of his skin, sleek and heated.

His lean fingers threaded through the dark silk of her hair. There was a subtle change in the kiss, in the way Zach held her. His lips were warmly tormenting, coaxing a melting yearning inside her that was poignantly sweet.

His hands slid down to cradle her hips, binding them intimately to his. Randy could feel his hardness burning into her thighs. Her pulse skipped erratically when his fingers shaped themselves around her, pulling her full and tight against his warm fullness for a never-ending moment.

And Zach knew then that if he didn't stop now, he'd never be able to. His palms slid over her buttocks once more, gentling and soothing. The pressure of his mouth eased. He kissed her lips, first one corner and then the other, and let his fingers trail up her spine before rolling to his side.

Even then he didn't let her go. He kept her captive within the bondage of his arms, stunned by what had just happened...and wondering if he dared explore it.

Randy's eyes opened, dazed and smoky. He could see the surprised awareness on her face, the same starkness of wanting that had driven him to this point. Her lips were parted. Moist and glistening from his touch. It was all he could do to keep from pulling her beneath him and losing himself in her mouth and body.

But something wholly unexpected happened inside him when her gaze slipped shyly away. He felt possessive and even more protective. She would have turned her head away, as well, but he wouldn't let her. His hand gently brushed her cheek, then curled around her nape. Resting his forehead against hers, Zach closed his eyes and waited for the throbbing in his body to subside.

For a long time the only sound in the tiny tent was the rasp of their labored breathing.

It wasn't long before Zach felt her gaze on his face. When she saw that she had his attention, she moistened her lips.

"Why—why did you do that?" Randy's eyes searched his. Her voice was controlled, which was more than she could say for her heart. She felt... guilty, for some wild crazy reason that was somehow mixed up with thoughts of Kevin. And she was confused over the hunger still winding through her. She lowered her gaze quickly, afraid of what he might see.

Zach stared at her. Her expression was guarded, but the slight catch in her voice unnerved him. It also had the curious effect of deepening the odd sense of protectiveness he felt.

Zach understood—not completely—but on a rather basic level, what she was asking... and why. Feelings like this had no part in their relationship, in their mission here. As soon as they found Garrett, it was over. Why start something that could never be finished?

He was at a total loss to explain. A part of him even resented her asking. He'd wanted to kiss her yesterday, he realized suddenly, after she'd led him off that damned ledge. He'd wanted to kiss away her tears and put a whole new expression on her face, an expression he had yet to see.

Was it because she was so much an enigma? Their embrace had caught both of them off guard. Her response surprised him. There had been no time to throw up the barriers she seemed so determined to protect herself with. Beneath her calm distant manner was the essence of a very warm woman. Was that why he'd kissed her? To see what lay beneath her icy exterior? But he already knew. He'd already seen and felt her fire, her passion. No matter how much she tried to hide her emotions, they were there.

He rolled away so abruptly Randy felt naked and exposed. She remained where she was, huddled beneath the covers, watching as he rose to his feet.

He shoved his fingers through his hair. "I don't know," he said finally. "It just happened, all right? It's too late to change it, so let's just forget it."

His voice was rougher than he intended. But Zach was suddenly angry—at himself for losing his head, and at Randy's uninhibited response. He caught a glimpse of her face, pinched and white, before she turned her head and closed her eyes. After a moment, she pushed aside the cover, got to her feet and picked up her clothes from the corner, all without a word.

She didn't bother to look at him as she passed by. "Breakfast will be ready in a few minutes."

"Randy—" He reached for her instinctively. She stepped deliberately out of reach before lifting her chin.

"Yes?"

His eyes narrowed. Her expression was distant and remote. She had coolly, calmly and with a detachment that astounded him, shut him out as if he had never existed.

He realized he wanted to apologize, but he didn't know how. After a moment, his hand dropped back to his side.

"I thought we'd check out the logging camp today."

"Fine." Her voice held no more emotion than his.

"And the cave, too, if there's time."

At least he'd succeeded in gaining her attention. Her breath came out in a hiss as she whirled on him. Zach didn't back down from her gaze, his own just as challenging.

"You'll never make it," she stated flatly. "I didn't want to alarm you after yesterday, but the trail into the cave is far worse than the climb here. You can stay here while I—"

"No."

"I'm not a tenderfoot, Marshal! I'm fully capable of recognizing if someone has been in the area recently."

"That has nothing to do with me coming along."

Her teeth came together with a snap. "What are you trying to prove then?"

He gave her a long, slow look. "Maybe the same thing you are."

Randy watched as he reached for his pants, resisting the urge to stomp her foot. His cryptic reply wasn't very satisfactory...and it was infinitely disturbing.

He glanced up and caught her scrutiny. "I want Garrett, Randy. And I'll do whatever I have to in order to find him."

Quiet as his voice was, it sent chills up her spine. His mouth was set in a harsh unyielding line. The light in the tent was muted and filmy, but his eyes were glittering pinpoints of light.

There would be no changing his mind. Randy knew better than to even try. "You'll have to decide before we leave then," she snapped. "We can't make it to the logging camp and the cave in the same day and get back here before dusk. Unless you're willing to travel at night. That probably wouldn't bother you since you're so squeamish about looking down. Personally, it's a risk I'm not willing to take."

She was baiting him. Zach wished he could have laughed at the picture she made standing there in her long underwear, her arms heaped with her clothes and spitting angry defiance. But in spite of his own bravado, the thought of traversing the trail to the cave— day or night—was something he didn't dare dwell on. And he knew from Randy's dig she was aware of it, too.

She also left him no choice, and she damn well knew it! "We'll go to the logging camp today," he said shortly. "Maybe we can stick around and stake it out for a while."

She nodded and stepped through the flap. Zach finished zipping his pants, his mind on Randy.

He knew he'd angered her with his dogged insistence. That wasn't what bothered him, though. He couldn't forget the way she'd looked just before she climbed from the sleeping bag. He didn't like knowing he'd put that expression on her face. In that brief moment when their eyes collided, there was no denying what she was feeling—the hurt and the vulnerability. He told himself it was better this way.

Improbable as it was, he was too damned attracted to her. That was one problem he'd never dreamed he would encounter. If he did what his body was urging him to do, he and Randy would never leave this tent.

And they'd never find Garrett, either.

No, he couldn't afford to forget why they were here. He had no business thinking of her as anything but what she was—his guide, his only link to Garrett.

THE DAY WAS AN OMINOUS reflection of their mood—dark and dreary. Thick clouds enveloped the peak just above the timberline.

Breakfast had been a dismal affair, and they were just about ready to leave when the crackle and buzz of the radio sounded. Randy had already sorted through their packs and removed the supplies they could leave behind. Zach was busy stowing the discarded items inside the tent, so she picked up the hand-held set and identified herself.

"Randy? It's Dan." The caller answered.

"Dan!" she exclaimed. "It's so good to hear your voice."

"Not as good as it is to hear yours. How are you, Randy?"

His anxious concern touched her. Her throat grew unexpectedly tight. "I'm okay," she whispered.

"The truth now, girl."

"Better than I expected." She smiled shakily, glad Zach was still inside the tent.

"And Garrett?"

"Nothing so far. We're going up to the logging camp today and the cave tomorrow."

Dan sighed. "It's the same at this end. We had to call off the aerial search because of the cloud cover." There was a short silence. "There's something else, too."

Her skin prickled. "What?"

"Yesterday two members of one of the teams were searching south of where you are. There was a bad fall..."

A bad fall...that was all she heard. Remembrance gripped her mind. The world spun crazily. It was a moment before Dan's voice began to sink in again.

"It was dusk and they missed their footing inside a ravine. One man is bruised pretty bad, and the other one broke his collarbone—"

"But they're okay?" Her voice was strained.

"They'll be fine," he assured her.

A burst of static followed and they were forced to end the transmission. Randy's palms were cold and clammy as she replaced the radio in her pack. The news of the fall had brought back too many memories of Kevin. She was immensely glad Zach had no intention of tackling the cave today. She wasn't sure she could have handled it.

A shadow fell over her. She looked up to find Zach towering over her.

"There was an accident?"

"Yes." Her voice low, she told him about the men in the ravine.

He grimaced and shook his head, his face impassive. After a moment he asked, "What was that about the aerial search?"

"It's been called off because of the cloud cover."

Zach swore softly.

Randy remained on her knees, gazing up at him. "I can't see where a helicopter is much good anyway," she said shortly. "The forest is too dense to see anything. And any sound up here carries for miles and miles. Even in the higher elevations, Garrett would have plenty of time to get out of sight."

It wasn't what Zach wanted to hear. He shoved his fingers through his hair, battling a frustration that was becoming a little too familiar. What if they'd all been wrong? What if Garrett hadn't headed into the wilderness? What if he'd hitched a ride from some unsuspecting motorist? He could be hundreds of miles away by now!

"Damn!" he muttered. "We'll never find him at this rate. And now there's two less people searching for him."

Randy bounded to her feet, filled with a seething resentment. She'd been a fool to think Zach Corbett had a heart after all—that he was anything but hard to the bone. He had stated his intentions quite plainly. He wanted Garrett, and he really didn't care about any-

thing or anyone else. As for that kiss this morning...as long as she did her part in finding Garrett,
she'd be a fool to think he had any other interest in
her.

"Is that all you can say?" she demanded. "I realize you don't know those two men who were injured,
but is it too much to expect a little concern? They were
out there trying to help you—"

Whatever else she might have said was lost. Her
breath was torn from her lungs when he reached out
and grabbed her shoulders.

"Don't you dare accuse me of not caring," he said
fiercely. "Those two men falling is regrettable, yes, but
I'm not responsible! Garrett *is* responsible for shooting my friend Larry. My God, he intended to kill him!
Do you ever stop to think about him? He has a wife
and two little boys, Randy. I had to tell Peggy he was
shot, and it was the hardest thing I've ever done in my
life. Now you can say that going after Garrett is a
personal vendetta—maybe it is. And maybe you don't
agree with me. In fact right now I'm not even sure I
want you to help me. But in my mind the only way I
can help Larry is by finding Garrett."

He let go of her so suddenly she nearly lost her balance. He grabbed his pack, slung it on his shoulder
and stalked off.

Randy gaped after him, shock and shame tearing
through her in alternating waves. Zach was right. She
had wronged him. She had given precious little
thought to his friend Larry when Dan had told her
about the two searchers. She'd been plunged back in
time, immersed in her own pain of remembrance.

And he was right about something else. Whether he knew it or not, his determination to find Garrett *was* a vendetta.

The shiver that ran through her had nothing to do with the chill, moist air. It frightened her to think just how far Zach would go to find Garrett. But she couldn't let him do it alone. She just couldn't.

Randy didn't stop to think or question her motives; she didn't dare. It was enough to admit that she was committed to Zach, right or wrong. Grabbing her pack, she ran after him.

She was out of breath by the time she reached him. "Zach." She caught his forearm. "Zach, please stop!"

He turned slowly. His jaw was tense, but other than that his face betrayed little emotion.

Beneath her fingertips, the muscles in his forearm were rigid and knotted. Randy doggedly kept her hand where it was. A dozen thoughts rose up inside her, but she couldn't get a word past the lump in her throat. She wanted to tell him that she hadn't meant to be cruel, that she hadn't meant to hurt him. Whether it showed or not—whether he admitted it or not—she knew she had struck a blow to his pride.

"What is it now, Randy?"

His quiet dignity was like a slap in the face. He stared straight at her, through her, creating a brittle tension that sapped her courage and was almost her undoing.

At her silence, his eyes narrowed. "Tell me something," he said slowly. "Tell me why—why you ever agreed to do this?"

He wasn't making it easy for her. But what had she expected after she had practically attacked him? Yet when she looked in his face, she saw no anger, no resentment. There was only a deep, scorching intensity in his eyes that warned her he saw far, far too much...

Her hand fell away from his arm. She floundered helplessly. He looked so strong, so tall and infallible standing there with the wind tossing his hair, the mountains at his back.

But she sensed his distance, his tension. For an instant her entire being was in chaos. She felt as if she'd been caught in the rampage of the wind, tossed in a dozen different directions all at once.

Everything had changed these past few days. Because of Zach, she had forsaken her vow never to return to these mountains. He had roused sleeping demons, demons from the past. He had made her think of Kevin again. He made her feel things she didn't want to feel...

She should hate him, she realized. She should hate him for bringing back all of her secret pain and fear....

"I told you once, Zach." Her gaze dropped. She focused on the pulse beating strongly in his throat, unable to meet his eyes any longer. "I had no choice. There was no one else. And because I—I felt I owed it to Dan."

There was a heartbeat of silence. The wind moaned a low, keening sound of loneliness. A wispy trail of fog tore past them and up the slope.

"And now?" His voice fell into the stillness. "Has that changed? If you had your choice, Randy—would you leave?"

Randy closed her eyes, despairing her stormy heart. *Damn you, Zach!* she cried silently. *Why do you have to make this so hard?*

She shook her head mutely. It was all she could manage.

"Why not?"

Because you touched me. Because you held me during the long, lonely night and kept the darkness away... Because you made me feel safe and warm and secure like I haven't felt in such a long, long time... Because with just one kiss you stirred something inside me in a way that even Kevin never managed...

That was the hardest admission of all to face. In all the time that Kevin had been gone, Randy had always felt that her love for him had never faltered.

But she felt linked to Zach, bound to him in some strange, indefinable way. It was a bond so fragile, so tentative and so new that she didn't fully understand it. But she could no longer deny its existence.

She felt his hand, warm and strong beneath her chin, compelling her to look at him. His expression had changed radically. No longer was he cold and distant. The question in his eyes, as well as the hint of uncharacteristic strain and uncertainty, made her want to cry.

"Because I want to help you," she whispered, and knew it for the truth. "I want to do whatever I can to help you in this."

For the longest time Zach said nothing. His grip on her chin tightened. His gaze dropped to her mouth. Gently...oh, so gently, he ran his thumb along the fullness of her lower lip. For a heartrending moment Randy thought he would kiss her again.

"Then let's not waste any more time," he said softly. His hand fell away and she registered a fleeting sensation of abandonment.

Randy had no sooner slipped on her backpack than she found her hand seized in his, their fingers mated in a burning clasp.

It was odd, she reflected hazily some time later, how secure that made her feel. Especially since they were headed deeper and deeper into the encroaching wilderness.

The mountain's shadow chased them down a small slope. Randy shivered and edged closer to Zach, a curious sensation winging along her spine. Were they being followed? Her head swung around, lifting sharply to a spiny ridge above them.

The eerie sensation deserted her as suddenly as it had come. Nonetheless, Randy kept her eyes trained high above, constantly on the move.

She was beginning to understand what Zach was feeling. It wouldn't do to let her guard fall and forget they were here searching for a dangerous criminal. No, it wouldn't do at all.

BY MIDMORNING they'd reached the logging camp. It was situated on the eastern slope of the mountain, several thousand feet below their campsite. Though the route was not a direct one, the trip wasn't as difficult as Zach had feared, nor did it take as long as he expected. His comment to that effect earned a rueful smile from Randy. She pointed out that the trip back up the slope would take nearly twice as long.

He was appalled to discover the camp had been abandoned roughly ten years ago. By the look of the place, he'd guessed a half a century earlier. There were less than a handful of buildings left, and none intact. Boards leaned crazily in all directions, ravaged by wind and weather. There were jagged holes in the roofs, if there was a roof at all.

He felt humble and frail here, yet for the first time he was beginning to understand the lure of the mountains. It was like traveling backward in time. He felt a million miles away from civilization, yet the sense of remoteness was more than physical.

The cloud cover had dissipated, swept onward by the relentless wind. Sunlight poured down to spotlight the snow-locked summit, highlighted in stark relief. For just an instant, Zach imagined standing there, in a world with no boundaries between earth and sky.

He let out his breath slowly. Yes, it was beautiful here. Beautiful...but daunting. Randy had called him a fool for ignoring his fear of heights and going after Garrett, and maybe he was. If nothing else, at least he would come away with a hard-won respect and appreciation for the land.

But before long, Zach considered the trip to the logging camp a total failure. There was no sign that anyone had been near the camp for years. In his mind, it was but one more day wasted.

And another day of freedom for Garrett.

He said nothing when Randy reminded him they needed to leave soon if they were to arrive back at camp before dark. He guessed they were about halfway there when she called a breather. He followed her with his eyes as she lowered herself to the ground. They were on a broad, rock-studded rib that was sheltered from the wind. His half smile held a trace of envy. His ego was still a little bruised by her agility. Zach eased down beside her with much less grace and, he was certain, infinitely more pain.

Their eyes met when she handed him a slice of apple. He took it, his frustration over Garrett slipping away.

His mind focused on the woman beside him. Last night and this morning, something had happened between them, something that had brought them closer together. Zach couldn't pinpoint the reason, but he knew Randy felt it, too—welcome or unwelcome. It might have been the isolation here in the wilderness, a basic need for human contact. But their world was now condensed to each other...and Garrett.

Zach was well aware he didn't need the complication of a woman on his mind. Not here, and especially not now. And yet he felt compelled to accept it.

"Randy."

She glanced over at him, a fingertip in her mouth to suck away the apple's stickiness.

His tone was very quiet. "Who is Kevin?"

The question shattered their peaceful interlude. Zach knew he had shocked her. He watched the color drain from her face, her expression utterly stricken.

Her lashes lowered. The silence seemed to drag on forever. Finally she spoke, her voice little more than a breath of air. "Why do you ask?"

He sensed the rigid control she was exerting over her emotions. It showed in the flatness of her voice. But she had yet to meet his eyes, and Zach found himself curiously irritated. *Because I want to know. Because I have to know.*

He said neither of these things. His gaze speared into her, silently willing her to look at him. "You said his name the other night." *While you were clinging to me. To me, Randy.* "In your sleep."

She opened her backpack and carefully replaced the knife she'd used to slice the apple. His jaw tightened. If Randy had her way, his question would remain unanswered. A surge of anger shot through him, but there was something almost pitiful about the set of her shoulders, the proud but rigid lines beneath the fabric of her jacket.

When she stood up, Zach stood as well. "Tell me, Randy."

She looked at him then, her face flooded with resentment. Just for an instant, he glimpsed a world of torment in her eyes that kindled a wave of regret for causing her such pain. But his need to know overrode all else.

A single step brought him before her. His hands closed around her shoulders, his grip gentle but firm. She would have wrenched away, but his fingers tightened enough to remind her she wasn't free.

"Please," he said softly.

It was odd how that one word seemed to make all the difference in the world. Time stood still while she stared at him, her gaze riveted to his. His heart wrenched when he saw her eyes grow suspiciously bright and moist.

This was tearing her apart. Zach felt her pain with every ounce of his being. She blinked once. Twice. Then her expression grew carefully bland. He was stunned at how quickly she was able to control herself.

The sound of her voice broke the tense, waiting silence. "Kevin was my fiancé."

Zach frowned. "Was?" He searched her ashen face. "You're no longer engaged?"

She shook her head. Her lips pressed together, as if to still a sudden tremor.

"He died." Her voice was wooden, but he felt the shudder that swept through her.

A half-formed suspicion winged through his mind. "Where?" he asked very quietly.

For a moment he thought she wouldn't answer. She stared up at him, her gaze on the verge of defiance. Then all at once, Zach felt her body lose all resistance. It was as if all the life had gone out of her. She gave a tiny jerk of her head, indicating the surrounding landscape.

He went very still inside. "Here? In the mountains?"

"Yes." Her lips scarcely moved.

Zach felt as if he'd been punched in the stomach. He was just beginning to understand the shadows he'd sensed inside her and the stark emptiness in her eyes. He couldn't tear his gaze from her ravaged face. For the first time, he truly understood what it meant to be sick at heart. "The accident you mentioned. Is that how—"

"Yes." She cut him off and drew a deep, serrated breath.

He also understood why she hadn't wanted to come here with him—and perversely, why she had. A dozen other unanswered questions tumbled around in his mind, but now was not the time. Randy was a woman who guarded herself closely, and he had pushed enough.

This time when she pulled away, Zach let her go. It was a choice he made reluctantly. There was a deep-seated need inside him, a need to soothe and comfort. Yet he sensed that Randy wouldn't welcome his comfort right now.

His eyes followed her as she moved several paces away, her back to him. Only yesterday he'd have branded her manner cool and aloof. Stubborn and prideful and maybe even standoffish. But now...

His heart caught. She was so alone, he thought. So alone. A matter of choice—or necessity? He hoped it was the latter, but he suspected it was the former.

"I'm sorry, Randy."

She turned slightly and gave a terse nod, but she refused to look at him.

The sudden quiet that had descended was almost unbearable. Even the wind had ceased its restless scouring of the earth. Zach hesitated, wondering if there was something else he should say or do. In spite of her brave facade, she looked hurt and defenseless.

Finally he picked up her backpack. "We'd better head back—" he began.

At that moment there was a low, ominous rumbling—almost like thunder. At first, Zach couldn't place the sound. The sky was too clear for a thunderstorm. Startled, he glanced up the steep embankment beyond Randy's head. For a paralyzing second, he could only watch in horror as a dozen boulders leaped down the slope, picking up speed.

The two of them stood directly in their path.

CHAPTER ELEVEN

ZACH DIDN'T KNOW he could move so fast. There was no time to shout a warning. He reacted without thinking, throwing his weight against Randy and wrapping his arms around her in an attempt to break their fall to the ground. But he hadn't counted on the momentum of his body. Earth and sky spun crazily as they were carried over the lip of a rocky incline. The sound of an involuntary cry knifed through him. Zach tightened his arms instinctively as they skidded and rolled toward the bottom.

He wasn't even aware when they tumbled to a halt. His heart pounded like a trip-hammer. Every part of his body felt battered and bruised. And Randy! She lay utterly still and limp beneath him, her backpack jammed at an awkward angle behind her head. His heart lurched. Was she dead?

There was a tiny, restive movement against his chest. At last he heard a muffled voice.

"This is starting to become a habit—a rather unpleasant one, at that."

Shaky as her tone was, it carried a trace of unlikely laughter.

Zach lifted his head. Her expression was an odd mixture of disgruntlement and pleading. For an instant all he could do was stare at her, overwhelmed at finding she was alive and unhurt. Randy frowned back at him indignantly and wiggled protestingly beneath his heavy weight.

Relief surged through him, and he laughed. It was a low, grating sound, but a laugh nonetheless. He slipped one hand behind the back of her head, his lean fingers sliding through her hair to cradle her cheek against his.

Zach squeezed her so hard, Randy thought her ribs would break. But it was a strangely pleasurable kind of pain, and so was the abrasive rasp of his beard against her cheek. Filled with the same giddy relief, her arms sneaked unthinkingly around his neck. She clasped herself to him with the same desperate strength.

After a minute, Zach drew back slightly, and gazed at her face intently. "Are you okay?" he asked hoarsely. His hand wasn't entirely steady as he pushed the hair off her cheek with the tenderness of a lover.

A part of Randy remained curiously detached, unwilling to think about their brush with death. It was easier—so much easier—to focus on Zach.

"I'm fine." Her voice was breathless and husky. She was still quivering from the disarmingly gentle touch of his hand. No longer was his body a heavy weight trapping her to the ground. She felt cold and bereft when he lifted himself away from her.

When he helped her to her feet, she followed the direction of his eyes. There was a small pile of rubble nearby, less than fifteen feet away. The rocks weren't huge, but big enough to maim. Add a little velocity to their size, and any one of them might have been lethal . . .

Zach voiced her thoughts. "That was close," he said grimly. "Too damn close."

Randy said nothing. She wrapped her arms around herself to ward off a sudden chill. Unable to help herself, her eyes veered back to the hillside.

Zach did the same. He stared upward, seeing once again the boulders bounding toward them, and experiencing once again a terrifying sense of helplessness.

Randy's hat was lying several yards uphill. He quickly moved away to retrieve it.

When he handed it back, she seemed totally preoccupied. Her gaze was lifted beyond him, retracing the path the boulders had taken, all the way to the top of the ridge. A jolt ran through his body. A terrible thought entered his mind, a thought he wasn't sure he wanted to acknowledge.

"Are you thinking," he asked very quietly, "the same thing I am?"

Her attention returned to him. "The rock is more unstable farther north. This isn't where I would expect a slide," she said slowly, then hesitated. "But I suppose it's possible."

"It's also possible someone had a hand in getting it started." Zach's voice turned hard as granite. His hand clenched. Randy could have been killed! He swore furiously. "If Garrett is behind this, he'll pay. Dammit, I swear he'll pay!"

Randy said nothing. An eerie chill of foreboding ran down her spine. What *had* caused the slide? The hand of nature . . . or the hand of man?

She shivered again. Either way, she wasn't sure she wanted to know.

THE MOOD BACK AT CAMP that evening was somber and subdued. Zach said very little. Darkness and clouds overcame them simultaneously. Tonight there were no stars or moonlight to cling to. Randy was surprised when Zach suggested they light the lantern.

She didn't refuse. Her mood was too uncertain and precarious. She feared the little lantern would glow like a beacon in the night, however, so she placed it in the tent and left the flap open.

Once they had eaten, Zach was up and down, sometimes pacing restlessly, sometimes sitting and staring into the gloomy shadows surrounding them. He wore that closed, intent expression Randy was coming to fear. She knew his mind was on Garrett. His anger, frustration and bitterness over the futility of their search filled the air with a tension that was almost palpable.

And she was falling victim to those very same feelings. She was just as restless, just as agitated. Only her reasons were much, much different. Had Zach thought even once about their stolen kiss this morning? She had thought of little else since then. If she was bitter, if she was angry, it was because Zach was consumed with wanting Garrett. And she was consumed with wanting Zach.

Randy wanted to shrivel up and wither away in shame. How was it possible? she agonized. With one kiss, he had stirred a wanton, wild hunger that shocked her. Just thinking of the way his mouth claimed hers made her go hot and then cold. Her eyes squeezed shut, but it did no good. She could see the shape of him—the broadness of his chest, the hardness of his arms—even with her eyes closed.

She had wanted the feel his tongue in her mouth, his hands on her breasts. She'd wanted to feel his skin against hers—not just his chest but all of him.

Her face flamed. Randy was glad the encroaching darkness hid her burning cheeks.

Kevin was dead. She had loved him forever, it seemed, with all that she possessed. In her mind, in her heart, she had never stopped loving him. In the time he'd been gone she had given little thought to love and desire. In her mind, they had always been one and the same. There could be no desire without love. But for the first time, Randy wondered if a woman could desire a man . . . and not love him.

She felt foolish. Randy had never considered herself naive, but she did so now. She was twenty-nine years old and this was all so new to her.

On and on her mind roiled. Yet one thought stood head and shoulders above the rest: it was so unfair, that she who had loved so intensely and so passionately, had never known the ultimate act. . . .

"What's that you're doing?"

Zach's voice startled her. Randy saw that he was standing beside her, eyeing the nylon rope in her hands. She flushed. Until that moment, she hadn't realized she'd been unconsciously fiddling with it.

"It's a climbing rope."

There was a short silence. "Will we need to use it tomorrow?"

They planned to leave for the cave at sunup. Randy hesitated, not wanting to frighten him needlessly, but not wanting to instill any false hope, either. "A lot of climbing can be done with very little equipment at all," she said finally. "It's carried mainly for safety—like using a seat belt in the car."

A hint of skepticism crossed his face. "I can't see where a rope would do much good if someone happened to fall."

Randy's smile was genuine, her first of the evening. "As long as it's done properly, a woman would have no trouble checking someone else's fall," she commented dryly. "Even someone who outweighs her by fifty or sixty pounds."

He smiled as well and crouched down beside her. Randy's heart began to pound. He was so close she could see the tiny lines fanning out from his eyes. He nodded at the rope lying loosely in her hands. "What kind of knot is that?"

She could feel the pressure of his knee riding gently against her thigh. Her throat grew so dry she could hardly speak. "One of the basic ones used in mountaineering. It's called a bowline."

He looked up at her. "Can you show me?"

Her nails dug into her palms. They were only a breath apart. If either of them leaned even a little closer... She laughed, the sound as shaky and tentative as she felt inside. "If it's come to this, you must be pretty bored."

His gaze sharpened. For an instant, his eyes seemed to reach clear inside her. "You don't bore me," he said very quietly.

And that was how they spent the rest of the evening. Randy showed him a dozen different mountaineering knots and he mastered none. He smiled once when she accused him of pretending clumsiness just so she would help him. There was an air of growing closeness between them, but it was marked with a tentative fragility. It was as if they were walking along the edge of a cliff. One step too far and it was all over. Their hands brushed, and they touched with their eyes, but that was as far as it went.

Zach stayed outside the tent when Randy announced her intention of turning in for the night, his mind in a quandary. This enforced intimacy with her was showing signs of slowly driving him crazy. Oh, he couldn't deny he liked being with her—even when they were arguing. A slow grin edged his mouth. He never ceased to be amazed when her fiery spirit cropped up.

Then there was her smile. It made his heart turn over with an emotion that was part pain, part pleasure. But she didn't smile or laugh nearly as much as he'd have liked. And he'd liked the feel of her hands on his tonight, slender yet deft and strong. He liked the way she cuddled against him at night as if they'd slept together for years. He had to remind himself he'd known her only a matter of days. It felt as if he'd known her forever.

Zach's grin faded. Despite their rocky beginnings, he liked her. He liked her too damned much. And she tempted him in ways he'd never dreamed of. Her bulky masculine clothing didn't matter in the least. He'd held her in his arms, and she was all lithe feminine pliancy. But he suspected she didn't welcome them any more than he did.

Did she still grieve for her dead fiancé?

Damn! He swore softly and dug the heel of his boot into the ground. He'd bet his last dollar she wasn't thinking of the man who had been her fiancé when

Zach kissed her, and he hoped to hell that wasn't sheer masculine ego talking.

Knowing Randy was inside the tent, shedding her clothes—and it didn't matter one bit that she slept in that damned long underwear!—made heat gather right in the pit of his stomach. Zach shifted uncomfortably when it spread to his loins. It was all he could do not to remember how she'd felt in his arms this morning, the way her lips had trembled against his like the wings of a bird, as if the intimacy was something never before experienced. But then she'd practically melted into him...

He stiffened as a most outrageous thought flitted through his brain. No, he thought in amazement. It couldn't be. Randy wasn't a kid. Why, she had to be close to thirty. And she'd been engaged, which in this day and age was almost the same as a marriage license. Even if she and her fiancé hadn't lived together, surely the two of them had...

Zach got up, swearing hotly but welcoming the cool rush of air that wrapped around him. If it was true, it was just one more reason to keep his hands to himself. A woman who'd saved herself for that many years wouldn't welcome a man who stormed into her life one week and left the next.

But she wasn't saving herself for you, a mocking voice reminded him. She'd been saving herself for her fiancé...for Kevin.

Zach shoved his hands into his pockets and kicked at a stone, his mellow mood gone. He whirled around and started for the tent, but what he saw stopped him as cold as if he'd run into a brick wall.

He thought he'd given her plenty of time to undress, but she'd used it instead to spread out and arrange their sleeping bags. The lantern cast a hazy glimmer of light in the far corner of the tent. He watched the shadow of her body glide toward the opposite corner and back to the center of the tent where she slid to her knees.

Her hands went to the buttons of her wool shirt. Zach stared as if he'd been hypnotized, which was silly, really, because he knew she wore a long-sleeved undershirt underneath. But he couldn't stop his imagination from a wild rampage when the wool shirt slid from her shoulders.

His breath caught as if he'd been punched in the gut. He didn't have to rely on his imagination after all. She was changing, pulling the undershirt up and revealing the taunt spareness of her ribs. Her arms continued their slow stretch upward. The pouting thrust of her breasts came into view.

She turned slightly, her body etched in a perfect, painfully clean silhouette. Zach's stomach muscles knotted. He felt as if his blood were steaming. In the back of his mind, he knew he should look away, but he couldn't. Damn, but he couldn't!

Her legs were long and sleek. She was slender, but not too slender, with gently rounded hips and exquisitely shaped breasts. He could see the slight rise and fall of her chest as she shed her pants. Did he only imagine her nipples tighten against the chill night air?

He went a little mad just thinking about it. He wanted to rip down the barrier between them; to touch and taste the naked bounty of her breasts with lips and hands. He ached to feel the silk of her skin, to turn her strength into yielding softness....

Where he found the willpower to wrench his eyes away, he never knew. He stood rigidly, eyes closed, hands clenched at his sides, fighting for breath...and fighting for control.

It was a long time later that he stepped into the tent, hoping that Randy was asleep. After what he'd seen, having her crawl into his arms and cling to him would shatter what little restraint he had left.

Randy had been waiting patiently for Zach since the moment she'd crawled into the sleeping bag. She was tired and she ached all over from being slammed against the ground, but she knew instinctively there would be no sleep for her, not until Zach joined her.

It was strange, she reflected with an odd quiver, how muddled her emotions were whenever she thought of this intense, driven man. He sparked her anger quicker than anyone she'd ever known. Why, her temper had been almost nonexistent until she met him. Yet she trusted Zach, and it both amazed and dismayed her to acknowledge how quickly that feeling had grown.

She lay staring up into the darkness, listening to the rustle of his clothing. She felt rather than heard him lie down beside her, then stretch and yawn. "You were a long time," she said anxiously.

There was a protracted silence. "I was just thinking," he said finally.

A pang swept through her. Randy didn't need to ask what he'd been thinking about—or rather, who.

"So was I," she whispered. *About you.* "I—I couldn't go to sleep."

Zach said nothing.

After a while, she leaned up on her elbows and peered through the gloom. "Can I ask you something?"

"Sure."

He sounded less than enthusiastic. Randy hesitated, wondering if she dared.... She finally just blurted it out. "I was just wondering...have you ever been married?"

For the longest time there was a debilitating silence, then she heard him mutter, as if he were talking to himself. "Cripes! Are you always this talkative at night?"

Randy was stung. She lay motionless as hot tears welled in her eyes. She brushed them aside, telling herself they were tears of anger.

It was Zach's turn to fall silent. He called himself every name he could think of, aware that he'd hurt her again. He sighed and reached for her, his heart filled with an odd tenderness and a bittersweet resignation. But this time Randy was having none of it. She stiffened and tried to wrench herself away the instant he touched her shoulders.

He captured her firmly, trapping her against the hardness of his chest, the length of his legs twined around hers. "Don't," he whispered, and it was the pleading in his voice that stopped her struggle. "Just let me hold you . . . please."

His lean fingers slid into her hair, then curled around her nape, compelling her to face him. Suspended in an agony of silence, Randy stared at him, yearning desperately to touch him yet not knowing if she dared. Since she had met Zach, there had been so many emotions . . . in so little time.

She felt the fleeting touch of a callused fingertip slowly tracing the quivering outline of her mouth. His touch was gentle, so achingly tender she wanted to cry. It came as a shock to realize she *was* crying.

He rested his forehead against hers so that they were only a breath apart. Softly, sweetly he kissed her mouth, a healing, soothing caress that took away the chill and shut out the lingering shadows of the night. It felt as if her heart had been encased in ice and had now begun the long, painful task of thawing.

"I'm sorry," he said into her mouth. "I shouldn't have said that, Randy. I didn't mean it the way it sounded, I swear."

It hurt to hear him say the words; it hurt to be with him like this! She could taste the salty warmth of her tears upon his lips. Why wasn't she ashamed of her weakness? Instead she let out a long, tremulous breath, slipped her arms around his neck and clung to him as if her life depended on it.

Zach closed his eyes and rubbed his cheek against the silky softness of her hair. He questioned neither his actions nor his motive. He only knew that right now, he needed her as much as she needed him, and nothing else mattered.

Time slipped quietly by. After a while, he remembered he had yet to give her an answer to her question. "I won't bite your head off this time," he said softly, "if you're prepared to give me a second chance."

She stirred against him. "What?"

He smiled. From the sound of her voice, she'd been on the verge of falling asleep. "You were curious about my marital status."

She lifted her head and pushed the hair out of her eyes. "Oh," she said in a small voice. "That."

"Yes. *That*." He knew she was wide-awake now. It was pitch-black inside the tent, but he sensed her waiting expectantly, practically bursting with curiosity. He was inordinately pleased at the prospect, and decided to stretch it out as long as he could.

A full five minutes must have passed before he heard her voice again, this time tinged with annoyance. "Well?"

"Well, what?"

"Have you or haven't you?"

"Been married?"

"Yes!"

In the darkness, his smile widened. His voice was deceptively lazy, even amused. "Who says I'm not married now?"

He heard her shocked gasp and laughed, picturing her wide-eyed dismay and knowing she was thinking of their torrid embrace this morning.

She started to scramble away but his arms tightened. "There's no need for that," he said with a chuckle. "I'm divorced, Randy, and I have been for quite some time."

"Oh." She seemed content to nestle against him again, but before long she spoke his name tentatively. "Zach?"

"Hmm?"

"What was she like?"

"Not like you," he said unthinkingly. "Not—" he hesitated "—strong."

Strong. He made it sound like a dirty word.

Zach felt her stiffen and tightened his hold on her. "Hey," he chided softly, "I didn't mean anything by that."

"Then what did you mean?"

The words were somewhat defiant. Zach gave a pondering sigh. What was he trying to say? Randy wasn't like Suzanne. Suzanne was like fine china, so dainty and frail he'd always been half-afraid to say a harsh word for fear she would break apart. She'd have gone to pieces on a trip like this, cried and begged to be taken home.

Randy was muscle and bone and strength and resiliency. And yet she was such a contradiction. Only moments ago he had kissed away her tears, held her trembling body close to his heart. Inside she was as fragile as a butterfly's wing.

Yet she had come back here, to these mountains that she hated so much. And that told Zach all he needed to know about just how strong this woman was.

"I'm not sure I can explain it," he said finally. "Suzanne is—a very dependent woman. Timid, I guess you could say. To her, marriage meant handing over control of her life from her parents to a husband. I was married to her for five years, and in all that time, I can't remember her making a single decision without consulting someone else. It was rather sweet, at first. I was flattered that she thought so much of me."

He fell silent for a few seconds. "But after a while, I knew I wanted something more. An equal, someone to share with. With Suzanne, I just felt...hell, I don't know! Stifled. Any little thing that went wrong was a catastrophe. I couldn't even talk to Suzanne about my work without being afraid she'd cringe and run crying into the bedroom."

There was something in his voice, a current Randy couldn't quite decipher. It wasn't disgust or mockery or arrogance, though. Guilt, perhaps?

"I remember once," he went on. "I had to protect a key prosecution witness in a big drug case. The trial went on for weeks. It was a touchy situation. We were constantly on the move because of all the death threats and I was hardly ever home. One night we were shot at. It was just a graze, but I had to spend a day in the hospital." He shook his head. "If you'd seen Suzanne you'd have thought it was the end of the world. She was practically hysterical."

Randy frowned, puzzled by the edge she suddenly sensed in him. "Under the circumstances," she said slowly, "I'd say it's understandable. She must have been scared to death for you."

"No," he said, and Randy wondered when she had ever heard such bleakness. "She wasn't afraid for me, Randy. She was afraid for *herself*. She went on and on about how helpless she'd be without me..." There was a world of emotion reflected in the deep sigh he gave. He sounded so tired, so defeated, that her heart caught painfully.

Her hand crept out to cover his where it lay on his chest. "You feel guilty, don't you?"

His answer was a long time coming. "Yeah," he said heavily. "I divorced her after that. We just couldn't give each other what we needed. It was a big blow to her, but I couldn't stay with her any longer."

"If you had, you'd only have encouraged her dependence," she observed gently. How could she have ever thought this man was hard and unfeeling? "And sometimes we have to believe things happen for the best. Besides, don't you think you deserved something for yourself?"

He hesitated. "It wasn't an easy choice to make, Randy. In the end, she went back to live with her mother in Washington, but it didn't stop me from feeling like I'd abandoned her."

Randy squeezed his hand, not knowing what else to say. There was a heaviness in her chest. She balked at branding herself jealous, but she knew she'd be lying if she said she felt nothing at the thought of Zach with another woman.

She bit her lip. "Do you still love her?" The question slipped out before she could recall it. She felt rather than saw his head veer sharply in her direction. She waited breathlessly, dreading his answer yet wanting desperately to know.

"No," he said just when she thought she couldn't wait any longer. "I never loved Suzanne the way I should have. She was tiny, quiet and soft-spoken—the exact opposite of my stepmother. In fact, there were times I wondered if that wasn't why I'd married her in the first place, because she was so different from my stepmother."

"Your stepmother? The one who locked you out on the balcony?"

Her disapproval was as sharp as a knife blade. What was this? Zach thought in surprise. His champion? A funny feeling speared his heart. He laced their fingers together where her hand still lay on his chest. *Oh, Randy,* he thought, *where have you been all my life?*

"That's the one." He smiled crookedly. "One was quite enough, thank you."

Randy wasn't going to let him get off so lightly, though. "She sounds like a fire-breathing dragon."

Zach's voice held no mirth. "She looks and acts like it, too. She's almost as tall as I am and probably outweighs me, too."

"What did your father see in her?"

"To tell you the truth, I have no idea. My mother died when I was four, and since my father's job took him away from home a lot, I think he thought I should have a mother, so he married Donna. But Donna was jealous and resentful of me right from the start."

His voice dropped. "When I was a kid, she terrified me. She never asked—she demanded. Things had to be done her way or not at all. She's cold, unyielding and the most domineering person I've ever known in my life."

It made Randy ache inside to think of a child growing up under such conditions. "I've been accused of having a will of iron a few times."

Not like this, Zach started to say, but something stopped him. Randy was not the church mouse he'd first thought her. She was stubborn and outspoken. How many times had they crossed swords already? The thought that Randy was anything at all like Donna was infinitely disturbing.

But he hated to shatter the closeness they shared right now. "I think we'd better call a halt to the inquisition or it'll be dawn before we know it. Before we do though, I have a question for you."

"Shoot."

"How did you ever get stuck with a handle like Randy?"

She groaned. "Anything but that one!"

"Sorry, but I promised only one question and that's the one."

She sighed and relented with as much grace as she could muster. Burying her face against his shoulder, she muttered the answer.

"What's that? I didn't hear you." He'd heard her perfectly well. The truth was, he liked seeing this shy sweet side of her.

She raised her head and gave him what he was sure was a blistering glare. "You're just doing this to get even with me for threatening to leave you on that cliff!" she charged with a loud whisper.

"That's more like it." He smiled his approval. "Time's almost up. Are you going to tell me where you got a name like Randy?"

"All right, but you have to promise you won't laugh."

"I won't."

"All right then," she said crossly. "It's short for Miranda."

"Miranda!"

"Yes," she hissed.

Zach laughed anyway.

HE WASN'T LAUGHING twelve hours later.

The day hadn't started out well, in spite of the fact that the weather promised to be sunny and warm. The clouds drifting along to the south didn't look at all threatening. It was for that reason he raised an eyebrow when Randy pulled both sleeping bags from the tent and began rolling one up.

"I thought we were coming back here tonight."

She didn't look up, nor did she stop what she was doing. "We are."

"Then why don't we leave this stuff here?" He swept an arm around their camp. "Why truck everything up there if we don't need it?"

She sat back on her heels and surveyed him coolly. She'd heard the hint of obstinacy in his statement. "I planned on leaving the tent and the stove and the fuel here. But I believe in being prepared for the worst, and if something happens, I intend to be warm."

Warm? He was plenty warm enough with his shirt and sweater. And it was sunny, for crying out loud! He clamped back a stinging retort and shoved his jacket into his backpack. But he'd be damned if he'd carry more than he needed. So with the toe of his boot, he shoved his sleeping bag back into the tent.

Randy jumped to her feet and plopped the lantern next to her pack, her intention plain. Her expression dared him to argue. "Suit yourself," she snapped. "It's no skin off my nose if you don't want to take it, but at least bring a change of clothes with you."

Muttering under his breath, Zach did as she asked. He even rolled up the sleeping bag and stuffed it into the pack.

Several hours later he was too numb to say much of anything. He could feel the sweat beading down his back from the exertion, but he felt as if he'd been plunged into a vat of ice.

The climb was everything he had feared—and more. They had been climbing steadily for longer than he cared to think about, skirting rocks as big as boxcars, scrambling along ledges and up little ribs. The rock beneath their feet was crumbly and unstable. He slipped several times, but he didn't dare look when his boots sent a shower of pebbles plunging down the mountainside.

High above, the summit loomed like a huge stone chimney. When they encountered a notch in the wall beside them, Zach slid down. He thrust his arms across his upraised knees and leaned his head back. Spots of yellow and green danced before his eyes. Waves of vertigo washed over him. He was totally off kilter, completely off balance.

Randy squatted beside him. She fumbled around in her backpack, then he felt something wonderfully cool and refreshing slide across his forehead.

"Are you okay?" she asked softly.

Hell no! he wanted to shout. But he didn't have the energy, and it was probably a good thing.

The towelette slid down and over his cheek. He closed his eyes in mute appreciation. "You feel light-headed?" she asked.

"Yeah," he muttered.

Her fingers, slender and smooth, felt for his pulse. "You're not used to the altitude."

His eyes opened. "The altitude?" His harsh laugh revealed his self-mockery. "Honey, if you want to put a label on it, why don't you tell it like it is?"

She smiled slightly and studied him for a moment. Her smile slowly ebbed. "Zach," she said quietly, "we can't stay here any longer."

As wretched as he felt, Zach heard the strained urgency in her voice. His gaze flitted to her questioningly.

"We have to hurry. Any minute now it's going to start raining. We don't want to get caught out in the open in a lightning storm."

She pointed above his head. Zach was stunned to find black sky oozing overhead. His jaw dropped open and he stared. How was it possible? Their camp had been so sunny and warm when they left.

At precisely that moment, there was a violent crack of thunder. A flash of lightning split open the seething mass of clouds. The air around them seemed to sizzle and hum. A peculiar sensation zinged through him, from his fingertips to his toes.

Randy tugged frantically at his arm. "Zach, please! We have to hurry. It's just a little farther."

He followed the direction of her finger. Ahead there was a huge outcropping of rock, and the only way to get around it was a lip that was scarcely wider than a sidewalk! With a horrified sense of inevitability, his gaze dropped to where jagged rocks lunged toward him, as if the mountain had yawned to reveal a gaping set of teeth.

He froze. "I can't," he heard himself whisper. "I can't."

But he hadn't reckoned on Randy. With a strength that would have astounded him at any other time, she grabbed his shoulders and shoved him down on his hands and knees. "You can!" she yelled fiercely. "Now I don't care if you crawl or walk or even if you fly, but move, dammit!"

And crawl he did, inch by painstaking inch. Thanks to Randy, he had no choice. She was behind him all the way, her shoulder butting into his hip and nudging him ahead, always ahead. Countless rocks gouged his hands and knees. The clouds opened up, pelting his face with a wind-driven sheet of rain like a hundred tiny needles. He alternately cursed Garrett and Randy for forcing him into this hellish nightmare.

He had no conscious awareness of when they finally reached the cave. Through a haze he heard Randy yelling in his ear, telling him they were inside. His lungs heaving, his eyes burning, he collapsed facedown. Behind him, he heard Randy breathing heavily. For what seemed like an eternity, he lay there, unable to believe he'd made it. If he'd been able to move, he'd have kissed the ground.

But all of a sudden, it hit him. Here they were, nearly at the top of a mountain, exhausted, cold and wet. And for what? What had been accomplished? A cynical voice inside answered. *Not a thing.*

Because they still hadn't found Garrett.

He rolled over and stared above him. The cave was a black hole in the side of the mountain, chill and damp and unwelcoming.

From the corner of his eye he saw Randy rise to her feet. That she found the cave even less friendly than he was evident in the way her gaze touched apprehensively on the stark stone walls. She stared into the forbidding shadows at the back of the cave, then quickly pulled her eyes away. She shivered and hugged herself.

Zach dragged the hair out of his eyes and sat up. "What the hell are we doing here?" he said aloud.

"You're afraid of the dark. And I'm afraid of heights. Quite a pair, aren't we?" His voice bounced off the ceiling. It sounded hollow and eerie, as eerie as his brittle laugh. "All this time and we haven't found even a trace of Garrett. We'll never find him—never."

He was only dimly aware of Randy shedding her backpack. She pulled out the lantern and lit it, then stepped gingerly toward the shadows in the rear.

Zach would have thought nothing could arouse him from his weary state, but he was on his feet like a shot the instant he heard a shocked gasp.

He grabbed Randy's arm. "What? What is it?"

He almost missed the note of cautious excitement in her voice. "I'm not saying you're wrong—"she raised a shaky hand "—but is that what I think it is?"

She raised the lantern higher and Zach caught the glint of metal. His gaze came to rest on a point some ten yards behind them.

There, in a deep niche high in the wall, lay a haphazard arrangement of canned goods.

"Someone's been here," he said, stunned. *"Someone's been here!"*

CHAPTER TWELVE

THE DISCOVERY PROVED to be a hollow victory. The cache of food—including flour, sugar, beans and some other dried goods—had been stowed recently; the hell of it was that they had no way of pinpointing how recently. It could have been yesterday. It could have been a month ago.

Hours later, Zach was still seething. He had no way of knowing if Garrett was still within reach. How many other caches of food did Garrett have? Garrett and his father had hidden out in these mountains for years! When would he be back? Tomorrow? A month from now? He was a fool to think they could ever catch him.

Outside, the rain continued in torrents. Zach slammed a fist against the wall and continued his restless pacing. He'd traced the cave's perimeter dozens of times already. The main chamber was huge and domed. A fissure dipped toward the belly of the mountain, but only a child could have wriggled through the opening. Randy sat against the far wall, facing the entrance.

"Zach."

His head jerked up when she spoke his name. When she saw that she had his attention, her chin lifted. "We're going to have to spend the night here. Only a

fool would try to head up or down this trail in a heavy
rain like this. By now it's probably impassable. And
the risk of falling rock is ten times what it usually is.''

So they were stuck up here. They couldn't leave, and
Garrett couldn't return . . . *if* he'd been here at all.

Randy's tone was guarded. She watched Zach
closely, as if she expected an argument.

Zach's expression softened slightly. His gaze traveled meaningfully to their packs, piled against a rock.
He nodded at the sleeping bag. "Aren't you going to
say 'I told you so'?"

She shook her head. Her smile didn't reach her eyes.
In fact, she seemed uncharacteristically uncertain of
herself.

"How long?" he asked after a moment.

She frowned.

"How long do you think this rain will last?"

"I wish I knew. In weather like this there's too much
interference to raise any kind of radio transmission, so
we can't look for help there." She sounded almost
bitter. "This rain wasn't in the forecast, but then that
doesn't surprise me. The weather is too unpredictable
up here. It can be clear as a bell one minute, and the
next hour there's a storm brewing."

So he'd discovered, Zach thought grimly. "We'll
just have to wait it out."

"Exactly." Her lips barely moved.

Zach went back to his pacing while Randy stared
out at the dismal curtain of rain. This was so much like
what had happened three years ago, it was frightening. Only it hadn't been rain that trapped her and
Kevin, but snow.

What if a cold front moved in?

Randy twisted her hands between her knees and
fought the shadowy hold of the past. She couldn't
suppress the icy shiver that reached clear to her soul.
As far as she was concerned, the sooner they left this
cave, the better.

THE HOURS CAME AND WENT with painstaking slow-
ness. Zach divided his time between practicing the
knots she'd showed him and pacing around the cave,
until Randy wanted to scream in frustration.

Outside the sky was a depthless gray. She couldn't
shut out the sound of the relentless wind, whistling
and wailing through granite notches. Churning clouds
whipped by in a frenzy. Fortunately the cave was
sheltered from the wind. The air was chill and damp
but nowhere near freezing.

She pretended not to see Zach's speculative glance
when she pulled yet another blanket from her pack
and threw it around her shoulders. She wore three
layers of insulated clothing below her down jacket, yet
she couldn't seem to get warm.

But there was no cold as penetrating as that which
came from within....

She was getting positively morbid! If only she could
stop thinking. If only she could relax! She hated her
cowardice and despised her weakness. She huddled
beneath the blanket; her fingers clenched and un-
clenched where she held it tight beneath her chin. She
stared straight ahead at the driving rain to keep from
looking at the low domed ceiling, the knobby stone
walls.

It was odd, very odd. Everything else had come
back to her, every landmark, every trail, every tree.

But she didn't remember this cave being so small. So... *close.*

Darkness settled in like a thick ebony shroud. The night's gloom intensified her feeling of being trapped. Randy crawled into her sleeping bag and prayed for daybreak.

Sleep was mercifully quick. But with sleep came dreams, and dreams sometimes became nightmares....

The darkness hemmed her in, pressing closer and closer, sapping her strength and robbing her of breath. They were trapped in a stark lonely world of blackness and cold, just the two of them, she and Kevin. There wasn't even enough light to see her hands in front of her face.

How long had they been there? She didn't know. And why did she suddenly feel she was being smothered, that the walls of their snow cave were closing in? She gasped for air, but each labored breath was like inhaling a lungful of ice.

Scrambling to her knees, she ripped off her mittens and lunged frantically around the small snow cave. No. Oh, Lord, no! A silent scream shrilled in her mind. The cave was collapsing!

She couldn't give up, not yet! She had to stay calm. She had to think. She had to save Kevin.

But she was alone. There was no one to help. No one to keep her from being swallowed up forever by the darkness and the cold...

Help us! Oh, please, somebody help us!

Zach awoke to a cry that curdled his blood. Beside him, he felt Randy thrashing wildly. In the darkness, his fingers instinctively grabbed for the flashlight at the same time as he bolted upright.

Harsh, sobbing breaths racked her slender form. She was shaking violently, her hands wrapped around her arms.

"Randy!" He scrambled to his knees and reached for her.

"Oh, God!" she moaned. "You have to find us. We'll die out here. Please, somebody help us!"

Zach grabbed her shoulders and shook her. Her lids fluttered open. He was stunned to the core by the naked anguish he glimpsed in her eyes, but the way she stared right through him frightened him as nothing else ever had. It was as if she were in another time, another place.

"Randy, wake up!" he said hoarsely. "You're all right, love. It's just a dream!"

Randy's vision swirled. She was only dimly aware of another presence. But that presence was alive and warm, and she clung to the voice and the touch of strong male hands as if they were her only link to life.

His fingers pressed against her jaw, guiding her face upward. The scream she'd swallowed turned to a muffled sob of relief when she saw Zach's face hovering above her.

"Are you all right?" His tone was urgent.

Her eyes were still half-wild. "I can't breathe," she choked. "God, I can't breathe!"

His heart wrenched as he listened to her struggle for breath. Both of his hands dropped to her shoulders. He gave a reassuring squeeze. "Take it easy," he soothed. "Relax."

He didn't pretend to understand the turmoil in her mind. Whatever had caused this debilitating fear of the dark was locked tightly away inside her. But this was not the time to question too deeply; there was time for that later. All he wanted right now was to drive the frightened light from her eyes.

With his thumb, he brushed the damp hair from her cheek. "Do you want the lantern on?" he asked softly.

"I ... yes. No! Oh, I don't know!"

She was still so scared, her mind blunted with fragments of her dream. She stared at Zach numbly, trying desperately to smooth the tattered edges of her emotions. But all at once she realized that Zach's touch—infinitely tender, infinitely gentle against her cheek—was doing what her mind could not.

Pride be damned, she thought helplessly. She wanted—no, needed—the warmth and comfort he offered. She flung herself against him, the desperate plea she held inside her coming forth unbidden. "Don't leave me, Zach. Please don't leave me. I'm so cold. So cold!"

The quiver in her voice caught at his chest. He gathered her into his arms, holding her with hands that hinted of comfort, not passion.

She burrowed against him as if she wanted to crawl inside him. "I thought I was over it." Her eyes squeezed shut. "I thought I'd never be afraid of the dark and the cold again. I thought I'd never have nightmares again. But it was so real. It was like it was happening all over again."

Zach pulled her closer still, feeling her shudders as if they were his own. "Do you want to talk about it?"

Her eyes flicked open to stare directly into his. "I can't," she said wildly. "I... please try to understand, it's not you." Her voice grew jerky. "If I could, I would, but I... I just can't. Not now."

Zach's chest tightened. In the hazy light given off by the flashlight, he saw the muscles in her throat work convulsively. Her eyes were dark with tortured memories.

"It's all right," he whispered. "You don't have to tell me anything you don't want to." He hooked his finger beneath her chin, gently but firmly demanding that she look at him. "But I'm here if that's what you want. Okay?"

"Okay." The word was no more than a breath of air. She tried to smile but her lips were trembling too much. Seeing her effort tugged at his heartstrings.

Zach switched off the flashlight and eased them both into the shelter of his sleeping bag. He arranged her body against his and tucked her head into the hollow of his shoulder, wondering if she was even aware of the way her fingers curled into the front of his shirt.

For Zach, the awareness brought as much pleasure as pain. It was impossible to hold her like this, to feel the yielding contours of her body shaped against his side, and forget that she was a woman, lovely and desirable. But he banished all such thoughts from his mind and simply held her, oddly humble and proud knowing that he was able to give the comfort she so sorely needed.

He trailed his hand up and down the length of her arm. She responded by melting against him and burying her face against the warm skin of his neck.

His mouth brushed gently against her temple, the silky curve of her cheek, the tender slope of her jaw. Zach loved the breathless sigh of pleasure she gave, the way her breath misted warmly against his neck. Time stood still while his mouth hovered at the corner of her lips. His senses were in chaos, his mind in turmoil. She was so tempting, so disarmingly vulnerable. Did he dare give in to the need heating his blood? Did he dare sample once more the innocent enticement of her lips, just for a moment...

The decision was made for him. Zach felt her move her head a fraction...

Their lips met. Tentatively at first, sweet and gentle and exploring. But when Zach would have drawn back, she slid her arms around his neck and clung to him as if he were all that she wanted in the world.

And that was exactly how Randy felt. It was a kiss of fiery sweetness, a kiss that raged out of control despite all attempts to contain it. She dug her fingers into the nape of his neck, tracing the tendons she found there and reveling in the feel of his skin. For an instant she felt wholly selfish, taking pleasure from the fusion of his mouth on hers, seeking strength from his strength.

Just a little longer, she told herself. It felt so good being held like this. When Zach touched her, the seeping, bitter cold melted into dark pleasure. If there was fear, it was for the moment this painfully sweet mating of lips would end.

He dragged his mouth away for a heart-stopping second, and she wanted to cry out her disappointment. But then he was there again, his body a warm, welcome weight against hers, his mouth tender and gentle and hungry all at once.

She yearned to feel his skin against hers, and suddenly he was there, his fingers sliding beneath the layers of clothes. She was rocked to the core by the pleasure she felt when his hands settled with gentle possessiveness on the narrow span of her waist. His tongue touched hers, and she kissed him back with a fervored intimacy that was like nothing she'd ever experienced.

His thumbs drew tiny circles on her skin, tracing the arcing line of her rib cage. Her body responded with a wild sweet will of its own. Her nipples were taut and tingling, straining for his touch. As if he knew exactly what she wanted, his hand stole upward to gauge the ripe fullness of her breast.

She drew in a sharp breath, the flood of sensations inside threatening to choke her. She'd never felt anything like this before, this demanding urgency of her own body. It was shocking. Arousing. Thrilling. She wanted to clamp his hand against her body, close her eyes and savor the delicious feeling of his palm claiming her flesh for all eternity.

Outside the cave, there was a low rumble of thunder. The air around them was full of the scent of earth and rain.

Zach tore his mouth away from hers. Closing his eyes, he battled silently for control, his breathing ragged and uneven. He wanted Randy so much he was shaking with it. In the foggy recesses of his mind, he wondered if Randy could tell how much he wanted her.

She moaned, a tiny sound of protest he longed to swallow with his mouth. A flash of lightning split the air. For an instant, the cave was as light as day. His eyes opened at the sound, and he saw that her face was flushed with desire, her eyes cloudy with need. He ached to see the sweet satisfaction of fulfillment there instead, but he knew if he didn't stop now, he'd never be able to.

Her fingers slid into the golden roughness of the hair that grew low on his nape. "Don't stop," he heard her whisper. "Oh, please, don't stop."

The yearning ache in her voice cut him to ribbons. *Damn,* he thought in angry despair. He should never have kissed her. Then he wouldn't want to... He bit back the thought angrily. That was the whole problem. He knew what he wanted, and yet he was wondering if it would be enough for either of them.

"Randy." His voice was low and tight. "This is no game. Do you know what you're asking?"

Under his intense scrutiny, Randy's gaze flitted away. Was this wrong? a voice inside agonized. To love the way his hand traveled over her, touching where no man had ever touched? Even Kevin...

But she couldn't think of Kevin—not now! To think of Kevin meant going back to the netherworld that threatened to smother her, the world she wanted to escape. To think of Kevin meant cold and fear and darkness....

Zach was light and heat and the vital energy of life. She could feel the heat of his body, the lifeblood pulsing through him. He smelled warm and musky and... and right now she needed someone to cling to.

She desperately needed the reassurance that she wasn't so terrifyingly alone....

She needed Zach. She needed him as she had never needed anyone in her life.

"I need this, Zach. I need *you*." Her fingers knotted in his hair. She bent and pressed her lips to the musky hollow of his throat, feeling the thunder of his rampaging heart. "Please," she whispered.

The world seemed to narrow into that one word. Zach knew, even if she didn't, what she was asking. He sensed a wild desperation in her, but he was caught squarely between heaven and hell.

Desire was nothing new to him. But trapped within his need for her was that strange, melting emotion he'd never before felt with any other woman, even Suzanne...especially Suzanne.

He wanted Randy more than he could ever remembering wanting anyone. More than that, he *needed* her. But like this? He was nothing but a crutch, a healing balm to drive away her demons of the night.

There was a heated rush of silence. Zach knew she could feel the hunger in his body, the tense yearning in the arms that held her close. And still he hesitated.

Lightning split the night, charging the air around them. In the aftermath, Zach couldn't close his eyes to what he had seen: the lingering traces of fear mingling with her uncertain expression, the unspoken question he glimpsed in soft blue eyes that refused to shy away. She was so strong, he thought again. But she'd never looked more vulnerable. And the sight of her lips, quivering and tremulous, tore right into his heart.

He was lost.

"Come here." He swept her against him.

Randy closed her eyes. Her breath rushed out in a sigh that he trapped with plundering lips. She clung to him blindly, absorbing his warmth like sunshine.

He loved the way she felt in his arms, so pliant yet resilient and firm. But he ached to feel every sweet inch of her molded against his hardness.

He sat up and tugged at her bulky layers of clothes. "Let's get these off you," he muttered hoarsely.

She sat up beside him, fumbling with the hem of her sweater. The storm outside grew more intense, filling the cave with sizzling flashes of light. Her hands were shaking as she drew the sweater up and over her head; the fiery intensity blazing in Zach's eyes both frightened and thrilled her. Her fingers were clumsy on the buttons of her shirt, and she felt his hand cover hers, strong and sure. Between her hands and his, the rest of her clothing followed. A thousand doubts and fears tumbled through her mind when Zach peeled off his shirt and began to work on his pants. In the hushed, waiting silence, the scrape of his zipper seemed overly loud.

She had one brief, terrifying glimpse of his nakedness before he slid in beside her. His limbs were long and netted with dark hair. His body was lean and hard, pared of all fat.

He wrapped her in his arms and pulled her tight against him. The heat of his body against hers was scorching. Randy heard a sharp intake of breath and vaguely recognized it as her own.

His hand came up to cup her cheek. His gentle touch seemed at complete odds with the tensile strength of his body. He raised his head and stared down at her. "This is a hell of a place for this to happen—a cold dark cave with only a sleeping bag for a bed." His eyes darkened; his voice lowered. "I wish it could be different." Against her jaw his fingers moved ever so slightly in the sweetest of caresses, conveying his regret.

She pressed her mouth into the warm roughness of his palm. "It's all right," she whispered. And suddenly it was, for with his touch, all her doubts and fears slipped away.

His hand slid down her throat. "I wish I could see you."

"Next time." But her smile was tremulous, the words filled with a bravado she refused to examine too closely. Their time was measured. When Zach caught up with Garrett, he would be heading home. And even if he didn't, he couldn't stay. His life was in Portland and hers was here.

Randy didn't care. Deep down, she had nothing to look forward to but countless other nights alone, a lifetime of them. She wanted this night—this moment—whatever the risk.

Whatever the cost.

She closed her eyes and twined her arms around his neck, wordlessly communicating that need.

His mouth came down on hers at the same instant his hand closed possessively over the thrusting curve of her breast. She loved the ragged breath he drew at the first tentative touch of her tongue against his. His arms tightened, making her quiveringly aware of the burgeoning thrust of his arousal. His kiss deepened, fierce and wild and urgent; his tongue dove swift and deep, seeking the dark honey within. A heady sense of power and exhilaration poured through her, surpassing everything she'd ever known. Every part of her came alive with an aching sensitivity.

They touched from head to toe. His body was lean and muscled and rough with hair. It seemed strange to lie against Zach with no barriers between them, yet her body melted naturally into his, displaying a will of its own. She sensed the hunger in him, just as she sensed he was holding back. He took his time, stealing her breath with kisses of fire and burning caresses. In the far corners of her mind, she wondered if he knew...

He pulled her hands to his chest, inviting her to explore his body the way he explored hers. Her touch wavered between shy and bold. She was fascinated with the thick mat of hair on his chest, twining her fingers in it and sliding her palms across his skin over and over. He kissed the corner of her mouth with a low chuckle that turned to a muffled groan when she began charting a forbidden pathway, straying ever lower. Her heart flew to her throat when she encountered the throbbing heat of his desire. She would have wrenched away but suddenly his hand closed over hers, warm and strong and sure, urging her back with seductive persuasion. Her fingers slowly uncurled. She discovered the straining fullness of him, his heat and shape and texture, until they both labored for breath.

When he could stand her sweet torment no longer, he pulled away and dragged her hands around his waist. Her tiny protest was lost between their lips. He kissed her over and over, each contact longer, more lingering. She felt as if she were sinking into a bottomless abyss when his lips slid with slow heat down to her breasts. Deep inside, a budding heat prickled and unfolded, spreading outward.

Her hands dug into his lean waist, as she felt his mouth on her breasts tugging, toying, teasing first one throbbing nipple and then the other until she bit back a cry of pleasure.

The heel of his hand, pleasurably rough, skimmed the hollow of her belly, tracing patterns on her quivering skin from navel to thigh and back again. Her heart raced double time. The place between her thighs felt heavy and feverish. Randy was shocked at how much she burned for his touch. She knew exactly what she wanted. Her hips arched up instinctively, and still he continued to taunt and tease, driving her to a fine frenzy, coming heart-stoppingly close but never quite reaching his ultimate destination.

His touch, when it finally came, was unbearably intimate...and unbearably sweet. Randy choked back a cry as his hand at last stole over the warm cove of her femininity. Gentle fingers parted her, finding her flowering core and initiating a mind-spinning rhythm that ripped the breath from her lungs.

Desire flooded her. She wanted his weight pressing into her, his fullness inside her filling the empty void he had created.

"Zach." His name was no more than a wisp of air, but it was a miracle she could speak at all. Her fingers dug into the tautness of his shoulders. "Zach, please."

He raised his head to look at her. His features were tense and strained. His eyes burned into her. Trapped in his turbulent gaze, Randy couldn't look away. The stark hunger reflected in his eyes should have frightened her, but all she could think was that in that moment, she would never be cold again. His hunger warmed her, reaching clear to her soul.

He shifted slightly, his searing arousal poised against her tender threshold. His mouth came down on hers. She caught at him, feeling the knotted tension in his arms as he lowered himself to her. Yet when he came inside her, it was with infinite care, so slowly and carefully she thought she would burst with the feelings that welled up inside her.

If his tender invasion caused any pain, she scarcely noticed. She found herself bathed in a flood of wonderfully sensuous feelings. She thrilled to the binding pressure of his hips against hers, the stretching fullness of his flesh inside her.

He began to move. Shivers raced through her. His tempo was slow and easy, the long silken friction making her arch her hips in sweet anticipation. She felt his breath rush past her ear. His movements gained power and momentum. His hands at her hips drew her more tightly into the cradle of his thighs.

Thunder crashed all around her—and inside her. She was drawn into the raging tempest, flung into the center of the storm. She was caught in a current, twisted and turned and swept to a height she'd only dreamed of. One final, soul-shattering stroke brought her to the pinnacle and over the edge. Then she was free-falling, hurtling downward through time and space, clinging to the only solid object in a wildly spinning universe....

Zach.

When she came back to earth, she was still cradled in his arms. She pressed her face against his shoulder. "You knew." Her breathless whisper broke the silence. "You knew this was the first time...that I'd never..." The sentence drifted away. There was no delicate way to phrase this. Randy knew the huskiness in her voice betrayed her.

Zach drew back so he could see her. He brushed the damp hair from her cheek. She met his gaze reluctantly, but her expression held a mixture of gratitude and wonder. He liked seeing her like this, so soft and sweet and shy. "Not for sure," he admitted. "At first I thought it couldn't possibly be...but I wasn't about to take the chance I was wrong." He smiled slightly. "You surprised the heck out of me, Randy Pierce."

Her eyes closed. Remembering his cautious tenderness the instant he came inside her made her throat grow tight. "Zach—" she whispered.

Warm fingers pressed against her mouth. "Shh," he said huskily. "You don't have to say anything else, Randy. I don't need an explanation—" his gaze grew intent "—nor do I want one."

She kissed the fingers pressed against her mouth, her eyes conveying the words she could not speak. When Zach turned and settled her against him, she kissed the bare skin of his shoulder, content to relax. She didn't want to think about tomorrow; nor did she wish to examine too closely what had just happened between her and Zach. When she was in his arms, there was no all-consuming darkness, no icy fingers of cold clawing through her. She felt safe, body and soul. And right now, nothing else mattered.

WHEN RANDY OPENED HER EYES the next morning, the cave was lit by filmy streamers of light. She came awake instantly, aware of a faint tingling along her nerves.

Something wasn't right. She felt as if a silent alarm had gone off inside her. She held her breath, trying to analyze the vague nagging feeling inside her.

Then she realized. The air outside was absolutely still. The rain had stopped. The storm was over. Then she heard the low, keening whistle of the wind . . .

Beside her, Zach slept peacefully. Last night came back to her in a shattering rush of remembrance. Heat flooded her entire body. She remembered the warm haven of his arms, and then he had made love to her. Oh, no. She'd practically begged him!

But there wasn't time for that now. Randy couldn't shake the feeling that something was wrong. She slipped from the sleeping bag and grabbed the radio, trying in vain to raise a radio transmission. All she heard was a faint hum. Her heart in her throat, she thrust the radio aside and dressed hurriedly, not even bothering to braid her hair.

Hazy sunlight greeted her when she stepped outside. Gazing at the patch of clear blue sky, she might have doubted last night's storm had ever occurred.

Randy began picking her way higher on the trail, her expression determined. The cave faced east; behind them was a solid wall that stretched skyward. To the north the summit loomed bleakly. It was in that direction that she headed.

She didn't have to go far to discover what she was after. The instant she stepped through a notch in the overhang, the wind slapped her in the face, stinging her skin and taking her breath away. It was cold and wet, blasting from the southwest—a sure sign of bad weather. As if that weren't enough, an ominous cloud bank drew nearer.

The hair on the back of her neck prickled. Randy felt as if she'd plunged into an icy crevasse. She whirled and ran back the way she had come. She stumbled and skidded, her usual surefootedness deserting her.

Zach was up and fully dressed when she burst into the cave. He shrugged into his parka, his face as dark as a thundercloud. "Where the hell have you been?" he demanded.

"Up near the summit," she panted. "Zach—"

"Near the summit? Alone?" A single step brought them toe to toe. "Are you crazy? Garrett could be out there!"

Garrett, she thought wildly. Garrett was the least of her worries right now. "We have to leave, Zach. We have to leave now!" She dropped to her knees and yanked at the zipper holding the two sleeping bags together.

Zach grabbed her arm and pulled her to her feet. "Dammit, Randy, didn't you hear me! You scared the living daylights out of me when I woke up and found you gone." If Randy hadn't been so shaken, she'd have heard the underlying torment beneath his harshness.

She tried to wrench her arm away but his grip was too strong. "You don't understand," she cried. "There's another storm coming. We can't stay here!"

Zach's eyes narrowed. "Why not? We did last night."

His utter calm made her want to scream with frustration. She took a deep breath and fought to control the feelings spiraling inside her. "This is different. We don't have enough food to last more than a few days and there's a cold front moving in!"

"A cold front?" He no longer sounded angry, just puzzled. His gaze slid to the radio lying against his backpack. "I didn't hear you call for a weather report."

Something inside her snapped. She ran outside the cave and pointed at the seething mass of clouds now passing overhead. Zach had no choice but to follow.

The wind sent her hair streaming out behind her. "We can't rely on the radio. We're too high and too far away, and if the weather is like it was yesterday, it's useless!" Tears spurted from her eyes. "Why can't you trust me? By this time tomorrow this whole peak will be covered in snow! We're not at Garrett's mercy up here, we're at the mercy of the weather. And if we don't head back down now, it's going to happen again!"

Zach was stunned by the hysteria in her voice. Everything inside him crystallized into a hard knot as a vague notion spun through his mind. He went very still inside. "What?" His voice reflected a calm he was suddenly far from feeling. "What will happen again?"

"It'll be just like when Kevin died!" she screamed. "The snow...the storm...I was caught up here in a blizzard once, and I won't do it again. Do you hear me, Zach? I won't do it again!"

She went a little wild then, tearing into him with a strength born of terror and fury. She was screaming, crying, cursing him, but the blind panic in her eyes shook him to the core.

It'll be just like when Kevin died.

Her cry tore through Zach like a death knell, over and over again. In its wake, his mind put together a fragmented picture of what had happened. Both she and Dan said she stopped climbing because someone close to her had been involved in an accident—a storm. That someone had been Kevin.

And Randy had been there.

The taste of self-disgust was like ashes in his mouth. He had brought her to this, he thought numbly. He had done this to her, and now it was up to him to try to undo the pain he had caused.

If only he could, he thought bleakly. If only he could.

Dimly he realized she was pounding on his chest. He caught her wrists in his hands. "Randy." She didn't even hear him. She was sobbing, still struggling against him and fighting to be free.

Zach closed his eyes, wrapped his arms around her taut, trembling body and forced them both to their knees. She was so rigid in his arms he felt she was about to shatter into a million pieces. He shook her gently until the glazed look disappeared from her eyes. A shudder tore through her, and she collapsed against him.

His eyes bleak, he held her head to his chest and wordlessly offered what little comfort he could. Hot tears wet the hollow of his throat; he felt as if they seeped clear to his heart.

After a moment, he spoke her name softly. "Randy."

Slowly she raised her head. She stared at him through eyes gone cloudy with pain. "I can't stay here,

Zach," she whispered tremulously. "Not with a storm moving in. Please, I just can't...."

The sight of her quivering lips tore into his heart. "I know." He brushed a stray curl of hair behind her ear, resisting the urge to linger. He wanted nothing more than to pull her down as he had last night and replace the dullness in her eyes with the light of passion.

His breath emerged as a long weary sigh. His hands dropped down to grip hers. He pulled her to her feet but retained his possession of her hands.

Randy blinked. "We're leaving?"

His grip on her hands tightened. "Just say the word and we're gone, lady."

Relief flooded her face, but Zach nearly groaned when her eyes grew unexpectedly moist once more. "Thank you," she whispered. His heart skipped a beat when she propelled herself upward and pressed her lips to his. Her kiss was sweet and fleeting...and sped straight from her heart to his.

He watched her somberly when she turned away. In that moment, he suddenly knew...this compelling urge for her was more than physical. Making love to her last night had pried his eyes wide open.

No, it wasn't her gratitude he was after. Deep inside, he knew instinctively that he wanted more from Randy—her thoughts, her desires, her hopes and dreams.

Maybe more than she had to give.

CHAPTER THIRTEEN

THEY SPOKE VERY LITTLE through the remainder of the day. Randy set a grueling pace that left little time for thought. They stopped only to gather up the supplies they'd left at their base camp. Darkness was complete when they settled in for the night. Randy slept in Zach's arms again, but that was all. They were both too exhausted for anything else.

Zach awoke early the next morning. He lay quietly, conscious of Randy's weight nestled against him and feeling strangely complacent.

His thoughts drifted to the day ahead. They were out of the high country now and expected to embrace civilization once again.

A twinge of unease shot through him. He had mixed feelings about their return. On one hand, he was anxious to see for himself how Larry was. A surge of anger shot through him as he recalled how Garrett had left Larry for dead. These past days of searching for Garrett had only increased his determination to find him. Zach didn't delude himself. His quest had turned into a personal vendetta. The need to find Garrett—to make him pay for what he'd done to Larry—hammered away inside him.

Then there was Randy. What the hell was he supposed to do about her? He couldn't stop himself from wondering what would happen when this was all over. She wasn't the kind of woman he could easily walk away from.

A faint tinge of bitterness crept into his mind. It would have been better if he had never touched her, if he had kept his distance as he originally intended. Yet he couldn't drive her image from his mind—the way she had looked that night, her eyes haunted and filled with terror. The memory cut into him still. She had been so frightened, so desperate for someone to cling to. To ignore that need would have been like cutting his heart out.

No, he couldn't shut away the burning remembrance any more than he could stop himself from feeling their coming together was inevitable.

When Randy awoke, they discovered that at some point during the night, it had begun to snow. In anyone else, perhaps, Zach might have expected a show of triumph. But Randy seemed curiously reluctant to meet his gaze, saying only that they'd better hurry.

Her reaction hurt. She hadn't spoken of the night they'd made love, except for their brief exchange afterward. Oddly Zach understood. What had happened between them was still too close, too fresh in their minds to examine with clinical detachment.

The snow slowed their pace considerably. They'd made radio contact yesterday and relayed the approximate time of their arrival. Coming so soon after the rain, the ground was slick and icy, but they reached the rendezvous point late that afternoon.

It was Randy who spotted the patrol vehicle first. There was a shout and a wave. As fast as the slippery terrain permitted, she stumbled forward, straight toward Dan Parker.

She fought a sudden rush of tears when he caught her against him. "I can't tell you what a relief it is to see you, girl." His heartfelt whisper rushed past her ear.

Randy closed her eyes and buried her face against his shoulder. It was all she could manage right now.

Dan drew back and pushed the brim of his hat up. He peered at her intently. "Are you okay?"

"I'm fine." Her smile was as wobbly as her voice.

Dan released her when Zach joined them. He offered the younger man his hand. "You two scared the living daylights out of me. If I didn't know how sporadic radio transmissions can be out here, I'd have thought the worst."

"That's exactly what happened." Zach slipped the backpack off and flexed his shoulders. "We got caught in a rainstorm the day before last and had to wait it out in a cave." His gaze flitted back the way they had come. Only the lower flanks of the mountains were visible. The peaks were smothered in a roiling blanket of clouds. His lips thinned. "Now it looks like we'll have to wait this one out, too."

Randy's back went rigid. His tone was ripe with disgust. His profile might have been etched in stone as he stared off into the distance. His expression was harsh and unyielding, and his beard-stubbled jaw only heightened the impression.

"We couldn't risk staying any longer," she said stiffly. "We didn't have the provisions."

Zach's gaze swung back to her. Dan's presence was forgotten. Their eyes collided and clashed fiercely for a never-ending moment. "I never said I blamed you," he said finally.

Didn't he? Randy wasn't convinced, and the agony wrenching through her was awful. She spun away to hide her pain, stumbling toward the patrol car.

The atmosphere during the ride back to town was anything but comfortable. There was no sign of snow down in the valley, but a steady curtain of rain fell from the sky. Randy stared out the window at the leaden gray landscape. It was Zach who told Dan about the cache of food they discovered in the cave, the rock slide and their prickly feeling that they were being watched. "Unfortunately," he finished, his voice hard, "we won't know if Garrett was behind it until we catch up with him."

Dan glanced at the other man. "You're not ready to call it quits, are you?"

For a moment there was no sound but the whine of the windshield wipers slipping against the glass.

"No." The word was delivered in a flat, passionless voice that was somehow frightening. "As soon as the weather clears, I'm going back. He's close. I can feel it."

Dan didn't argue. He'd experienced the same gut instinct too many times to dismiss it lightly.

No one was surprised when Zach asked to be let off at the hospital. When Dan pulled to a halt near the entrance, Randy was only hazily aware of his low-voiced conversation with Dan.

He got out. The slam of the car door sliced through her. *How can he do this to me?* a voice inside screamed. He was being so cool—so cold!—as if these past few days were nothing to him....

Her door was yanked open. A rush of moist air and drizzle spilled into the interior. A long arm shot in front of her. There was a slight tug on her shoulder, and she found herself staring straight into Zach's face.

He hunched down on the curb. "Will you do me a favor?" he asked softly.

Her eyes roved over his features. He no longer looked angry and tough, only weary...so utterly weary something inside her melted. She nodded, her throat suddenly tight.

"When I flew in, I left my bag at the sheriff's office." He glanced briefly at Dan for confirmation.

The other man inclined his head. "Randy's car is still there, too."

Zach's hands slid down to grasp hers. "I want to see Larry and stay with his wife, Peggy, for a while. Could you get my bag and pick me up here later?"

His gaze was rife with unspoken messages, messages she wanted to close out but couldn't. Her heart began to pound. She understood the question in his eyes very clearly. He wasn't shutting her out. He wanted to stay with her. *He wanted her.*

Kevin, she thought helplessly. *Oh, Kevin, please forgive me.*

The pressure on her hands increased. "Please, Randy." His voice was very low, rough with need.

She couldn't refuse him. Heaven help her, she couldn't. "Okay," she whispered.

Zach leaned forward and pressed a brief hard kiss on her mouth. "I'll see you later then." She watched him rise and walk toward the hospital entrance. Her eyes never left his form until he disappeared through the double doors. With a tired sigh she slumped back against the seat.

It was then she saw Dan's eyes fixed on her in the rearview mirror.

No, she thought numbly. Oh, no! There was no doubt that Dan had heard Zach's request and drawn his own conclusion. Waves of shame and regret washed through her.

"Dan," she said helplessly. "Oh, Dan, I . . ."

He twisted around in the seat so that he faced her. "Don't look like that," he said gently. "There's no reason to feel guilty."

She fought the urge to stuff her fist into her mouth and burst into tears. "But I—I don't know what to say. I don't know how to—"

He shook his head firmly. "Don't, Randy. If something happened up there between you and Zach Corbett, that's between the two of you. Stop being so hard on yourself. It's way past time you moved on with your life." A wistful smile touched his lips. "I've always loved you like a daughter, Randy. And all I ever wanted was for you to be happy. That hasn't changed and it never will."

There was a gnawing ache in her breast. She didn't deserve his understanding, his caring. But she clung to it with all that she possessed.

She drew an unsteady breath. "You always know what to say, Dan Parker. I guess that's just one of the reasons you've always been so special to me." She bent forward and kissed his lined cheek. "Thank you," she whispered.

SEVERAL HOURS LATER, Randy was back at the hospital, flipping through a magazine in the waiting room while she waited for Zach. He was in Larry's room with Peggy. Earlier, Peggy and Zach had coffee with Randy downstairs in the cafeteria before returning to Larry's room. Zach and Peggy had asked her to come and meet Larry, but she'd declined, afraid Larry might not be up to it and not wanting to intrude.

According to Peggy, Larry was improving rapidly. There were plans to transfer him by helicopter in several days to a hospital back in Portland. A few more days there and he could look forward to being released.

Still, it was clear that Peggy had been through hell the past week. As they had talked, Peggy's voice occasionally grew thick with tears as she talked about how frightened she had been for her husband's life. His chances had been fifty-fifty the first forty-eight hours.

Randy's heart went out to her as she listened, but it was Zach's hand that Peggy reached for. Randy found herself caught up in viewing him from a far different perspective. He was, she knew firsthand, an easy man to lean on. Yet it seemed odd for a moment to see him in the role of friend and protector, rather than the hunter. How many times these past few days had she thought him ruthless and driven?

But she wasn't being fair, a voice protested. If he was sometimes harsh, it was because he had to be. But he had held her hand, kept her warm and shielded her from the dark. And he had introduced her to physical love with sweet, tender gentleness, gentleness that she knew no man—even Kevin—could have surpassed. The admission was difficult—and painful.

So far she'd managed to keep her mind free of that night in the cave. Zach wasn't to blame for what had happened. She had wanted him to make love to her. Thinking about it again kindled a tingling fullness in her breasts. She remembered his mouth and hands raining fire on every inch of her, the tender-rough friction of his skin sliding slowly against hers, the filling heat of his body inside hers driving her mindless. It had felt so good. More, it felt so right.

The ultimate act. The ultimate intimacy...the ultimate betrayal. She was helpless to prevent a part of her from feeling she'd betrayed Kevin.

But another voice reminded her that Kevin was dead, lost to her forever.

So where did that leave Zach? Their fates were intertwined—but only here, only now. She couldn't let herself get close to him. She couldn't! Because soon he would be gone.

Nearby there was a slight rustle. Randy looked up to find Zach's tall form filling the doorway.

"Hi," he said softly.

"Hi." Randy shoved her hands into the pockets of her jeans, feeling inexplicably shy and nervous.

He ran a hand over the stubbly surface of his jaw. His slow, rueful grin made her heart turn over. "I'm surprised you and Peggy had the nerve to be seen with me. I must look like hell."

There was a tight knot of awareness in her stomach. His eyes looked almost translucent against the dark shadow of his jaw. His shirt was open at the throat, revealing a wild tangle of curly brown hair.

No, she thought fuzzily. He looked wonderful to her. Raw and masculine and very, very sexy. But he looked so tired. She wanted to lay her hand against his cheek and smooth away the faint grooves etched beside his hard mouth.

"What are we waiting for then? There's a perfectly good shower at my house." Light as her voice was, she couldn't control the slight quiver in it. "I think I could even manage to find a razor."

"Hey, is that a complaint I hear?" With a low laugh he caught her hand and dragged it to his cheek.

Her fingers shaped the square configuration of his jaw, loving the pleasantly rough sensation of his skin against her palm. A rush of emotion squeezed her chest, so intense it was almost painful.

"No," she whispered, and suddenly there was a whole new pulse of feeling thrumming away inside her.

His eyes darkened. He pulled the hand on his cheek down between their bodies and reached for her free hand. With slow deliberation, he weaved her fingers tightly through his.

His eyes captured hers. Penetrating. Intent. "Are you sure about this?"

The vibrant urgency in his voice stunned her. Zach was so tall, so strong and confident, all the things she wasn't. But when he touched her, it was almost as if she could feel his strength and conviction flowing into her.

Her eyes searched his. When she finally spoke, her voice was little more than a breath of air. "Are you?"

His fingers squeezed hers. "Yes. Oh, yes."

It was all the answer she needed. She smiled, a slow, sweet smile that took his breath away. "Then so am I," she said softly.

ZACH WAS FEELING downright complacent. A steaming shower and a hot meal—neither of which he swore he would ever take for granted again—made him feel he was part of the human race once more.

While Randy fixed dinner, he'd built a fire in the huge stone fireplace in the living room. She had seemed a little nervous at first; Zach had a very good idea it had a lot to do with the presence of his suitcase in her bedroom. But she'd finally begun to relax when he teased her unmercifully about feeding him dried food again.

If she had made excuses, if she had tried to deny what had happened between them that night in the cave, something inside him would have snapped. That night had changed him forever. He didn't know how or why she had come to mean so much to him, but she had.

It was crazy to be here with her like this. Deep in his heart, Zach knew it. It left a bitter taste in his mouth to remember how she had called for Kevin, dreamed of him and cried over him.

She hadn't forgotten this man from her past. In some strange, indefinable way, Kevin still held her. Yet *he* was the one she reached for; *he* was the one who held her close through the long lonely night. And every time he touched her, it was harder to let go.

They washed and dried the dishes together. Afterward he pulled her down in front of the fire. He sat on the floor with his back propped against the sofa.

Randy curled into his arms naturally and without thought as if they'd been doing so for years. The atmosphere was quiet but altogether comfortable, broken only by the occasional hiss and crackle of the fire. He felt a twinge of guilt that Garrett was so far from his mind, but even that thought was swiftly suppressed.

"Zach?"

He felt the whisper of her breath across his cheek. "Hmm?" He toyed with the hair streaming over her shoulder. It clung to his fingers greedily, as if it possessed a will of its own.

"Tell me about...where you live."

Zach blinked. His fingers stilled. "Where I live?"

"Yes. I mean, do you have a house? An apartment?" She spoke quickly, even hurriedly, as if she were anxious to get it out. "I was just wondering...what it's like."

He quirked an eyebrow. "Is this a subtle way of checking out my financial status?" She batted him playfully on the chest. He grinned, then went on. "I bought a house about three years ago. It's about fifteen years old now, nothing fancy, but lots of wood and glass."

"Is it in the city?"

"On the outskirts. It's rural without being remote. There's lots of fir trees and a small creek that runs just the other side of the property line. I like it," he finished softly.

"It sounds nice."

He slanted her a curious glance. She sounded almost wistful. "I don't have half the view that you have here, with the mountains practically at your doorstep." He chuckled. "In fact, I'd have no problem with a view like this as long as I knew I didn't have to—"

She jerked up so abruptly Zach was caught totally off guard. "Don't envy me," she said fiercely. "I hate living so close to those mountains! I'd leave if I could. Sometimes I'd love to just pack up and go as far away as possible and never look back."

Zach cursed himself for the pain he'd unwittingly inflicted. He'd spoken thoughtlessly, even carelessly. He'd completely forgotten that's where she'd lost Kevin.

He sat up and stretched out a tentative hand, gently rubbing the flannel-covered valley of her spine. "I'm sorry," he said quietly. "I just wasn't thinking—" he hesitated "—of what you told me about your fiancé."

Randy shivered and hugged her knees to her chest. She needed no reminders.

His hand continued its up-and-down motion. "There's something I don't understand, though. If you hate it here so much, why don't you leave?"

Beneath his hand, he felt her stiffen. No more than a few inches separated them, yet Zach felt that distance growing with every second that passed.

She turned her head away. "It's not that easy."

He studied her quietly, pricked by her withdrawal but refusing to let it dissuade him. "It's only as hard as you make it."

Her head whipped around. "That's easy for you to say!" she flared. "I—I'd feel like I was running away! You just don't know—"

"That's right," he challenged sharply. "I don't, so why don't you tell me?" He pulled her around so that he could see her. She met his silent demand without flinching, her expression carefully blank.

His grip on her arm tightened. "Tell me," he said quietly. "What's keeping you here? Your store? You could sell it or hire someone to manage it."

The silence was suffocating. Randy stared at him through dark and tormented eyes.

"Please," she whispered. "Don't do this. Please just let it go."

Her voice was raw. It sliced into him like a knife blade.

His hands fell away from her. Zach sighed, battling a burning frustration. He was getting nowhere. If he kept at her, Randy would only pull further and further away.

He said nothing when he felt her scramble to her feet. He chose instead to stare into the flickering flames of the firelight, sure that if he looked at her he wouldn't be able to hide his bitter hurt.

For the longest time, Randy remained where she was. She stared at the back of his head. At the rigid set of his shoulders. She wanted to say...so much. How could she explain what she didn't know herself? Everything was tightly locked up inside her; she knew Zach well enough to know that if she said anything—anything at all—he would offer comfort. And she had the craziest notion that if he touched her she would burst into tears...and never stop.

And so she stood, fighting the storm in her heart. Fighting herself...and him.

"Why don't you go to bed?" Zach spoke without looking at her. "I'll be along in a few minutes."

His curtness shattered her. Randy whirled and fled, sure she would die of shame if she stayed a moment longer.

Zach closed his eyes when she was gone. He knew he'd hurt her. But it was no less than she had wounded him. He wanted to believe that Randy would come around, that she would trust him. And deep down, he suspected she would . . . in time.

But time was the one thing they didn't have.

He rubbed the back of his neck wearily, giving in to the fatigue of the day and the tension of the night. With a sense of strained inevitability, he picked himself up, shut off the lights and headed towards Randy's bedroom. How the hell could he act as if nothing were wrong? It might be best for both of them if he simply spent the night on the sofa. But there was a sliver of light shining under the door. He nudged it open and paused.

Randy gave no sign that she'd heard him. His eyes ran over her quickly. She stood before a heavy pine dresser, still fully dressed. Her eyes were closed and her head was bowed low. One hand was clutched to her breast. The utter bleakness in her pose caught at his chest.

He crossed the room and laid his hands on her shoulders. Her head lifted slowly, as if she dreaded what she might find. In the mirror, they silently confronted each other.

The anxious distress on her face stabbed into him. She looked like a lost lonely little girl. Without a second thought Zach pulled her around to face him.

A finger beneath her chin demanded that she look at him. "Are you okay?"

Randy nodded, trying in vain to swallow the huge lump in her throat.

His gaze dropped to the hand she still held to her breast. "What's that you have?" he asked curiously.

She bit her lip. Her eyes flitted away. She looked almost guilty, he observed with a frown. He let a small smile curve his lips. "Well?" he prompted.

Her fingers slowly uncurled. Her palm opened for his inspection.

Zach's smile withered. There was a night light in her hand.

"Randy." He pulled the light from her hand and deliberately set it aside. Calmly, gently, but with implacable firmness, he spoke. "Sweetheart, you don't need that. Not when I'm here."

It was true, she thought numbly. But the realization was anything but comforting. Instead it kindled a flash of near-panic. Zach was here now, but for how long? Soon he would be gone . . . soon.

Zach, she thought wildly. *Oh, Zach, what will I do when you're gone?*

With a soundless cry she flung herself against him. Strong arms closed around her, pulling her up against a warm solid body. She clung to him, wordlessly accepting the safety of his arms.

Seeing her like this wrenched his heart. He held her crushed against his body as if he wanted to absorb her into himself, stroking her back, nuzzling the silky hair at her temple.

At last he slid his fingers into her hair and tipped her head back. Some of the tension had left her body, but her lips were still trembling ever so slightly.

And Zach could think of only one way to stop the quivering.

His head lowered slowly. She kissed him back, tentatively at first, then with mounting fervency. Her hands curled into his shoulder and she clung to him helplessly.

He sensed the wild urgency in her, the need to touch and be touched. In his own way, he was just as desperate as she.

Ever since that night in the cave, he'd been besieged with doubt. Was she thinking of Kevin, wanting Kevin even as Zach had kissed her? Even as he loved her? The thought tormented him. He yearned for her to see *his* face, not Kevin's. Zach longed to hear her cry out his name in the heat of possession, and that need was deep and driving.

His hands slid beneath her shirt, seeking the silky warmth of her bare skin. "Open your eyes, love." The hoarse command betrayed the tremendous control he exerted over himself. "Open your eyes and look at me."

Her lids fluttered open. Her eyes widened. He knew she'd glimpsed his fierce hunger, but there was no turning back. His fingers wound into her hair. He kissed her with his eyes wide open, watching as desire chased the shadows from her face. He kissed her over and over, his tongue swirling far and deep, bold, breath-stealing exchanges that parodied the act of love. His blood pounding thickly, he lifted her from the floor and drew her hard and tight into the cradle of his thighs.

In his haste to undress her, one of the buttons on her shirt flew across the room. Her nails scraped the hair-roughened skin of his belly as she fumbled with this belt, but the slight tingling brought more pleasure than pain. They were both shaking when they fell to the bed.

Her response drove him wild. He reveled in watching her come to life beneath his hands, writhing beneath his tender touch, catching her small breathless cries with his lips.

For Randy, his hands on her body—touching, pleasuring—obliterated all else from her mind. Her senses were spinning, her breathing ragged. Her entire being was concentrated on Zach, his tongue curling around her nipples, his fingers between her thighs taunting and teasing, sending her to the brink of madness. Then he was with her, inside her, his sleek strength surging boldly into her warm welcoming depths.

It was even more glorious than before. Her body arched. She needed no urging to lock her thighs around his hips and seek the rhythm that would send them both to heaven. When the spasms of completion spun her away, she wrapped her arms around his neck and hung on for dear life, fearful of losing such sweet, piercing pleasure. His hands on her hips tightened. One final plunge and he sent them both plummeting over the edge.

When it was over, he lay with his head buried in her shoulder. She listened as their hearts thundered against each other. It was wonderful to lie here like this. He made her feel sheltered and secure, as if nothing or no one could ever hurt her again. Her fingers combed through the dark gold of his hair, feeling the rigidness slowly seep from his body.

"Zach," she murmured. "Oh, Zach, I..." She wanted to tell him all that she felt, but mere words failed her.

Slowly he raised his head. His fingers smoothed the hair from her love-flushed cheeks. His lips brushed the hollow below her ear, the curve of her jaw, finding her mouth long moments later. The urgency was gone from his kiss. Instead his mouth conveyed such aching tenderness that Randy felt she was melting inside. And Zach knew then that this moment—this woman—was all he'd ever wanted.

It would have been perfect . . . if only she was his.

CHAPTER FOURTEEN

RANDY SPENT THE NEXT MORNING at the store with Chuck. As she expected, all was well. She experienced a twinge of guilt when Chuck flipped open the accounting books on her desk, remembering Zach's words the night before. He was a wonderful salesman and an excellent manager. He handled the store perfectly well without her, which was probably a good thing.

The rainfall stopped late that afternoon. It wasn't long before the sky was blazingly blue and clear. No doubt the snowfall had ceased in the higher elevations as well, so Randy had already begun preparations for another trip. She knew that as soon as the weather cleared, Zach intended to pick up the search for Garrett once more.

He had dropped her off at the store that morning and taken her car over to the hospital to see Larry. At noon he called her from Dan's office, but she didn't see him until later that evening.

His mood was somber while they ate. But when he said nothing, she decided to broach the subject herself.

"What time do you plan on leaving in the morning?" she asked quietly.

His eyes flickered. He stared at her, his cup suspended in midair. Slowly he lowered it to the table. "How did you know?"

She smiled slightly. "You won't let Garrett get away. That's been obvious right from the start."

The look he bestowed on her was long and thoughtful. "Can you blame me?"

She hesitated. "No," she said finally. "But I wish you didn't have to do this." She picked up their plates and carried them to the sink.

Zach regarded her quietly. There were times when Randy couldn't hide what was in her heart. And there were other times he was certain he could run around in circles trying to figure her out.

This was one of those times. If only he knew what true meaning lay behind her words. He wanted to believe she cared about him, but he wasn't sure he dared. In spite of what they had shared last night, he wasn't convinced he was more than just a crutch to her.

When Randy turned around, his gaze was riveted on her. His eyes were dark with an emotion she couldn't quite fathom—or perhaps she didn't want to. "Would you go . . . if I asked you not to?" Her voice emerged whisper thin.

Zach's gaze sharpened but then he sighed. "I have to. It's my job."

She wiped her hands on a dish towel and turned to face him. Her expression was faintly accusing. "It's more than that."

"You're right," he said slowly. "This time it is."

Some nameless emotion squeezed her heart. Was this how Zach's wife had felt? "Your work," she said unsteadily. "Is it always this dangerous?"

He shook his head. "Only on rare occasions," he said briefly. "Most of the time it's pretty routine."

"But you've already been shot once!"

His laugh had a faint edge to it. "Lightning never strikes in the same place. Surely I wouldn't be that unlucky twice."

"Don't, Zach! Don't say that. Don't even think it!"

Her vehemence startled him. He rose and pulled her rigid body into his arms. "Hey," he said softly. "It'll be all right. You'll see. I'd never let anything happen to you."

"It's not me I'm worried about! I—I felt like this the first time." She hated the quaver in her voice, but she couldn't stop it.

He tipped her face up. "Like what?"

She took a deep shuddering breath. "Like something terrible is going to happen up in the mountains. I know it sounds crazy, but maybe you're right and we were lucky. What if something goes wrong? What if—"

At precisely that moment the phone rang. Randy hesitated, an eerie feeling winging up her spine. It was Zach who moved the few steps to retrieve it.

Somehow she wasn't surprised when the call wasn't for her. Zach's conversation with the caller was brief. A dreaded sense of inevitability crept through her as she waited. She had the feeling her worst fears had just been realized.

His features were edged with barely suppressed excitement when he hung up the phone. "Dan wants us over at his place right away." He grabbed her hand and was already pulling her out the door. "There's been some news about Garrett."

ALL THE WAY TO DAN'S, Randy prayed that Marian wasn't home. It was only her certainty that Dan would never have placed her in such a sticky spot that allowed her to leave the safety of her own home in the first place.

Thank heaven she was right. Dan met them on the front porch and told Zach his wife was away for the evening. Randy was aware Dan meant the words for her.

Still, it took all the strength she possessed to walk into his house again. She hadn't been inside since before Kevin had died.

Nothing had changed. It was all so familiar she wanted to scream with rage and pain. The window seat in the corner was still stuffed with quilted pillows. The sight touched her heart. How many hours had she and Kevin sat there, playing games and laughing? Her gaze slipped to the mantel above the fireplace. She nearly came apart. Kevin's college graduation photo still occupied a place of honor there.

Dan led the way into the kitchen. Randy followed on wooden legs.

Zach began to pace around the room. It was only by concentrating on his presence that she was able to calm the whirlwind of emotions inside her.

Dan dropped an official-looking document on the table and beckoned to Zach. "One of my deputies just brought this by. Seems a hunter named Les Carter just got back today and saw Garrett's picture in the newspaper. He went to set up camp last night and had a little run-in with a man who told him to get the hell out or else. Carter didn't like the looks of this guy and decided to call it quits and head back instead."

Zach's eyes were glittering. "Garrett?"

"The description matches. And Carter is ninety-nine percent sure that's who it was."

"And this was last night?"

Dan nodded.

"Where?"

Dan said nothing. His gaze veered unerringly to Randy.

Zach's eyes narrowed. Something was happening here; the atmosphere in the room was suddenly stifling. The sheriff's expression was no less tense than Randy's.

This time it was Randy who spoke. "Where, Dan? Where did this happen?" Her voice was whispery soft. If she had shouted, the demand in her voice couldn't have been more implicit.

It seemed eons passed before Dan spoke. "The abandoned gold mine on Mount Hope," he stated quietly.

An unspoken message passed between them. Zach didn't understand the significance of the mountain peak they spoke of. Yet whatever hidden meaning there was, it had a tremendous impact on Randy, though she made a valiant effort not to let it show. The hands she placed on the tabletop weren't entirely steady. He could almost feel the tremor that ran through her body.

And all of a sudden Zach knew that Kevin had died on Mount Hope.

Indecision warred within him. How could he ask Randy to go back there? To confront all her remembered heartache? She had done so once already, and he had witnessed firsthand its ravaging effects . . . and they hadn't been on Mount Hope.

Yet he had no choice—no choice but one that might forever haunt them both.

The silence was endless. No one seemed to know what to say, what to do. It was left up to Zach to pick up the threads and pull them together, though he felt like an insensitive clod.

"We can't afford to be wrong." His voice sliced into the stillness. "But we need to keep all bases covered in case Garrett heads back to the cave after those supplies." He looked at Dan. "Is it possible to send someone back there in case he shows up?"

"I've already got somebody rounding up volunteers." Dan paused. "Sending a helicopter in would leave you wide open to Garrett, which means you'll have to go up on foot." He grimaced. "I'd feel a hell of a lot better if you let me arrange some backup."

"Too many people might tip Garrett off," Zach reasoned slowly. "If he knows we were after him before, maybe he'll think we gave up. But if we send in the whole damn cavalry, he'll be long gone before we ever get to him. It'll make the job a hell of a lot easier if we can catch him by surprise."

"Two men. That's all I'm asking."

Zach took one look at his set face and made a quick decision. "One. One man besides me and Randy." He sat back and waited.

Dan glared at him. "You won't change your mind, will you?"

Randy sat motionless through the exchange. Her initial shock had vanished; she was a little amazed at how calm and accepting she now felt.

"Zach's right," she injected quietly. She reached for a pencil and the contour map spread out in the middle of the table. "Too many people up there would ruin the element of surprise. But if we go up on the west side, there's a ridge above the mine—" she circled a spot on the map "—that should keep us out of sight."

Zach traced a line on the map. "Is this where you mean? We'd come in above him and then head down toward the mine?"

"Right."

"It makes sense to me," Dan said slowly.

"Then that's what we'll do." Zach glanced between Randy and the sheriff. "Let's plan to leave at sunup tomorrow—"

The back door swung open and a figure stepped inside. Three startled pairs of eyes swung in her direction. Marian stopped short. "Pardon me," she murmured. "I didn't realize there was someone here with you, Dan." Her gaze reached beyond her husband, touching on the slender form still seated at the table.

Marian's jaw snapped shut. All at once the air in the room was vibrating.

Randy froze. Her insides wound into a knot, hard and tight.

Through a haze she heard Dan's voice. "Marian," he stated calmly, "I know what you're going to say, but this is business."

"Business!" she hissed, glaring at Randy. "I don't care what it is."

Dan stepped toward his wife. "If you'll just go in the other room, we'll be finished here in a few minutes."

Randy was caught in a web from which there was no escape. She wanted to tear her eyes away and run until she dropped, yet she couldn't look away from Marian. And suddenly all she could see was Kevin, shivering uncontrollably...

Marian knocked aside Dan's arm and pointed at Randy. "No! I won't leave, I tell you. This is my house and I won't have that bitch in it! I swore the day my son was buried that I'd never forgive her, and now you've brought her here!"

Zach jumped to his feet so violently his chair crashed to the floor. "Wait just a damn minute here," he said hotly. "This might be your house but you have no right to call Randy—"

"Don't, Zach!" The pleading cry was accompanied by the touch of surprisingly strong fingers curling around his forearm. "Please," Randy begged, "don't hurt her more than she's already been hurt."

Zach opened his mouth, but Dan had already grabbed Marian's arm and begun dragging her from the room. "Zach, I think you two had better leave now. I'll see you both in the morning." He had to shout in order to be heard over Marian's spiraling voice.

"How could you do this to me! To bring her here— *here*! Because of her, my son is gone. She took him up to the cursed mountain and he never came back. She killed him—she killed our son. She killed Kevin!"

There was a resounding echo in Zach's head. Kevin... *Kevin*.

Comprehension dawned with a dizzying rush. It was suddenly so crystal clear, he wondered how he'd ever missed it: the elusive kinship between Dan Parker and Randy, the seething undertones he'd sensed when the three of them encountered Marian in Dan's office the day of his arrival. Dan had even told him Randy had stopped climbing because she lost someone very close to her.

That someone was Kevin . . . Dan Parker's son.

ZACH HAD NO CONSCIOUS recollection of leaving Dan's house and going back to Randy's. Once they were away, she was like a zombie, her eyes downcast, not saying a word. She roused only when he took her hand and led her from the car. She stood quietly while he stripped her coat from her and switched on the lights in the living room. Her listlessness was unnerving. She should have been spitting mad, seething with resentment; at the very least, he'd thought she would be shaken to the core over Marian's vileness. Why didn't she let go of her feelings, whatever they were? At this point, even tears would have been welcome.

His touch was cool and gentle as he took her face between his hands and made her look at him. "Talk to me, Randy." He saw her swallow, saw a haunting emptiness etch across her pale features before her lips pressed tightly together. His gut twisted. He knew she was struggling, and there wasn't a damn thing he could do to help her.

Just when he thought he could stand the unbearable tension no longer, she closed her eyes and reached for him. Her arms snaked around his waist. She clutched him to her with a desperate strength. Her voice was muffled against the hollow of his throat. "I—I don't even know where to start," she choked.

Zach edged over to the sofa and pulled her down beside him. When she grabbed blindly for his hand, he experienced a tightness in his chest that brought as much pain as pleasure.

His touch immeasurably gentle, he smoothed the hair behind her ear. "Tell me about Kevin," he said quietly. "He was Dan's son, wasn't he?"

"Yes. Dan and—and Marian's." Her voice caught, then steadied. A part of his mind registered the strength of her willpower; still another told him he'd never seen anyone more vulnerable.

"We lived in the house next to theirs," she went on. "Kevin was just a few months older than me. We—we did everything together. Kevin was always there, as far back as I can remember. I think we both always knew we'd get married someday."

Zach tipped her face to his. "Yet he never touched you," he observed softly. He ran this thumb across her lips. "Why, Randy?"

Hot color flooded her cheeks. "I . . . neither one of us felt right about it," she explained breathlessly. "I'd never have been able to look Dan and Marian in the face, and I think Kevin felt the same about my parents. And then later, we decided to put off getting married for a while. He wanted to be a doctor, you see. First there was college and later medical school. He was gone most of the year." Her lashes dropped, shuttering her eyes. "It was hard being separated, but at least I was busy, since my father turned the store over to me a year before they moved to Arizona. And

Kevin and I had had so much time together already. We thought we had so much more."

The wistfulness in her voice twisted his insides like a rusty knife. The possessiveness he'd felt these past few days was undercut by a flicker of doubt. Did she regret that he had been the first—and not Kevin? Zach wanted to pull her face to his and demand an answer. But if he ever hoped to call this woman his own, he needed to mend wounds, not inflict them.

All of a sudden an icy coldness seeped through him when he caught the words "Mount Hope."

"Kevin came home one weekend in September. He'd climbed a few times with me, but he wasn't the enthusiast that I was—he didn't have the time for one thing. But this particular Saturday he wanted me to take him up to see the gold mine there. The weather was beautiful. We were in shirtsleeves most of the way up."

Her hand was still linked with his. Zach could see the white-knuckled grip of her fingers; he could feel the tightness invading her entire body. He had to strain to hear her voice.

"While we were nosing around inside the mine, Kevin fell and twisted his ankle. He could hardly walk. I wanted to hike down for help, but he insisted he could make it. Only... he couldn't. By the time I realized he'd never make it down on his own, it was too late to leave him."

Zach's arm slid along the back of the sofa. He brought her head to his shoulder. "A whiteout?" he asked softly.

She nodded weakly. "We'd rarely seen snowfall so early in September, but I—I thought I'd come prepared just in case. We had a tent, food and water and sleeping bags. But this was awful, Zach, the worst I've ever seen. Between the snow and the wind, by morning the tent was nearly buried. We had to dig a snow cave for shelter."

Her voice grew raw. "I thought the storm would never end. I tried to leave once to get help for Kevin, but I couldn't tell up from down, right from left. I was lucky to find my way back to Kevin . . . God, it was so cold . . . so dark! I lost track of the time. I didn't know if it was day or night . . . ."

Zach's throat was clogged with emotion. His arms tightened. He held her, feeling her pain pour into him.

Her fingers knotted in his shirt. "The storm lasted for three days. The search party was ecstatic because they found us almost as soon as they were able to start searching. But for us it was already too late." Her voice broke. "Kevin was gone."

Zach went very still inside. "And Marian Parker blamed you. Because Kevin died . . . and you lived."

Her eyes squeezed shut. It was all the answer he needed, and for an instant he was consumed with a burning resentment toward Marian Parker.

The words were out before he could stop them. "Tonight at Dan's. How could you let Marian attack you like that? You didn't say anything, Randy. You just sat there," he said fiercely, "and I know you're stronger than that. Why didn't you fight back?"

Shock held her motionless for an instant. Randy drew back, stunned by the anger she felt in him. "I know what you think," she whispered. "If Marian is striking out at me, it's because of love. Because she's been hurt. She lost her only son, Zach, her only son."

Zach jumped to his feet in frustration. He was scarcely aware of pulling Randy up along with him. "And so did Dan, but he's not going around throwing poison darts at you! It's no wonder you're afraid of the dark yet. You can't forget how Kevin died, because Marian won't let you!"

"You don't understand," she said dully. "If I hadn't taken Kevin up to Mount Hope that day, he would still be alive."

"You don't know that!" Zach argued. "Anything could have happened since then. A car accident. A plane crash. Anything!"

But Randy shook her head over and over, her expression filled with such self-condemnation that a feeling of numbed disbelief supplanted his anger.

"You see?" Her tone was harsh. "You were right about me after all. You didn't think I knew what I was doing. Did you know you were taking your life in your hands when you let me take you up into those mountains? The danger wasn't from Garrett, Zach. You went up there with a kill—"

"No. *No!*" It was a cry of outrage, a cry of anguish. His hands caught at her shoulders, stealing her breath and effectively silencing her. His arms closed around her with a grip that was almost bruisingly fierce, but tinged with desperation.

With a low moan he thrust his fingers into her hair and pulled her head back. He didn't know when he'd felt so helpless.

"Don't do this to yourself," he pleaded. "Don't do this to me. You weren't responsible for Kevin's death and you can't continue to blame yourself, no matter how Marian feels. It was an accident, a tragic accident, and it scares the hell out of me to think it could have been you.''

Zach was shaking and so was she. He crushed her to him again, scarcely aware of his actions. Her muscles went weak and she sagged against him. He sensed her silent struggle to control the violent upheaval inside her. There were no tears. God, he wished there were! But suddenly she was clinging to him as fiercely as he clung to her.

He closed his eyes and forced his voice past the unfamiliar tightness in his throat. "If I'd known at the start what this would cost you, I wouldn't have let you set foot in those mountains again." He hated feeling so torn in two. "And now Garrett is up on Mount Hope. How can I ask you to come with me tomorrow?"

Her hands pressed against his chest. She lifted her head to gaze at him, knowing everything she felt was like an open book. She had no desire to ever return to Mount Hope. Yet she had this unreasoning fear that something terrible might happen to Zach if she didn't.

She was probably the last person to keep him safe. But she had to try. She had to.

She searched his harshly planed features. "I'm scared," she admitted. Her gaze fell, and she focused on the strong column of his throat. "But unless you don't want me along, I—I want to be with you tomorrow."

He gave a low impatient exclamation. "Of course I want you along. But I'm scared, too, because I don't want you hurt by anyone or anything—past or present." He tipped her face up to his, his expression intent. "I trust you, Randy."

Her eyes filled with tears. *I trust you, Randy.* She didn't realize until that moment how much she needed to hear him say that.

If only she could have been relieved. Instead, Zach's words kindled a fear far deeper and much more potent than any she had ever known. Kevin had trusted her, too. Kevin had *died* trusting her.

How could she live with herself if something happened to Zach?

AT THAT PRECISE MOMENT, Dan Parker pulled a small suitcase from the closet and dropped it onto the bed. The spring of the locks sounded overly loud in the stillness of the room.

The slight rustle at the door warned him of Marian's presence. He spared her no glance as he moved from the dresser to the bed and back again. In some distant corner of his mind, he realized he was blocking her out . . . as she had blocked him out these past three years.

"Dan." She took a tentative step forward. "Dan, what are you doing?"

His thoughts were colored with a rare cynicism. She hadn't shouted or screamed. Perhaps he should be grateful.

It was odd, he decided. He didn't feel much of anything.

"I'm packing," he said evenly. And he continued to do so.

"Packing?" she echoed. "But . . . why?"

"Why? Because I'm spending the night at my office. We're sending a team up to Mount Hope tomor-

row after that federal escapee, John Garrett. I'm going
with them."

Marian's face turned white. "That's why that federal marshal and Randy were here? Why didn't you
tell me you were going?"

"I just decided."

"But that could be dangerous! And to Mount Hope
yet . . . Dan, how can you do this?"

His lips twisted bitterly. "And what about Randy
and Zach Corbett? They're taking just as much risk,
maybe more. But I suppose it's asking too much for
you to think about either one of them, especially
Randy." The suitcase snapped shut. "When this is
over, I'll be back for the rest of my clothes and find
somewhere else to stay."

She stared at him. "You're leaving me?" She
sounded incredulous.

"Yes."

"Why?" she cried. "Why are you doing this? My
God, Dan, you're throwing away almost forty years of
marriage."

"I never said that." His voice was sharp. The puzzled hurt in Marian's eyes lanced into him. "I need
some time to think. I need some time alone."

"You need time away from me. That's what you
mean, isn't it?" She collapsed into the chair by the
door. "It's because of what happened tonight, isn't it?
Because I lost my temper. I—I'm sorry. I didn't mean
to shame you in front of—"

"Marian," he injected quietly, "I felt many things
tonight, and shame was the least of them. Shame is
what *you* should be feeling."

She had the grace to drop her eyes beneath his drilling stare. Her hands wrapped together in her lap. "I don't see how you can do this to me, Dan. We've had a lifetime together. I—I thought you loved me."

"I do, Marian. It's why I've stood by you these last three years, hoping that one day you would realize what you were doing to yourself. To me." There was a heartbeat of silence. "And to Randy."

At the mention of Randy's name, her eyes blazed. Dan cut her off with a curt gesture. "When Kevin died," he stated very deliberately, "I lost my only son. That hurt me as much as it hurt you. But I told myself that I still had you, that we still had each other."

He shook his head. "But you never saw it that way. I watched you close your friends out. I suffered when you closed me out. I tried to get you to see a counselor to try to work it out, but you always refused. And sometimes I felt—" he swiped at the lone tear oozing down his cheek "—that Kevin was the only one who had ever counted with you. Because once he was gone, *I* didn't seem to matter anymore.

"You've given Randy a terrible burden of guilt, Marian, and it hasn't lessened over time. Does it satisfy you to know that? Does it make you happy? You just couldn't let go of Kevin, and because of you, she can't, either."

Marian's face was ashen. "Dan, you make it sound so..."

"Ugly? That's what it is." His voice turned harsh. "But then I'm not telling you anything new. We've had this conversation a hundred times before and it's never made any difference. Why should it now?" He watched her for a moment. "You refuse to see what you've done to that girl, Marian. And the woman I married could never have been so cruel.'' He picked up the suitcase and started past her.

"Dan!'' She clutched at his sleeve. ''What—what's going to happen to us?'' she whispered.

For an instant his eyes held a trace of wistfulness. ''I wish I could say that's up to you.'' His sigh seemed to hold the weight of the world. ''But right now I don't know, Marian. I just don't know.''

The door opened silently. It closed just as silently behind him.

CHAPTER FIFTEEN

DAN WAS WAITING in the parking lot the next morning.

Randy hit the ceiling when he told her he intended to go with them. She argued, she pleaded, she cajoled, but Dan remained stubbornly insistent.

Finally Zach pulled her aside. They stood together in the watery light of dawn. He laid a hand on her shoulder. "I don't like it any more than you do," he said softly. "But before you say anything else, let me ask you something. How would you feel if I said you had to stay behind?"

Randy's shiver had nothing to do with the cool morning air. "I don't think I could stand it," she confided. "Waiting and wondering and not knowing—" she hesitated "—I guess it's what I was trying to say last night. In spite of how I feel about Mount Hope, staying here would be worse than being up there again."

"I think," Zach said quietly, "that's how Dan feels."

Randy bit her lip. "I know you're right," she admitted. "But with Dan along, I'll worry even more."

"I know." He studied her, his expression sober. "I wish I could tell you that he's perfectly capable of handling anything that might come up. I wish I could say that about myself." He smiled slightly. "But I doubt if anyone is ever completely self-sufficient."

And that, Randy thought with an unexpected pang, was something she was just beginning to discover. She felt as if he'd landed a blow at the center of her heart. When Kevin died, she hadn't let herself lean on anyone, not even her parents. The only way she could cope was by taking her feelings—and her heart—and thrusting them into cold storage.

But when she had met Zach, the ice around her heart began to thaw. First he'd made her feel inept; then angry and defensive. But at least he had made her feel. And just as in a case of frostbite, the process of thawing her heart was painful.

Did she love Zach? *Oh, please, no!* She couldn't. Because soon he would be leaving. *Leaving...*

His thumb brushed lightly over her cheekbone. "The next few days won't be easy for any of us. But all we can do is hope for the best."

Hope for the best. How simple that sounded. But Randy was afraid to hope...and just as afraid not to.

ALL THAT DAY the trio moved deeper into the wilderness, pressing on toward their goal. The air was crisp and cold, the sky clear and blue, laced with billowy clouds. The sunlight winking down on them seemed almost mocking. Wind-driven snow clung to the trees, giving them a ghostly aspect. Every so often a tingle of apprehension ran up Randy's spine, but she was determined to ignore it.

The looming shape of Mount Hope dominated her vision, its craggy summit locked in a heavy sheath of snow. Every step brought her closer... and that was something she couldn't ignore.

They maintained a tense silence throughout the day. No one seemed inclined to small talk. They stopped once to examine a crazy pattern of footprints in the snow, but the tracks belonged to some kind of animal, most likely deer.

Late in the afternoon they reached a small sheltered clearing on the sloping flanks of the mountain. Dan looked exhausted, though he hadn't uttered a word of complaint. Randy decided to call it a day, her gaze veering directly to Zach's, as if she expected an objection. He merely nodded and slipped his backpack to the ground. Between them, it wasn't long before the tent was up and a small pot of freeze-dried stew was simmering on the stove.

"How long will it take before we reach the ridge above the mine?" Zach's voice broke the silence over dinner.

In spite of herself, Randy's gaze lifted skyward. As if by some cruel hand of fate, evening sunbeams streaked through the clouds, turning the summit a hazy shade of pink and gold. Just as quickly, the hole in the clouds closed and the snowy landscape took on a dismal shade of gray. It was like looking through a dirty glass window.

She set her metal plate on the rock she was perched on, her appetite gone. She didn't look at Zach when she spoke. "Midafternoon tomorrow."

Beside her, Dan rubbed his chin thoughtfully. "Maybe we should think about making camp there tomorrow night and sneaking into the mine at dawn the next morning."

Zach nodded. "Sounds good to me." He picked up the rifle at his side and looked at Randy. "You know Garrett is armed. You're not afraid to use this if you have to?"

Randy had the strangest urge to throw back her head and laugh hysterically. She knew her way around firearms, and because of that, they held no fear for her. But did Zach really think a rifle would protect her—any of them—from the dangers here?

Ever since she'd learned of Garrett's escape, she'd been battling a persistent, niggling feeling that something terrible would happen up here. She'd thought when she and Zach returned the first time perhaps she'd been wrong. But now that feeling was sharper, stronger than ever.

Someone on this mountain would never leave... never. She felt as if she were involved in a deadly game of Russian roulette. Which of them would it be? Her? Zach? Dan? Or Garrett?

The list of pawns had grown by one... or had it? Garrett might not even be here. The gruesome reminder made her head spin. He might be ten miles away. A hundred. Which left only the three of them...

She swallowed. "I'll use the gun if I have to."

Zach's gaze bored into her. "Good," he said quietly. "Because when Dan and I go after Garrett, we're going in alone."

Randy blinked. "Alone," she repeated dumbly. "You mean you want me to stay behind while you—"

"That's right." Zach cut her off abruptly. "I want you to stay behind at the ridge."

"But I might be able to help you. Zach, I'm a crack shot. Ask Dan."

"I've put you in enough danger already. I won't take any more chances where you're concerned."

His unrelenting tone brought her surging to her feet. Hands on hips, eyes flashing, Randy urged and pleaded for the second time that day—again, to no avail. She was just about to turn her back and stomp off into the tent when inspiration struck.

"You can't leave me behind," she said sweetly. "Remember I told you about the trail to the cave?"

Zach's eyes narrowed. He rose to his feet and faced her, suspicion miring his expression. "What about it?"

"The trail leading from the ridge to the mine skirts the west wall of that pinnacle." She pointed toward the peak. "It's only about half as long, but I'd say it's about twice as steep. And," she added mildly, "about twice as narrow."

Zach blanched. Randy had a hard time holding back a sound of triumph, but just when she was about to win the battle, he crossed his arms over his chest and cocked an eyebrow.

"If I did it before, I can do it again. I'll just hold Dan's hand instead of yours this time."

Randy's mouth dropped open. His smug grin was infuriating, but the glint in his eyes warned her he wouldn't change his mind. Without another word, she grabbed the lantern, whirled and stalked into the tent.

She was still fuming when Dan crawled into the tent some time later. It was a tight squeeze with three sleeping bags spread out, and she instinctively scooted toward the outside wall. But she frowned when it became apparent that Zach was remaining outside.

"Isn't Zach coming in?" Low as her voice was, she couldn't quite hide her vexation with him.

Dan slid into the bag on the opposite wall. "He's going to stand watch for a while. I'll go out and relieve him in a few hours. If Garrett really is close by, we'd better not take any chances."

He flicked off the lantern, plunging the interior into darkness. Randy experienced a pinprick of guilt. Was Zach being stubborn or was she? She wasn't afraid, not with Dan just a few feet away, but it was Zach she wanted near. She couldn't stand the thought that he might be angry with her. Was it so wrong to want to help him? And Dan? She'd felt so helpless when Kevin died; she didn't want that again.

As if he sensed what was on her mind, Dan's voice drifted through the darkness. "Zach's right, you know. If Garrett's at the mine, you're better off being as far away from there as possible."

Randy turned and propped herself on her elbow, peering through the shadows. "I know he's only trying to protect me," she admitted wearily. "But what about you two? I—I can't explain this feeling I have, Dan. But it's almost as if I know if I'm not there, something terrible will happen. I'd never be able to live with myself if I knew I could have prevented it." Her voice grew thready. "My God, Dan, I still can't face Marian. It's hard to think of her hating me any more than she already does, but if you're hurt, that's exactly how she'll feel."

"I won't let that happen, Randy. I promise you that."

Forceful as his tone was, there was something in it Randy couldn't identify. She was still puzzling over it when Dan's voice came again.

"Besides, there's something you should know, and I'd rather you found out from me than someone else." There was a tiny pause. "When this is over, Randy, I . . . I'm not going home."

Randy's heart thudded. He couldn't be saying what she thought he was! "I'm not sure what you mean," she said faintly.

His sigh seemed the loneliest sound in the world.

"You're the last person I should have to explain this to," he said heavily. "I'm leaving—moving out for a while. I need some time to think. Marian isn't the same person she was when Kevin was alive. She's changed. She's hard. Tough where she was always so gentle. I've tried everything I can to make her see it, but she can't. Or maybe she won't. And I—" he hesitated "—I'm not sure I can live with her anymore. That's something I'm going to have to decide."

There was a shocked silence. Randy could scarcely believe her ears. There were a million layers of hurt in his voice. She sensed his hopeless frustration and her heart reached out to him.

"I'm sorry," she whispered. "Oh, Dan, I don't know what to say. . . ."

He stretched out a hand and touched her shoulder. "There's no need to say anything," he told her gently. "And for God's sake, don't blame yourself for this. I'm not sure I can ever make you realize how much I regret the way she's hurt you. She's shut both of us out, and all I can do is pray that she realizes it before it's too late."

Despite his words, his tone told the story only too well. He thought it was too late already. Randy listened to his murmured good-night. Dan turned over onto his side and soon his breathing grew deep and even.

Not so with Randy. The longer she lay there, the tighter her chest grew. *Don't blame yourself,* Dan said. But she did. If Marian had changed, it was because of her... *her.* The knowledge rammed into her like a knife.

The tent was suddenly airless. Scarcely aware of what she was doing, she fumbled with the flap and ran outside. She stood with her hands pressed to her cheeks, drawing lungful after lungful of stinging night air.

Randy was unaware of Zach's presence until she felt his strong, gentle hands close around her arms. She was turned bodily, cocooned in the safety of his sheltering embrace. She was helpless to do anything but bury her face against the hard column of his neck and cling to him, needing his strength and warmth.

At length he withdrew slightly and tipped her face back. In the moon-washed darkness, his profile was tough and rugged. But the touch of his finger on her jaw was almost unbearably gentle. Randy had no thought of pulling away. There could be no pretense between them now, no lies or half-truths.

"What's wrong?" Zach asked softly.

"When we get home again—" she ignored the voice that taunted *if* they got home again "—Dan's leaving Marian."

A wave of shock washed over Zach. "Leaving her? You mean he's divorcing her?"

She stumbled over the words. "He—he says he doesn't know yet what he's going to do."

Zach's eyes narrowed. "I see," he said slowly. And he did, only too well.

His fingers bit into her shoulders. "When are you going to stop this?"

His tone was rough. Randy started in surprise, then stiffened. She tried to pull away but he wouldn't let her.

"You let Marian blame you for losing her son. Now with Dan's marriage on the rocks, you're blaming yourself for that, too."

"I don't *think* I'm to blame," she stated evenly, "I know I am. It's as if... as if I started some kind of chain reaction. It's this whole situation with me that's driven Dan and Marian apart. Don't you think I know that? Marian wouldn't be the way she is today if it weren't for—"

"Don't say it!" Zach warned fiercely. "Don't even think it, because it's not true. If anything started a chain reaction, it was Kevin's death, not you!" He saw her flinch at his bluntness but plunged on anyway. "The way Kevin died doesn't matter. Don't you see that? It's the fact that Kevin is *gone* that's caused Marian to be the way she is!"

Randy stared at him numbly.

Zach shook her gently. "Do you think I can't see what's happened? You can't leave here because of Marian. She's keeping you here as surely as if she'd put a noose around your neck."

Randy began to quiver. "You don't understand," she cried softly. "It's as if my own mother turned against me. How can I pretend that hasn't happened?''

His harsh features softened. "I don't have all the answers, Randy. But you can't go on the way you have been. You'll end up just like Marian if you don't start living for yourself again."

Her expression turned bitter. "It's easy for you to sit back and give advice, Zach. Exactly what do you propose I do?"

"You already have the answer to that," he told her levelly. "You could do what you've wanted all along. You could leave."

Her laugh was a false and brittle sound. "I can't live with my parents again, Zach. They look at me and they see Kevin and Dan and Marian. And I look at them and I see pity. I won't have anyone feeling sorry for me, Zach, I won't!"

He hauled her up against him. "I'm not telling you to go with them! I'm asking you to come with me. To forget Kevin and Marian. When this is all over, come with me!"

The silence was horrendous. Randy couldn't look away from him. She could have wept at the wordless plea she glimpsed in his eyes. If only it was that easy, she thought in despair. If only....

She wrenched away from him and pressed her fingers to her temples. This was too much, and all at once. "I can't," she whispered. "Oh, Zach, I just can't. Don't you see?"

The silence seemed to vibrate between them. Zach held himself very still. Only the tempest in his eyes betrayed his emotions.

"It's Kevin, isn't it?" he asked softly, almost whimsically. "After all this time you're still in love with him."

"No. No, that's not true, Zach, I swear! I—I've accepted his death—"

"Have you?" His jaw clenched. "I thought there was something between us, Randy. I thought I was more than just a crutch. Was I wrong?"

She flinched beneath his silent accusation. What could she say? Her emotions were a hopeless tangle. How could she explain what she didn't fully understand herself? *Come with me,* he said. But for how long? Life was fleeting. No one knew better than she. And in that same way, love was sometimes fleeting...though not for her, never for her. How long would Zach want her? A day? A week? A year?

She was afraid of the way Zach made her feel. The need he aroused in her was frightening. It was more than physical, and that frightened her most of all. Maybe she was afraid of loving again...and losing. And she had brought nothing but pain to those she loved.

Her hands fell to her sides. She floundered helplessly, afraid of revealing too much, just as afraid not to. "You're pushing me," she cried, and her voice was as raw as she felt inside. "You're pushing me and I resent it! Dammit, I—I don't know what you want from me!"

The words were a mistake. She knew it the instant they broke from her lips. Something flickered over his face, but whether it was pain or anger she couldn't be certain. He fixed her with a look so penetrating and intense she wanted to cry out and run as far away as she could.

And Zach knew it. He wanted to help her, God knew he did. But she simply wouldn't let him. She was strong, yes. But not as strong as he'd thought. Because she couldn't forget..or forgive herself.

His thoughts turned bitter as he thought of Kevin. How could he compete with love everlasting? Yet he clung selfishly to the knowledge that he had been the first man to make love to her. He had claimed a part of her that belonged to no other man...even Kevin. Yet it was a bittersweet triumph, because he wanted her heart.

But her heart was already taken. He wouldn't ask her to come with him again. Because he knew she wouldn't change her mind.

Zach knew she was watching him, just as he knew this was tearing her up inside the same way it tore at him. But for once, he was oblivious to her pain.

Just for an instant, he battled a siege of violent emotions. He resented Kevin, even while he despised himself for doing so. He was furious with Randy for refusing to see that she had a future, as well as a past. And he felt greedy; he wanted to pull her in his arms and brand her with his touch so she would never forget him. He yearned to make love to her, to take all of her and store it away inside him for the time when he would not have her.

But Zach did none of those things. Instead, he turned his back on her and stared into the stark blackness of the night. "You'd better get back to bed," he said very quietly. "We'll need to get an early start in the morning."

Randy remained where she was, unmoving. His posture was rigid and tense, like a soldier. She knew she'd hurt him, and the pain that realization wrought was excruciating. Tears burned her eyelids. "Zach, please try to understand...."

"I do." The words cut across her like a whip. The edge in his voice revealed his frustration; it was like a blade turning in her breast. "Good night, Randy."

The phrase echoed in her brain until she wanted to scream aloud. She felt as if a cold arctic wind had blown across her heart. He whispered good-night...but this was goodbye.

They both knew it.

No ONE HAD MUCH TO SAY the next day. What little conversation there was was between Randy and Dan, or Dan and Zach. It was as if a deadly pall had descended over the group. The weather, so clear and sunny yesterday, was a dismal reflection of their mood. A mass of pewter clouds crawled above the mountain peaks like an invading army. The surrounding world was dull and colorless, cast in varying shades of gray. Even the snow, so pristine and immaculate the day before, had lost its brilliant sparkle.

Beside her, Randy heard Dan laboring for breath. She glanced at him sharply. His face was white except for two spots of color on his cheekbones. The huge frosty puffs of breath he blew out dissipated with the wind.

Evergreens crowned the slope they were on, seeking a tenuous hold at every turn. She grabbed Dan's arm and pulled him up against a tree trunk that was bent and misshapen from the relentless wind.

"We're stopping," she said firmly.

Dan shook his head. "No," he gasped. "I won't hold you two up."

Her voice brooked no argument. "Five minutes won't make any difference one way or another." She called to the tall figure plodding on ahead. "Zach!"

There was no sign he heard her.

"Zach!" She didn't care if she sounded like a shrew. "We're taking a break."

He turned around and gave her a thin-lipped stare. He didn't retrace his steps but remained where he was.

Randy's mouth tightened. She pulled her thermos from her pack and poured hot coffee into the cup. She passed it to Dan and sent a fulminating look at Zach, but he never even noticed. Implacable intent tightened his features as he scanned every direction. He was once again the cold harsh stranger who had but one ruthless goal—John Garrett.

If she hadn't been so preoccupied with Dan, she might have noticed how tense Zach was. He tucked the rifle under his arm, his long fingers curling familiarly around the dull steel barrel. It was as if every cell in his body were tuned as a bowstring, tautly alert.

After a moment he walked back to her. "Let's go," he said curtly.

Randy whirled on him. "Dan needs a rest!" she hissed. "Can't you see that?"

Their eyes collided. There was a flicker of something in his that passed for an apology. His expression softened slightly as he glanced at Dan. Then once again his gaze lifted beyond their heads, searching the area behind them.

"I know that," he murmured without ceasing his relentless perusal. "But this area is too open right here. Let's wait until we get past there." He nodded over his shoulder.

Dan waved aside her protest. "He's right, Randy. Besides, I'm all right." His smile was a little weak, but to her relief, she noted some of the color had returned to his face.

They plodded onward. The glacier ahead of them was slit by a jagged crevasse. Randy kept as far away from it as possible, eyes scanning for signs of others. All was silent except for their labored breathing and the crunch of their boots biting into the heavy sheath of snow.

It happened so quickly there wasn't a thing she could do to stop it. Once minute she was walking near Dan, less than four feet away. He edged slightly forward and she heard a low rumble. The world tipped crazily and she stumbled. The landscape ahead of her slid away, and Dan with it. It was as if some unseen nether god of the underworld had reached up and snatched him into its grasp.

"Dan!" The wind ripped away her scream of terror.

Zach suddenly appeared and hauled her up beside him. "My God," he muttered, white-faced. "Where the hell is he?"

Randy's blood was like ice. "The snow we just had—it hid another crevasse!"

He started forward but Randy grabbed his arm. "Wait!" she cried. "Let me! I'm lighter!"

Her hands shaking, she grabbed the rope coiled over one shoulder and around her chest. Quickly she tied it around herself, dropped the other end into Zach's hand and threw herself to her stomach. She crawled forward inch by painstaking inch until she reached the place where Dan had fallen.

The snow was solid there. Her heart in her throat, Randy scrambled to her knees and peered into a narrow snow-choked chasm. "Dan!" she screamed. "Dan, can you hear me!"

The silence was deathly. *No!* The voice in her head ricocheted through her mind. Fear knotted her stomach. This couldn't be happening! First Kevin, and now Dan! How could fate be so cruel...

"I'm right here, Randy," The voice came from just below her. It was weak but steady.

Her tears turned to tears of relief. Zach appeared beside her, and together they saw what looked like a huge lump of snow shake and shiver.

Dan was wedged into a crack about fifteen feet below them. "Are you hurt?" she called anxiously.

"I must have wrenched my knee. Dammit, wouldn't you know it!" Dan sounded more angry than anything else.

Randy turned to Zach. "We have to get him out of there, Zach. Now!"

Her eyes were wild. Her frantic tone warned of hysteria. Zach's heart caught painfully. Kevin had hurt his leg, too, he recalled suddenly. The parallels between Kevin's injury and Dan's were just a little too similar and too much for Randy to handle, he realized.

He pulled off his glove and laid his hand against her cheek. Her eyes clung to his and he felt a surge of emotion. She needed him, he thought fiercely, as much as he needed her. She just wouldn't admit it.

"We will," he promised softly. His eyes fell to the rope still knotted around her waist. "Let's get that off you and around Dan—"

Suddenly there was a sharp crack—the staccato rap of rifle fire.

"I don't think so," a voice said from behind them. The gritty sound sent a prickly sensation up Zach's spine. "I've got another use for that rope and it doesn't involve saving *Dan* here. So get on your feet *now*," the man ordered. "Both of you. And turn around, real slow-like."

In that moment, a peculiar sense of inevitability washed over him. Zach knew, even before he turned around, that they had finally managed to find their quarry.

They were no longer the hunters . . . but the hunted.

CHAPTER SIXTEEN

FEAR CLUTCHED Randy's insides. The man before her was massive. Stringy long hair hung down to his shoulders. Most of his face was obscured by a bushy red beard. Huge beefy hands curled around a rifle aimed straight at Zach.

It was John Garrett. Randy would have known it instinctively, even if she hadn't seen the mug shot in Dan's office.

From the corner of her eyes, she saw Zach jerk his head over his shoulder, indicating Dan. "We've done nothing to hurt you," he said evenly. "Why don't you help us get him out? He might be injured."

Randy's eyes darted from one man to the other. She knew what Zach was doing. Feigning ignorance of Garrett's identity in the hopes that they could catch him off guard.

But Garrett was having none of it. He grinned, displaying unsightly yellow teeth. "Is that a fact? Seems to me I'd be doing myself a favor if I let the sheriff rot there forever."

Garrett's expression was malevolent. "As for you two—" his gaze encompassed both Zach and Randy "—I know you're with the law. I watched you for days. It didn't take long to figure out you were on my tail."

Zach's fists clenched. "The rock slide near the logging camp. That was your doing, wasn't it?"

"It might have happened anyway." Garrett's laugh was an ugly sound. "I just helped it along."

"And the cave?" Zach demanded. "You were there, too, weren't you? You stashed supplies there."

"That's right." Garrett appeared to take perverse delight in taunting Zach. "If you'd arrived a few hours earlier, you might have caught me by surprise. Course you wouldn't have lasted very long." Thick lips formed a twisted parody of a smile. "But you wouldn't quit and now you'll have to pay."

Beady black eyes glittered obscenely. Meaty fingers stroked the trigger of the rifle meaningfully. The action left Randy in no doubt as to his meaning.

Zach didn't back down under his fierce demeanor. "Why don't you give it up, Garrett? If you kill us, the court will just go that much harder on you."

"The court? What the hell do I care about the court?" Garrett sneered. "Besides, I killed one man already."

"No! You didn't. He's still alive, Garrett. The federal marshal you shot is still alive."

Dan's shout drifted up to them. "He's right, Garrett! The time to stop this is now!"

Zach's eyes never wavered from Garrett's twisted features. "Think," he urged. "If you hurt any of us your sentence will be that much harsher—"

"The hell it will! I won't be caught, you hear? I can hide out in these mountains for years and no one will ever find me."

"Can you? We found you, Garrett. We found you and it only took a matter of days."

At Zach's silken taunt, Garrett went livid. "Then maybe I ought to take you with me, you bastard! I'll take you with me and if anyone comes near me I'll—" Suddenly he stopped. An eerie silence prevailed.

"No," he amended softly, and Randy didn't know when she'd heard such a chilling sound. His gaze cut toward her. He grinned, and she had only a fraction of a second to translate the full import of that wolfish grin.

"I won't take you." It was Garrett's turn to taunt Zach. He never took his eyes off Randy.

Zach went white.

"I'll take *her*." His hand clamped around Randy's neck. He jerked her to his side. "What do you say, lawman? Anybody dares come near me and guess what happens to this sweet little partner of yours?" His fingers squeezed painfully. Randy gasped.

"God damn you, Garrett." Zach's voice was low and furious. "Keep her out of it. She's not one of us. She's just a guide—"

"Shut up!" Garrett whirled and leveled the rifle at Zach's chest.

Randy's heart lurched. Zach wanted nothing more than to retaliate. She could see it in the glitter of his eyes. But what chance did he have against a giant like Garrett, especially when he was at point-blank range of Garrett's rifle? She wanted to get down on her knees, cry and beg for Zach's life, but terror held her paralyzed.

"Don't!" she managed to choke out. "Please don't hurt him, please! I—I'll go with you! I'll do anything you say!"

Zach stepped forward. His voice cracked like a bullet. "Randy, no! You don't know what you're—"

Cold hard steel jammed into his chest. "I told you to shut up!" Garrett's snarl sent terror zinging through her veins. Zach's jaw closed with a snap. His eyes were pure frost.

Garrett chuckled, a low grating sound. "You hear that, mister? She wants to come with me." He dragged Randy forward. Keeping the rifle trained on Zach, his grimy fingers reached out and stroked her chin. Bile rose in her throat.

His hand fell away. "Get that rope off and hold on to it," he commanded. "Then your friend is coming with us for a little walk."

Randy's nerves were stretched to the breaking point. She was trembling so that she could scarcely unwind the rope from around her waist. When she finally finished, the rifle barrel veered sharply behind them. "Move!" Garrett barked out.

Zach stepped forward, his features set in mutinous lines. Randy started to run up next to him, but Garrett jerked her back to his side. She didn't know what he intended to do with Zach, but there was a horrible fear gnawing away inside her.

She didn't have to wait long to find out. They moved a short distance up the slope to where a young fir tree jutted from the snow. Garrett clamped a hand on Zach's shoulder and shoved him to his knees. "Get your coat off!" he shouted.

Zach's lips tightened. His eyes never left Garrett's face as he pulled his parka off and dropped it next to him.

Garrett's eyes gleamed. "Now sit down and get your back to that tree. Then put your hands behind you."

Randy felt herself being yanked forward. "Get his boots and socks off," Garrett ordered. "Then tie his ankles together. When you're done, take his wrists and tie his hands behind the tree."

A terrible notion washed into her mind. Surely Garrett didn't intend to... "Why?" she demanded. "Why should I?"

"Because if you don't I'll leave you here with him, that's why! Just do it, woman, now!"

Randy's blood ran cold. "But you've taken his parka and his boots. He'll freeze without them!"

Garrett's lips pulled into a feral smile. "Smart girl," he smirked. The smile faded. "Now get down there and tie him up. And remember, I'm watching every move you make, so no tricks!"

He pushed her to her knees. Randy stared at Zach, her eyes wide with horror. She almost wished that Garrett had chosen to shoot him instead. It would have been a far more humane sentence of death. Zach gazed back at her, no trace of emotion on his face. How could he be so calm? she thought wildly. So damned accepting? She felt as if she were about to break into a million pieces.

She yanked off her gloves mechanically. She stripped her mind of all thought. It was the only way she could force herself to lift her hands and bring the rope around Zach's ankles. Her fingers worked automatically, looping, knotting and tightening. When she was through with his ankles, Garrett bent over to examine her handiwork. Apparently satisfied, he jerked his head, a silent indication for her to start to work on Zach's wrists.

She stepped behind him and lowered herself to the snowy ground. Her heart bled for him. She'd never felt so helpless, even when Kevin lay dying next to her. It wasn't until he was near the end that she had finally abandoned the fragile thread of hope that they would be rescued. But there was no hope for Zach— and Dan—at all. Dan could never get out of the crevasse without help. And hypothermia would claim Zach in a matter of...

Exactly where the idea came from, Randy never knew. But all at once she remembered the night she had shown Zach a number of knots used in mountaineering...and suddenly she prayed that he would remember, too. If only she could pass some kind of message to him! But with Garrett so close, she could say nothing without him overhearing.

"I'm done." It took little effort to fill her voice with venom. She rose to her feet and gazed at the spot where Dan was still trapped. "What about the sheriff? You're leaving him there, too, aren't you?"

Garrett gave an evil grating laugh, but Randy scarcely noticed. She was too caught up in her own excitement. Her ploy had worked. He gave only a cursory glance toward the coil of loops around Zach's wrists. Still wearing that leering grin, he nudged Zach's parka directly in front of Zach's outstretched legs with the toe of his boots. Zach's boots and socks came next. "Sleep warm and cozy tonight, lawman." His gaze veered toward Randy and he laughed again. "I know I will."

With that Garrett hitched the rifle over his shoulder then grabbed her arm and began pulling her along behind him. Randy twisted her head around for one last look at Zach, but even that was denied her. Garrett grabbed her painfully around the neck and forced her attention ahead of them.

It didn't take long for Randy to realize they were headed toward the gold mine. She thought of breaking away, of trying to make a run for it, but she quickly discarded the notion. She was an easy target here on the glacier. And once they traversed the ridge and followed the narrow trail down to the mine, there was nowhere to run. All she could do was hope that Zach would figure out how to free his wrists.

She stumbled a little on the slippery rock. Her gaze fell to the gaping chasm to her left. A wave of hopelessness swept through her. Did it really matter if Zach freed himself? It wasn't a question of whether or not he would come after her; with every breath in her body, she knew that he would. It was a question of whether he could make it. Would his concern for her safety override his fear of heights? If he made it this far, he would have to brave this treacherous trail. Alone... *alone*.

Randy was exhausted by the time they reached the mine, yet it was more a weariness of the mind than anything else. It wasn't until then that she realized she'd left her backpack behind, and the radio with it. On the way here, it occurred to her she might be able to radio for help if she got the chance. But now even that option was closed to her. She leaned against a rocky slab and closed her eyes, battling a wave of despair.

A shadow fell over her. Her lids snapped open. Garrett stood before her. "You didn't do too bad for a woman," he drawled. "I expected to have to haul you most of the way up here." Randy stiffened when he looked her over from head to toe. "Are you really what that lawman said? A guide?"

Randy didn't flinch beneath his gaze. She suspected that Garrett was a man who would abhor any sign of weakness and wouldn't hesitate to use it to his own advantage. "Yes," she said tightly.

"Then you've been here before."

Randy briefly took in the small treeless clearing blanketed with snow, the gaping hole in the side of the mountain that marked the entrance to the mine. She gave an involuntary shiver.

Garrett pulled off his hat and wiped his grimy forehead. "I ought to be madder than hell that you brought those two up here." He stared at her broodily. "But the fact is—" he grinned salaciously "—I might get to like having you here."

Randy wet her lips nervously. She knew she was grasping at straws, but the hungry look on his face frightened her. "Look," she began in a low voice. "Why don't you just let me go? I won't tell anyone where you are. I'll even pay you, I swear."

She thought she was onto something when his eyes lighted up. "Oh, I like money all right. Why do you think I robbed those banks? And I sure as hell don't like to work for it."

"Then let me pay you—"

But he was shaking his head. "No," he said curtly. "I ain't sure what I'm gonna do with you yet. I know what I'd like to do with you—" the leering grin reappeared "—but that can wait. For now I've got work to do, and I don't want to have to keep my eye on you every minute. If you've been here before, you know there's only one way out. So I don't need to worry about you getting past me."

His smug satisfaction made her furious. But her anger turned to something else entirely when he grasped her arm and pulled her toward the jagged opening of the mine. She blanched. "Don't put me in there!" she cried. "I'll stay right here, I promise. Please, I won't go anywhere!"

They stumbled through the dark forbidding entrance. "Damn right, you won't," he grunted. He dragged her down into the tunnel with seeming effortlessness, though she continued to pull back and resist.

He jammed her back against a cold stony surface. "You just stay put, you hear?" His foul breath struck her face. Randy turned her head aside and said nothing. "I can make this tough on you or I can make it easy as pie. Either way," he warned, "it's your choice."

Randy swallowed dryly, watching as Garrett retraced his steps. The tendrils of terror clinging to the fringes of her mind began to recede. He hadn't taken her deep within the bowels of the mountain, thank God. It was cold and dank in the passageway, but at least there was a sliver of light gleaming through the entrance above.

She slumped back against the wall. Silence hung heavily all around her. It was inevitable that her thoughts turn backward. Here, she thought numbly, was where the horrible nightmare with Kevin had begun. How was it possible that she had returned here—that she had come full circle?

The parallels were uncanny. She thought of Dan, trapped and hurt in the crevasse. It was altogether possible that all of them—she, Dan and Zach—might end up stranded here on Mount Hope, with little hope of rescue.

But the longer she sat there, the more she realized.... She'd been so terrified of returning here, afraid of being bombarded by memories of Kevin. Yet now, her mind was filled with Zach. He was all she could think of. Was he all right? Had he managed to locate the knot she had deliberately left looser than the others? It hurt to think of Zach sitting helplessly in the frigid mountain air. And then there was Dan. God, it hurt to think of them both!

Her throat grew painfully tight. She couldn't lose them. Not here, not now...*not again.*

She prayed that Zach would free himself before it was too late...for all of them.

ZACH STARED OFF at the place where Garrett and Randy had disappeared from sight. He could hear Dan yelling, but between the distance and the wind, he couldn't make out the words. He was terrified, he realized, yet it wasn't fear for himself that gripped his chest. It was fear for Randy.

What would Garrett do with her? His blood ran cold just thinking about it. Would he use her as a bargaining tool? Or would he decide she wasn't worth the trouble and kill her? And what would happen to her in the meantime?

A violent eddy of wind tumbled a tree only inches away from his bare feet. The gust was so fierce it left no mark in the freshly fallen snow. Then there was a low keening moan. A shock wave went through his entire body. It was as if he could hear Randy's desperate cry for help. And there was nothing—nothing!—he could do to help her.

The wind lashed his face, slapping his hair in and out of his eyes and making them sting. It was the wind that would kill him, Zach realized with an eerie sense of calm. Like a frigid curtain of death, it wrapped its icy tentacles around him and through him. Already his feet were numb. He could scarcely feel his toes. Even his fingers...

His fingers. Behind his back, Zach flexed them slightly, and it was then he felt something.... Was it only his imagination or was there a slight slack in the rope? He remembered Randy's expression just before Garrett jerked her away. There had been something in her eyes—something pleading.

Surely she hadn't... Zach's mind balked but his body had a will of its own. He stretched out the fingers of his right hand and touched a smooth knotted coil, trying to work his fingers between the loop. The effort was clumsy and fumbling because of his chilled skin. His tentative tug on the knot produced no response and his heart sank. He tried again. And again and again...

The rope dropped away from his wrists.

Zach grabbed for the rope around his ankles. "Randy." Her name tore out of his throat. The sound was half laugh, half sob. "Oh, Randy, I love you."

It took several minutes, but finally his ankles were free. He snatched his gloves, boots and socks. He wished he dared take the time to chafe some warmth into his frozen flesh, but he didn't dare.

Pushing himself onto his feet, he started toward Dan and the crevasse. "Dan!" he shouted. "Dan, I'm coming!" His feet were still numb and he stumbled once. Snow filled his clothing, but he picked himself up and lurched forward.

"Dan!" Panting, he dropped to his stomach at the edge of the crevasse. "Are you all right?"

Dan peered up at him. His face was white with fear and worry. "God, man, what the hell went on up there?" he rasped. "I heard Garrett yelling at you to get moving and then I didn't hear anything!"

Zach was busy tying the rope around his waist as he'd seen Randy do. "Garrett had Randy tie me up back there." He jerked his head over his shoulder. "Then he took off with her."

"How the hell did you get away?"

A grim smile touched his lips. "Randy left a knot slack enough for me to loosen and get free." He tossed the rope into the slit. "Tie that around you and let's get you out of there."

Five minutes later, Dan collapsed facedown on the ground next to him. Zach hauled him to his feet. It was impossible not to notice Dan's grimace of pain when he tried to stand. Zach's arm tightened supportively around the older man's shoulders. "You can't travel with that knee." He gave Dan no chance to argue. "Let's get you out of this wind and off that leg. Then I want you to get on the radio and get somebody up here to get you out of here."

Faded blue eyes anxiously scanned his face. "You're going after Randy?"

Zach nodded. "If Garrett's holed up at the mine, that's probably where they're headed."

It seemed to take forever to find a place to leave Dan. Zach finally found a notch in a crumbly conglomerate that was sheltered from the wind. Dan's skin was a sickly shade of white. His entire body shook with cold and strain and fatigue. Zach made him as comfortable as he could. He hated leaving him alone, but he knew he had no choice. Dan started to argue when Zach put up the tent, until Zach told him it would make his position easier to spot from the air.

Dan grabbed his arm just before he left. "Bring her back, son. But whatever you do, be careful." The lines around his mouth tightened. "These mountains can be deadly."

Zach squeezed his shoulder reassuringly. But when he left the older man behind, dread lay like a heavy stone in his stomach. He didn't trust Garrett with Randy, and he was afraid of what he might find. Perversely, he was just as afraid he *wouldn't* find her.

His gaze lifted. Mount Hope rose before him like a huge black specter. The summit lay hidden beneath a roiling blanket of seething clouds. His thoughts grew bitter. No wonder Randy hated it here. There was the threat of death, danger and destruction all around.

It was that thought that drove him on. All he could think of was getting Randy back, safe and unharmed. And mercifully, Garrett had been careless. Apparently he was so sure he'd never be followed that he made no effort to hide their tracks.

How much time passed, Zach didn't know. Nor did he care.

Despite the cold, a fine layer of perspiration coated his skin. His lungs burned with each stinging mouthful of air he hauled in. Still he pressed on, his face a relentless mask of steely determination...until he reached the sheer wall of the pinnacle. A narrow shelf jutted out from the rock face, plunging and twisting downward, then veering around a jagged outcrop. Randy had told them the mine lay just beyond.

But the ledge was everything Randy had said—and more. Zach's mouth was dry with fear. His heart slammed against his ribs. There was no way to negotiate the ledge without confronting the gaping chasm that fell away to the left. It looked as if it plummeted clear into the bowels of the earth. The thought ripped through him. How could he do this? One slip, an instant's carelessness, and his life would be forfeit.

You have to, a voice inside prodded. *What if something happens to Randy? What if Garrett hurts her? What if he kills her? Could you live with yourself knowing you might have been able to stop it?*

And Garrett would win. *He would win.*

Zach's eyes squeezed shut. He gathered every scrap of courage he possessed. *Hold on, Randy,* he urged silently. *I'm almost there, love. I'm almost there.*

The first step was the hardest. Zach's jaw was clenched so tightly his teeth hurt. In places the ledge was scarcely wider than one of his boots. He moved at a snail's pace, despising himself for the way he clung to rocky little knobs for support. Around the outcrop of rock, the ledge broadened out into a small clearing. It was here that Zach halted, his nerves scraped as raw as his hands.

Nearby he heard a thunk, like a chunk of wood being thrown. Zach went very still inside and out, all his senses ready and alert. He dropped to a crouch, his hand sliding under his coat to draw his revolver.

Muscles tense, he risked a quick look at the clearing. An ugly hole in the side of the mountain marked what must be the entrance to the mine. Directly in front of it a ring of stones encircled the blackened ash of a camp fire. Against the mountainside was a small stack of wood.

There was no sign of Randy. Garrett stood with his back to him. Hands on his hips, he stared at the entrance to the mine. Zach's eyes narrowed. Had Garrett imprisoned her inside the mine? He pictured her huddled on the ground in the cold and the dark. Emotion caught at his chest, knowing how terrified she would be. Reason warred briefly with compassion. On the other hand, it would make it easier to handle Garrett if Randy was out of harm's way.

That was the extent of Zach's planning. He knew it was now or never when Garrett began to walk toward the mine entrance. Like a soldier primed for action, he slipped out from behind the rock.

"Hold it right there, Garrett." His voice ripped through the silence.

Garrett turned slowly. The disbelief etched on his grizzled face was gratifying, but Zach didn't take the time to savor it. There was a rifle propped next to the woodpile, and it was there that he directed his steps.

But before he reached it, there was an echo of footsteps from behind Garrett. Randy appeared in the mine entrance. The light momentarily blinded her, but her voice reflected her joy when she caught sight of him. "Zach!" she cried. "Oh, Zach, I knew you'd—"

Garrett lunged for Randy. Zach cursed furiously. There was no time to get off a clean shot at Garrett before Garrett grabbed Randy's braid and jerked her in front of him. His arm snaked around her neck; he locked his elbow under her chin and pinned her back against him.

Garrett's thin cruel smile curdled his blood. "Who's giving the orders now?" he jeered. "Drop that gun and kick it away!"

Zach saw red. Randy's eyes were huge and frightened above the bulk of Garrett's arm. But he slowly began to lower the barrel of the revolver, praying Garrett would believe he was giving it up and let Randy go.

Garrett's arm tightened. Randy's ears were roaring. Her vision started to blur. She clawed at Garrett's arm, desperate for air.

Zach flung away the revolver. A surge of loathing tore through him. He had to fight to keep from hurling himself at Garrett. The animal instinct in him demanded vengeful satisfaction for what Garrett was doing to Randy...and what he had done to Larry.

"How commendable," Zach mocked, "using her for a shield. Do I really scare you that much?"

Garrett's face flushed beet red. "Shut up!" he bellowed. "You hear me? Just shut up!"

His taunt had hit home. Triumph spurted in Zach's veins. It was working! He shifted his stance slightly, his pose one of almost indolent ease. But inside, every nerve was screaming and ready for action.

"Who's gonna make me!" he sneered. "You? You're a coward, Garrett. If you were any kind of a man, you wouldn't need to rely on her for protection."

Garrett bared his teeth. "You don't scare me, lawman."

Zach laughed.

It was just the edge he'd hoped for. Garrett went wild. He thrust Randy aside. She stumbled to the ground. Arms wide, his face contorted, Garrett charged like a raging bull. From the corner of his eye, Zach saw Randy half-sitting in the snow.

"Get out of here!" he yelled to her. He neatly sidestepped Garrett's lumbering body.

Randy scarcely heard. She scuttled backward, but that was as far as she moved. Her heart in her throat, she couldn't take her eyes off the struggle taking place before her.

Garrett's eyes were lit like a madman's. Zach knew the other man had the advantage in size and weight, but he was counting on Garrett's fury to make him reckless.

The ploy worked beautifully. Garrett struck out blindly, again and again. Zach dodged and feinted, circled and dodged. But he hadn't counted on the stones circling the fire. He tripped and stumbled and Garret was on him. They crashed heavily to the ground.

Zach gave a lithe twist of his body and bounded to his feet. Crouched and ready, he watched Garrett stagger upright.

They eyed each other warily, each finding something in the other he hadn't expected. Their chests heaved; their breath sounded like harsh rasping sobs in the frigid alpine air.

Then all at once something changed. The atmosphere tightened to a screaming pitch of awareness. At the exact same moment, both men spotted the rifle still propped against the woodpile, just beyond Randy. Zach's mind was off and running, silently gauging. Garret was closer, but he was tired and winded . . .

Garrett lunged.

From somewhere there was a strangled cry. Randy scarcely realized it came from her throat. She surged upward and forward, reacting on instinct alone as she thrust out her foot.

But it was too late. Garrett was not to be thwarted. With one arm he thrust her aside. There was a sickening crack as her head connected with a solid wall of rock. Oddly there was no pain. She dropped to the icy ground like a puppet whose strings had been cut.

"No!" Something burst in Zach's brain. It all happened in a split second, but Zach's body was already in motion, driven by raw fury. His entire being was racked with a murderous rage. Garrett had barely gained possession of the rifle before Zach's foot sliced up beneath the barrel. It sailed end over end before sinking deep into the powdery snow yards away.

Zach leaped onto Garrett, tackling him and sending them both flying to the ground in a shower of snow. They wrestled, rolling wildly over and over. Neither seemed to notice how close they had come to the jagged outcrop of rock where Zach had hidden.

But suddenly they were there, grappling and punching, twisting and fighting. Both struggled to their feet; Zach still didn't know the ragged chasm was only inches away.

Garrett's lips pulled into a twisted smile. He launched himself at Zach, and their struggle renewed in deadly earnest....

Randy was still out cold. She didn't see Garrett's look of horror as he lost his footing, or Zach's frantic grab for him.

And she never heard the horrible echo of Garrett's scream as he plunged over the edge...to his death.

CHAPTER SEVENTEEN

THERE WAS A SOMBER-LOOKING assemblage waiting at the airport. A dozen men—some in uniform, some not—milled around the helicopter pad, their faces tense and drawn. The ambulance and crew stood ready and waiting. They spoke in hushed tones, occasionally glancing upward to scan the western sky.

One figure stood apart from the rest of the group, thin and slight, hunched against the frigid bite of the wind. She never moved. She spoke to no one. And she alone never took her eyes from the leaden gray sky.

It was she who noticed the dot on the horizon drawing nearer. Her ears strained to hear the dull roar of the helicopter.

"Here they come!" someone shouted.

Suddenly it was there. The air was filled with the throbbing whine of the rotors. The helicopter swept in a wide arc, skimming the treetops before slowly drifting down. It landed in a flurry of dust.

There was an oppressive silence after the pilot cut the engine. Then several men ducked forward and slid open the side door.

Marian's heart climbed to her throat. One of the men stuck his head out and beckoned to the paramedics. "We've got a head injury in here!" he shouted.

Fear wrapped around her like a shroud. *Dan,* she thought wildly. *Oh, Dan, no!*

Someone ducked through the opening. *Dan.* For the longest time, Marian stood rooted to the spot. Someone helped him to the ground; she noticed the way he favored his knee. Yet he was alive, and nothing else mattered. The profound relief that flooded through her made her weak, yet somehow she found the strength to put one foot in front of the other.

And Dan did what she'd never expected. Limp and all, he met her halfway.

Marian didn't care who saw them. She wrapped her arms around him and clung to him blindly. All she could think of in that moment was how much she loved him and how close she had come to losing him— through her own folly.

"I thought I'd never see you again." Her voice trembled. "I heard the call go out on the scanner from the helicopter. I called Mitch, but he said the transmission he'd received was choppy. He knew someone had been hurt, but that was all. And I was so afraid I'd lost you, too!" The words were torn from deep inside her. "Oh, Dan, I know this isn't the time, but I . . . I have to tell you how wrong I've been. I knew it as soon as you left. I—I know how much I've hurt you and—" Tears choked her voice. She was unable to go on.

"I'm all right, Marian." Dan's tone was gruff with emotion. He touched her hair. He looked as if he wanted to say more, but before he could say anything, there was a flurry of motion behind him. Marian's eyes flitted over his shoulder to the tall man who'd just jumped from the helicopter. She recognized Zach Corbett. He turned immediately and reached inside the craft.

Marian caught sight of a tangled dark braid dangling over the end of the stretcher. Randy's skin was colorless, her lips bloodless.

Marian started to shake inside. How many times, she agonized silently, had she wished Randy would disappear off the face of the earth? All along she had told herself she didn't care. But she did. God help her, she did.

She didn't know how much until that moment.

The wave of shame and regret that swept through Marian almost brought her to her knees. ''No,'' she whispered. ''Oh, no, not again . . .'' She couldn't tear her eyes away from the stretcher being loaded into the back of the ambulance.

She was almost afraid to look at Dan for fear of what she would find in his eyes. When she did, his gaze was riveted to her. It took a tremendous amount of willpower to force another sound past the lump in her throat. ''Is she all right? Oh, please, Dan, tell me!'' Her voice caught. ''I—I'll never forgive myself if she's—''

He stifled the flow of words with his fingers. ''I think she'll be okay, Marian. But she had quite a blow to the head, and she's been in and out ever since.''

One of the deputies stepped up and cleared his throat. ''Sheriff, the medics said you'd better stop by the hospital to have your knee x-rayed.''

Dan gave an absent nod. His eyes flickered back to his wife. "Marian," he said softly, "will you come with me? When I'm done there we'll head home."

Her eyes grew suspiciously moist. Her smile was watery…the most precious sight he'd ever laid eyes on. Her fingers squeezed his.

It was all the answer Dan needed.

A LONG TIME LATER Dan slowly made his way down a wide hospital corridor. He'd left Marian in the waiting room downstairs. He'd asked if she wanted to come with him to Randy's room, but Marian murmured she thought it might be best for all of them if she waited until later to see her.

Dan hadn't pressed her. This time he understood.

Randy's room was dimly lit. Somehow Dan wasn't surprised to find Zach sitting at her bedside. Her head was angled toward the window, but he could see that her eyes were closed. She gave no sign that she'd heard the door open, but Zach rose and came toward him.

Dan's eyes were on Randy. "How is she?" he asked quietly.

"It's just as we suspected—a concussion." Zach smiled slightly. "They gave her something to sleep. The doctor wants to keep her overnight. A few days' rest and she'll be good as new." His eyes never strayed from her.

Dan blew out a sigh of relief. "I guess I knew it all along," he murmured, "but it sure feels good to know for certain." He laid a hand on the swinging door. "As long as she's asleep, I won't stay."

Zach followed him into the hallway. "How's your knee?"

"I tore a little of this and a little of that, so I'll have to wear a brace for a while. The doctor said as long as I take it easy the first few weeks it shouldn't give me any problem later on." He gave a short laugh. "Looks like I get a vacation whether I want it or not."

"Will you be . . . at home?"

Dan nodded. There was a moment's uneasy silence. He glanced toward Randy's hospital room. "As awful as this whole thing with Garrett has been," he said slowly, "I think it's finally made Marian open her eyes."

Zach said nothing.

"Well," Dan murmured after a moment, "I'd better get back to Marian. I think I'll stop by and see Randy in the morning, so I'll probably see you then—"

"I won't be here in the morning, Dan." Zach's gaze seared into his. "I'm leaving here in less than an hour. I've arranged to drive back to Portland tonight."

Dan's jaw dropped. "You're leaving without telling her goodbye?" He jerked his head in the direction of Randy's room.

Stark disapproval underscored the surprise in his tone. Zach winced. "Believe me," he stated heavily. "It's better this way."

"Better?" Dan's jaw clenched. "Are you sure you don't mean easier—easier for you to walk away?"

Zach didn't flinch beneath the other man's angry gaze. "Is that what you think?" he asked tightly. "That I'm walking away from Randy?"

"Hell, yes! She's in love with you, man! Don't you know that?"

Zach slumped against the wall, the pose one of utter weariness. "No," he whispered, and there was a world of agony in his voice. "I don't. And to tell you the truth, Dan, I'm not sure if Randy even knows what she wants. But she doesn't seem to think it's me."

For a moment Dan simply stared, stung by Zach's air of defeat. "You can tell me it's none of my business," he said finally. "But how do you know that?"

"How else? She told me. Oh, not in so many words, but I asked her to come with me when this was all over. She refused."

"Then change her mind!"

Zach couldn't hide his bitterness. "I've tried. It's guilt over your son that's keeping her here, Dan. We both know it. I can't push her into something she feels isn't right for her, and neither can you. If she ever leaves here, it has to be her choice. And to tell you the truth—" his voice fell "—I'm not sure I'd want it any other way."

Dan stared at him, at the gaunt planes of his face. He looked raw and beaten. Dan's heart wrenched. Nothing hurt worse than love denied...nothing.

He squeezed Zach's shoulder. "Don't give up," he urged. "You haven't lost her yet."

Zach's smile held no mirth. "How can I lose her," he murmured, "when I'm not sure she was ever mine to begin with?"

WHEN RANDY AWOKE, the fuzziness was gone from her mind. Even before she opened her eyes, she knew she was in a hospital room. She remembered ghostly shapes hovering over her and whispering voices— sometimes crisp and efficient, sometimes low and urgent. But at least her head didn't ache so much . . . her head!

She sat up with a gasp. The sunlight was blinding. She squinted against it, but her fingers instinctively sought out the sore spot on the side of her head.

Firm but gentle hands pressed her back onto the pillows. "Whoa, there," chuckled a soothing feminine voice. "We'll have you up and around soon enough, young lady."

Randy peered up at a pretty young nurse. "But my head—"

"Is still right where it should be." The nurse laughed and guided her fingers to a long lumpy bandage angled above her right ear. "See? You had a pretty good-sized gash there that had to be shaved before the doctor could stitch it up. But your hair covers it so no one will ever know it's there but you." The nurse smiled at her. "You slept through breakfast, but I'll see if I can get something for you to eat."

The words were anything but reassuring. With them came a frightening rush of memory. The last thing she remembered was Zach falling—that was when she must have cut her head. Then there was a scream . . . it wasn't her imagination. She knew it. So who had screamed? Garrett? Or Zach? The bloodcurdling sound echoed in her mind. She pressed her hand to her mouth.

"No," she whispered. "Please not Zach."

She quizzed the nurse when she returned with a tray, but the nurse knew nothing. She scolded gently over Randy's lack of appetite, but she was too frightened to eat. The nurse had just removed the tray when the door creaked again.

Dan gave a rueful grin and hobbled into the room. Heedless of the sudden pounding in her head, Randy pulled herself into a sitting position, wrapped her arms around him and hugged him fiercely.

"How are you? she whispered. "Are you okay?" Dan drew back and quickly explained about his knee.

She gripped his hands, unwilling to let him go. "And Zach? He's all right, isn't he? Most of yesterday is a blur. The last thing I remember is Garrett lunging for the rifle—"

"Garrett went over the ledge, Randy. He's dead. And Zach is fine." He squeezed her fingers reassuringly.

Relief made her weak. She sank back onto the pillows gratefully. A chair scraped against the floor as Dan pulled it up to the bedside. After a moment she drew the blanket to her chin. She couldn't look at Dan as she spoke, nor could she withhold the question any longer. "Is he here?"

In the silence that followed, her fingers plucked at the binding. "No," Dan said finally. "He went back to Portland last night."

Randy's lungs burned with the effort it took not to cry. She wanted to say something—anything—to break the lengthening silence. But she couldn't force a sound past the lump in her throat.

Dan leaned forward and placed his hand over hers. "He stayed until he knew you were all right, Randy."

She closed her eyes before he could see the threat of tears. So Zach had stayed, she thought bleakly. Well, that was more than she expected; more than she deserved. After all, she'd given him no reason to stick around. Perhaps she should be grateful...instead she only felt empty.

Dan left then, promising to return tomorrow. Randy felt suddenly drained, emotionally and physically. She nodded listlessly, wanting nothing more than to retreat into the blessed oblivion of sleep once more. Her body ached as she rolled over onto her side....

But it was nothing compared to the ache in her heart.

THE DOCTOR SIGNED Randy's release the next morning. She dressed mechanically; her body felt slow and cumbersome. When she was done, she dropped down on the edge of the hospital bed.

It was odd, she mused silently, how the prospect of going home held little appeal. She had always hated being confined to bed, even when she was sick.

Her thoughts took an abrupt turn. Perhaps it wasn't so odd after all, for Zach had made love to her there. Could she ever sleep in her bed—her lonely bed— without thinking of the intimacies they'd shared there? Without remembering how she'd slept in his arms, how he held her tight and kept the night shadows at bay? The thought was like a knife twisting inside her.

Zach, Oh, Zach, what will I do without you?

Just then there was a knock on the door. Dan poked his head in. She beckoned him inside.

He smiled approvingly. "The nurse at the desk said you're being released this morning."

Randy summoned a weak smile. "Looks like you came just in time. Are you willing to play chauffeur?"

"As a matter of fact—" he echoed her faint smile "—I am." Something flickered in his eyes, something she couldn't decipher. She watched as he went to the door and opened it. He motioned to someone standing just beyond.

Marian walked into the room.

Shock held Randy motionless. She could only stare as Marian advanced slowly toward her.

The older woman looked as scared as Randy felt. Her heart jerked painfully. It was as if a little piece had just been chipped away, yet it had the curious effect of making everything inside her go numb. She told herself it was the only way she could get through this.

Marian didn't stop until she stood directly before her.

The silence heightened to a whining pitch. It was as if the entire world were holding its breath.

"Marian." The name sounded alien on her lips. She wet them and tried again. "Marian, why are you here?"

For the longest time Randy didn't think she would answer. "I'm here," Marian whispered at last, "because I couldn't stay away any longer."

The door clicked shut. Neither woman seemed aware that Dan had left them alone.

Strangely enough, it was Randy who looked away. Her body was stiff. She felt she would snap with the slightest pressure. She spoke, her voice clipped and very low. "Your decision? Not Dan's?"

Marian's wounded look stabbed into her. It made her feel so guilty she had to remind herself that this woman had shown her no quarter. She had every right to be wary of Marian's motives.

"I know that's what you think." Marian's denial fell into the tense silence. "But it's not true, I swear. Dan told me he thought I should wait a few days but I—I just had to see you."

Her distress was genuine, her tone imploring. Randy couldn't refuse when Marian pointed to the spot on the bed next to her and asked if she could sit there. Once she was seated, she laid her hands on her knees and closed her eyes.

"This is so—so hard! I mean…I knew it would be, but I hoped—I hoped to handle it better. There's so much to say and I don't even know where to begin!"

The ice encasing Randy's heart began to thaw. Seeing Marian like this—her composure so fragile— was jarring. It also did nothing to help her own fraying nerves.

"Marian," she said gently. "I think I know what you're trying to say, so there's no need for you to do this." Unthinkingly she reached for Marian's thin hand.

"There is," Marian said quickly. "Not just for you, Randy, but for me." Her tone was strong and sure, yet she clung to Randy's hand as if it were a lifeline. She looked up at her with a small smile. "You always had the most amazing knack of cheering me up, for knowing just what to say. It was one of the things I loved most about you."

Randy's throat grew tight. "Until Kevin died."

Her smile withered. "Yes," she admitted. "But I've only just realized it wasn't you who changed, but me. It never even occurred to me until Dan told me he didn't think he could live with the woman I've become. It took his leaving me before I really took a good look at myself—" she faltered slightly "—and I didn't like what I found."

Randy's expression softened. "But Dan's back now, isn't he?"

Marian nodded. Her smile made a brief reappearance. Then her eyes grew cloudy once more. "I was so scared when the three of you got back yesterday. There was a report that someone had been hurt, and I was so relieved when I discovered it wasn't Dan. And then I saw you, so white and lying so still. For a minute I was afraid you were dead. And suddenly I knew how much I'd hurt you, how much I'd wronged you."

She clutched her hand even more tightly. "Oh, Randy," she choked out, "I'm so ashamed. How can I tell you how sorry I am?"

Something came apart inside Randy. There were tears running down Marian's thin cheeks. Randy didn't realize until that moment that her own were just as wet. She reached out and gripped Marian's other hand, her smile watery. "You just did," she whispered.

It was this scene that Dan saw when he peeked tentatively into the room. He let the door close behind him. With an air of infinite patience, he handed each woman a tissue. "Maybe I should ask the nurse for a bucket." He tried to make a joke of it, but his voice was rough with emotion.

He cleared his throat and glanced at Marian. "Have you told her the news yet?"

Marian shook her head. Still dabbing at her cheeks, she reached for Dan with her free hand. She smiled mistily up at him. "I thought we'd tell her together."

Dan's expression grew incredibly soft. He pulled her up beside him and wrapped an arm around her shoulder, then turned his gaze to Randy. "We've decided to sell our house, Randy." There was a brief pause. "It's really too big for just the two of us," he began slowly.

"And it's time we moved on," Marian finished with surprising firmness.

Randy was still digesting the news. "I'm...stunned, to tell you the truth." She laughed shakily. "It seems like you two have lived in that house forever."

Marian exchanged a glance with her husband. "Our entire marriage," she murmured. "We have a lot of good memories—" for an instant the moisture reappeared in her eyes "—but we both think it's time for a change."

Randy blinked. "So what will you do? Buy a smaller house?"

Again that silent look passed between them. It was Marian who answered. "Actually we don't know where we'll settle after the house is sold."

"But it won't be here in Bend," Dan injected quietly.

Marian's hand slipped into his. "No," she agreed. "Dan's decided to retire after Christmas. We thought we might buy a trailer and do some traveling. So the next time you talk to your folks you might tell them not to be too surprised if Dan and I show up on their doorstep," she warned with a smile.

As she spoke, Randy's mind traveled fleetingly backward, to the day she'd first met Zach. She recalled Dan telling her that the best thing for all of them would be to leave this town and never look back.

She'd known all along that he was right.

She glanced from one to the other. "I'm glad for both of you," she said softly. "And I don't think you'll ever regret it."

Marian came forward and hugged her. "It was the hardest decision I've ever had to make," she admitted, drawing back. "I've been so caught up in the past—in losing Kevin—that I didn't realize I still have a husband. And we both have a lot of years left."

Her gaze sought Dan's over her shoulder and she smiled. But when she turned back and spoke again, her voice wavered. "This almost destroyed my marriage," she whispered. "Don't let that happen to you."

Randy's mind spun. Zach. She was talking about Zach.

At that moment the nurse stepped into the room. "We've got some papers for you to sign anytime you're ready."

When the nurse was gone, Marian tipped her head to the side. "Why don't you come and stay with us for a few days? They told us at the desk the doctor said

you had orders to take it easy for the next few days."
She squeezed her shoulders. "Please, Randy. We'd
love to have you."

Randy hesitated. The idea was tempting, but something held her back. Marian and Dan had just come
through a very trying experience. They needed some
time to mend; some time together.

She shook her head and gently declined. "I appreciate the offer, honestly I do, but I think…I think I'd
like some time alone right now."

Dan frowned. "Are you sure?"

"Very sure," she said softly. "I think it's time that
I did some thinking—" a faint smile touched her lips
"—and made some choices."

CHAPTER EIGHTEEN

RANDY SPENT THE NEXT few days quietly. She stopped in at the store, but only briefly. A wry smile curled her lips every time she thought of Chuck—he didn't seem to mind her absence in the least. On the contrary, he appeared to be thriving on his newfound job expansion. As for the times when she was alone, it was because she wanted to be, not because she had to be.

Several days after her release from the hospital, Randy spent the afternoon with Dan and Marian, helping Marian with the much belated task of sorting through Kevin's belongings. Sitting on the floor in Kevin's old room, they talked and laughed and reminisced. She held Marian while she cried in her arms, but it was a time of healing for both of them.

It was much later, while Randy lay in bed, that Zach's words about Kevin spun through her mind. *It's Kevin, isn't it?* he'd said. *After all this time, you're still in love with him*. But she wasn't—she wasn't! Whenever she thought of Kevin, she could bring back the memories, but not the feelings.

Her heart was filled with just one man. She was bound to Zach . . . in a way she'd never been bound to Kevin.

"No," she said aloud, then more forcefully. "No! It's you I love, Zach, *you*!"

And she did, with every beat of her heart. He had come into her life as unexpectedly as a fierce windstorm, and he'd left in much the same way.

By morning Randy had come to a decision. She knew exactly what she had to do...and she prayed she had the courage to do it.

THREE DAYS LATER Randy peered out the window of a taxicab. It was evening, and she'd left the busy city center and freeways of Portland behind. Towering fir trees bordered the side of the two-lane roadway, following the dips and curves of gently rolling hills. But a steady drizzle seeped from the sky, the kind of rain Oregon was so famous for. For Randy, it made the peaceful pastoral setting seem almost cold and unwelcoming.

The cab turned onto a narrow paved road. It was just as Zach had said—rural without being too remote. The vehicle rolled to a halt in front of a house that was long and low, built of natural cedar. Cathedral windows looked out over the wide expanse of lawn. From a corner deep within the house, a lamp glowed.

"This is it, lady." The cab driver sounded disgustingly cheerful.

Oh, yes, she echoed silently. This is it. She was here in Portland. Parked in front of Zach's house...

The driver turned and looked at her expectantly.

Randy climbed out of the cab. Her legs felt like jelly. Her hands were shaking so that she could scarcely pull the bills from her wallet. Finally she gave up. When the driver delivered her suitcase into her hands, she thrust what she knew was an exorbitant amount at him. "Here," she said hastily. "Keep the change."

The cab sped away. Randy stood for a moment, clutching her suitcase. She couldn't remember when she'd felt so frightened and insecure.

It took every ounce of courage she possessed to walk up the sidewalk. Two steps later, her stomach began to knot. Her breath came in jagged spurts. What if Zach wasn't home? What would he think if he came home and found her perched on his doorstep, like a forlorn little waif? Maybe she should have called. She had entertained the notion and then decided against it—not because of any great desire to surprise him—but because she had refused him once already. She didn't think she could take it if his pride dictated that he turn his back on her.

She reached for the doorbell and heard its summons inside the house. But it was as if the sound came from a very great distance.

She stared at the dark imposing doorway and waited. Time was suspended in an agony of silence. A thousand doubts swelled inside her. What if Zach didn't want her here? What if he regretted what had happened between them? She knew he cared, but did he love her? He'd asked her to come with him, but he hadn't said he *loved* her. What if his feelings weren't as strong as he thought...as she hoped? She'd sacrificed her soul...and for what? The gamble of a lifetime?

The door opened.

She stared at Zach.

Zach stared at her.

Her heart tripped over itself. He looked much the same as he had in the mountains, dressed in jeans and a chambray shirt. Only his clean-shaven jaw was different. She wanted to reach out and touch it, slide her fingers along the skin stretched over his cheekbones, knowing the texture would be pleasantly rough against her fingertips.

"Hi." Her voice was faint. She mustered what little remained of her shaky confidence. "I'll bet you're surprised to see me."

Zach smiled. Surprise. The word didn't even come close to what he was feeling. "Hello, Randy." He opened the door wider in silent invitation.

Once she was inside, he relieved her of her suitcase, then motioned her toward the living room. Randy descended the few steps into the sunken room, marveling that her legs even held her. Yet she was too jittery to sit, so she remained where she was.

Zach had moved to stand in front of a massive rock fireplace.

Randy glanced around. The leather furnishings were comfortably appealing. The beamed ceiling conveyed an air of rustic simplicity. The room spanned the width of the house. The spacious dining area at the far end opened onto a large deck. She swallowed a pang. Beyond, the deepening night sky framed a thick row of fir trees and the small stream Zach had told her about.

"This is nice," she said softly. "I like it."

"Thanks." As easy as his reply was, his gaze resting on her was dark and solemn.

For just an instant, her suitcase, still sitting by the door, caught her attention. Had he left it there deliberately? Randy tried desperately to still the whirlwind of emotion inside her.

She saw Zach slip his fingers into the pockets of his jeans. His eyes never left her face. He watched her as if he were waiting . . . and no doubt he was.

"I suppose," she said at last, "you're wondering why I'm here."

His smile was so slight it was almost nonexistent. But all he said was, "How did you find me?"

"I have Dan to thank for that. He pulled a few strings and managed to get me your address. I thought about calling you," she added quickly. "And then I decided it might be better if I just made the trip myself and tried to explain . . ."

Damn. *Damn!* It wasn't coming out at all the way she'd hoped, but now there was nothing to do except get everything out in the open.

"I was so hurt when you left without saying goodbye—without saying anything." The words began pouring out in a ragged jumble. "But I've done a lot of thinking since then. And it didn't take long to realize that you were right all along. I could have left Bend after Kevin died, but I didn't. Maybe it was my way of doing penance, a way of punishing myself. But now that I can finally look Marian in the eyes again—"

"Marian!" The low exclamation broke from his lips. An expression of wary disbelief crept into his features. "Don't tell me she's responsible for you being here."

"In a way, she is, Zach. She—she came to me and told me how much she regretted blaming me for Kevin's death."

His lips compressed. "As if that makes up for what she put you through."

"I had to forgive her, Zach. Because it's the only way I could ever be truly free. I *am* free. That's why I put my house up for sale and sold the store to Chuck."

"You sold the store?"

He sounded incredulous. Whether that was good or bad, Randy couldn't tell. She couldn't work up the courage to look at him.

"Yes." Her throat tightened. "You said once that I was still in love with Kevin. But I'm not, Zach, I'm not!"

Tears burned her eyes. "I won't lie. I fought my feelings for you tooth and nail. I didn't *want* to feel anything, because it hurt so much. I didn't want to—" she stumbled over the words "—to love you. Maybe I did feel like I was betraying Kevin, but if I did, it was only at first. But it wasn't true when you asked me to leave with you, and it's not true now."

Her vision was misted by tears when at last her eyes sought his. "Kevin is a part of my past," she whispered. "But you . . . you are my future. I'm here right now, because there's nowhere else I'd rather be. Please, Zach." Her lips began to quiver. "Please don't send me away."

Zach felt the break in her voice as if it were a physical blow. The sound tore right into him. Her eyes were huge and glistening, full of longing. The naked vulnerability reflected on her features made his heart turn over.

He reached for her. "Oh, Randy." Her name was half laugh, half groan as he brought her close to his heart, right where she belonged. He knew what it had cost her to come to him; it only made him love her that much more.

"I can't believe that you're here. But now that you are, you'd better believe I'm not about to let you go." He framed her face with his hands. "You," he said softly, "are here to stay."

Randy was trembling inside from the way he looked at her, the gentleness in his touch. It was going to be all right, she thought weakly.

Zach tipped her face to his. He looked deep into her eyes...straight into her heart. "Do you have any idea," he asked quietly, "how much I love you?"

The intensity of both his look and his tone rocked her soul. A rush of joy swept through her. Her arms slipped around his neck, her fingers knotting in his hair.

"And do you have any idea," she choked out, "how much I needed you to tell me that?"

Zach drew back just enough that he could see her. "Yeah," he said softly. "As a matter of fact, I do."

The words fell into a hushed void. Randy stared up at him, touched by the anxious uncertainty on his features. He was waiting, she realized numbly, for her.

She pressed her mouth to his. "I love you," she whispered, and once started, she couldn't seem to stop. She clung to him, her heart and eyes finally spilling over. It was an emotionally charged moment for both of them. But through the tears, she smiled.

Zach couldn't think when he'd ever seen anything so beautiful. It was a smile he would carry in his heart forever.

THE FIRE BURNING in the hearth sent a shower of sparks up the chimney. The dancing flames filled the room with a soft glow and cast flickering shadows on the wall. Two figures lay nestled in the corner of the sofa, quietly talking.

With her head leaning against Zach's shoulder, Randy told him about Dan and Marian's decision to sell their house.

Zach shook his head. "I still can't believe Marian finally came around," he murmured. "After all this time."

Randy was silent for a few seconds. "I think Dan leaving her must have shaken her up enough that she finally took a good look at herself." One corner of her mouth lifted. "It sure shook me up."

That it had, Zach agreed silently. He experienced a pang recalling how devastated Randy had been that night. He slid his fingers through the silky fall of her hair. "You think things will go okay for them?"

She twisted around so she could look at him. "This may sound odd," she said slowly. "But I think this whole experience has brought them closer together." She smiled. "I think things will be better than ever for them."

Her smile made Zach's breath catch. The shadows were gone from her eyes, and so was the haunted emptiness. Her face was filled with a radiance he'd never dared hope for...and it was all for him.

He lowered his head and brought her mouth to his. There was no desperate urgency to the kiss they shared; instead it was filled with the infinite sweetness of fulfillment.

"What about you?" he murmured. "Do you think you'll like living here?"

Randy's gaze was drawn toward the window at the front of the house. Far below, the twinkling lights of the city peeped through the darkness. Her eyes shifted toward the dining room. She saw that the dismal clouds had disappeared. Dozens of stars were scattered high above the treetops.

She brought Zach's hand to her face. "I'm going to love it here. But not as much as I love you," she whispered.

His thumb stroked her lower lip. "You don't mind my work? It's not dangerous on a daily basis, but those occasions sometimes do arise."

She nuzzled her cheek against his palm, aware of his slight frown. "We all have to take risks, Zach. And I'd rather take mine with you—than without you."

Zach's expression grew incredibly tender. The heartfelt emotion shining from her eyes made his throat ache. He claimed her mouth for another kiss. When their lips finally parted, he rested his forehead against hers. Randy was rather startled to see a teasing glint in his eyes.

"I have a confession to make, Randy."

"Already?" She matched his lightness, watching as he rose and moved toward the dining room table.

When he returned, he dropped an envelope into her lap and sat down again. "What's this?" she asked, puzzled.

"Open it and see."

She did as he asked. Her eyes widened when she saw what was inside. "It's a plane ticket! You were coming to see me—and you planned to fly!" For all that the words were an accusation, they lacked any heat whatsoever. In fact, Randy sounded perfectly delighted.

"Unfortunately, yes."

She glanced back at the ticket. "Hey," she murmured. "There's no return date."

"That's because I didn't know when I'd be returning." A silly grin edged Zach's mouth. "But I did know I wasn't coming back without you. And believe me, I was prepared to use whatever means I had to to get you back—fair or foul."

She wrinkled her nose. "Kidnapping is against the law, Zach Corbett. I shouldn't have to tell you that."

He chuckled. "I was hoping it wouldn't come to that. If worst came to worst, I was going to remind you that you might be pregnant. In fact, I even hoped you might be."

"Pregnant!" Randy gasped. "Do you think so?"

Zach shot her an amused glance. "Neither one of us was exactly prepared to do anything to prevent it, so you tell me."

"No, I...it's too soon to tell," she stammered. She scarcely noticed him laugh at her reaction. She glanced down at her tummy, her expression rather dreamy.

He laid a possessive hand on her abdomen. "Something tells me you like the idea."

"I do. I mean . . . I've always wanted a family, and I'm almost thirty now. I'd love to have a baby. Your baby, Zach."

He loved her shy breathlessness. "We could work on it on our honeymoon."

The husky pitch of his voice made her shiver. His mouth trailing kisses along the length of her neck made her middle go heavy and tight. Her fingers slid into the golden roughness of his hair. "And where will that be?"

Her body slipped down on the sofa. His followed. He kissed the hollow behind her ear. "Somewhere close," he murmured. "Let's honeymoon somewhere close."

"That's just so you don't have to fly." Randy felt a laugh bubbling up inside her. She couldn't resist teasing him a little. "I guess Australia is out then, huh?"

Zach sighed and propped himself up on his elbows. "Anything you want, love, is fine with me."

"Really?"

"Really."

"Then let's not bother packing." She pulled his head down to hers. "Because I already have everything I want—" She smiled against his lips. "Right here."

Harlequin Superromance.

COMING NEXT MONTH

A compelling novel of deadly revenge and passion
from Harlequin's bestselling international
romance author Penny Jordan

POWER PLAY

Eleven years had passed but the
terror of that night was something
Pepper Minesse would never
forget. Fueled by revenge against
the four men who had brutally
shattered her past, she set in
motion a deadly plan to destroy
their futures.

Available in February!

HPP-1A

The Pirate
JAYNE ANN KRENTZ

At the heart of every powerful romance story lies a
legend. There are many romantic legends and
countless modern variations on them, but they all
have one thing in common: They are tales of brave,
resourceful women who must gentle and tame the
powerful, passionate men who are their true mates.

The enormous appeal of Jayne Ann Krentz lies in
her ability to create modern-day versions of these
classic romantic myths, and her LADIES AND
LEGENDS trilogy showcases this talent. Believing
that a storyteller who can bring legends to life
deserves special attention, Harlequin has chosen
the first book of the trilogy—THE PIRATE—to
receive our Award of Excellence. Look for it in
February.

AE-PIR-1

Harlequin Superromance®

LET THE GOOD TIMES ROLL...

Add some Cajun spice to liven up your New Year's
celebrations and join Superromance for a romantic
tour of the rich Acadian marshlands and the legendary
Louisiana bayous.

Starting in January 1990, we're launching CAJUN
MELODIES, a three-book tribute to the fun-loving
people who've enriched America by introducing us to
crawfish étouffé and gumbo, zydeco music and the
Saturday night party, the *fais-dodo*. And learn about
loving, Cajun-style, as you meet the tall, dark,
handsome men who win their ladies' hearts with a
beautiful, haunting melody....

Book One: *Julianne's Song*, January 1990
Book Two: *Catherine's Song*, February 1990
Book Three: *Jessica's Song*, March 1990

SRCJ-1R